Fun Together

Hillary Noelle

No AI was used in the creation, design, or editing of this book.

E-book ISBN: 979-8-9990262-1-7

Paperback ISBN: 979-8-9990262-0-0

Cover Design by Austin Drake - Bottle Cap Creative

Developmental Edits by Katie Wolf

Line and Copy Edits by Emily McNish at Fairy PlotMother

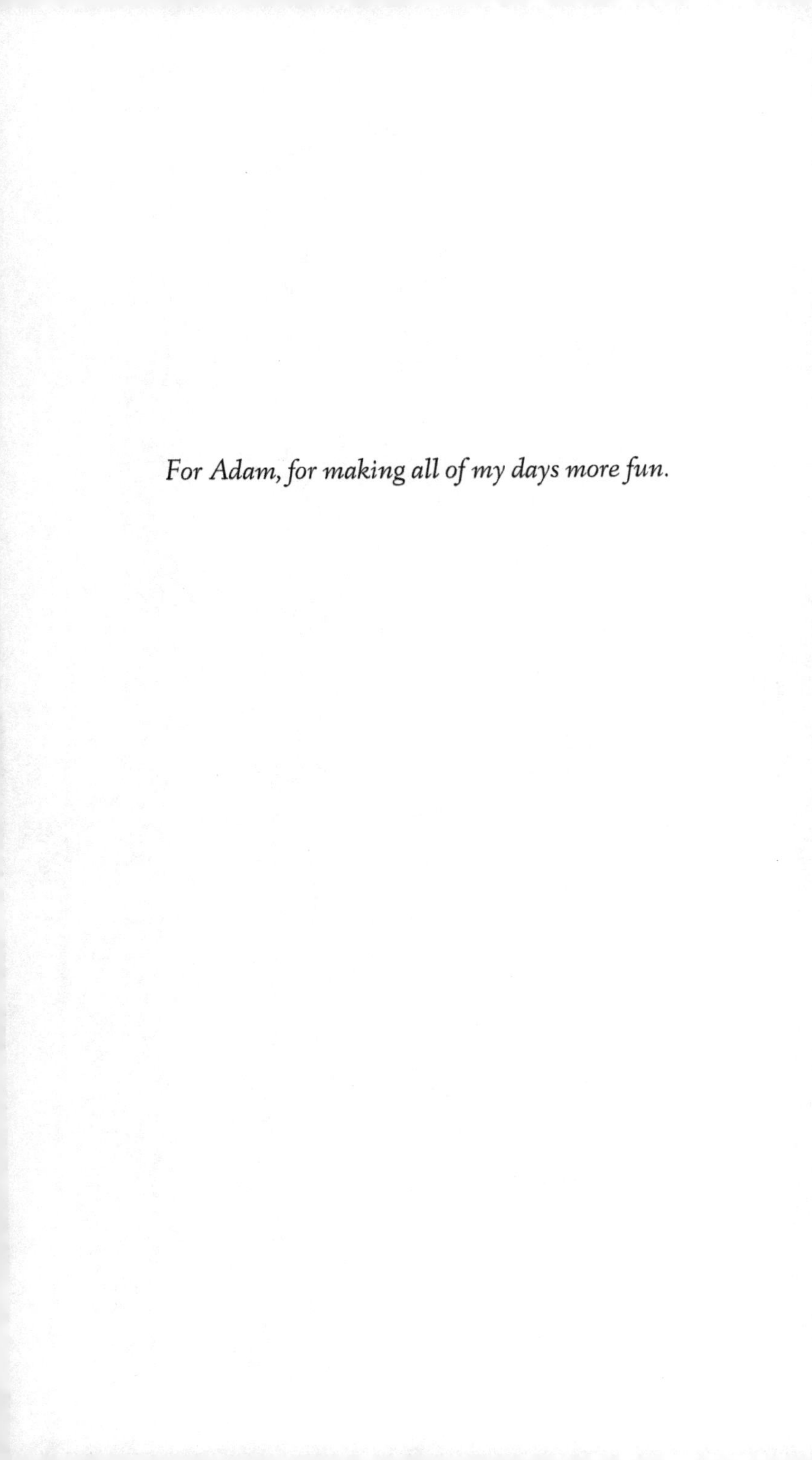

For Adam, for making all of my days more fun.

CONTENT NOTE

Fun Together is a romantic comedy in every way, and it's my singular goal in life to make you giggle and kick your feet while reading this book.

However, I did want to point out potential content that may be difficult for some readers. There is mention of parental abandonment in Chapters 39 and 46 if you would like to avoid this topic.

If you have any questions, please don't hesitate to reach out to me via the contact form on my website.

THAT EXTRA SHOT of espresso was a terrible idea.

But when boredom takes over, there's only one thing that'll make the afternoon go by, and it's coping via caffeine. It's one of the last Summer Fridays left this year, when the corporate overlords of Millionfish Enterprises allow us to leave at noon. I'm sure everyone is probably out enjoying the muggy August afternoon.

Everyone except me. It's 2:30 and a tumbleweed of sticky notes just rolled past my cubicle.

Before Alexis left for the day, she asked that I stay and wait for a package from Sharper Image to be delivered. Sometimes she sends me home with products to test for employee "gifts," and she didn't tell me what it is this time, but I'm sure it's some kind of productivity-boosting gadget she heard about on a podcast. Back in November, they gave each of us one of those light therapy lamps that are meant to simulate natural sunlight after employees mentioned they were struggling with coming and going to the office when it's dark.

I've become a seasoned pro at spending these Friday

afternoons alone at the office, so I've already done the usual things I do to pass the time at work (besides my actual job). I re-organized my inbox. I trimmed my split-ends with a dull pair of office scissors. I watched Damon Salvatore fancams for thirty minutes straight.

Enter the emergency iced latte that's now harassing my nervous system. I'm pretty sure I can hear the vibrations of the blood circulating through my body, rumbling deep in my ears. In my overactive imaginings, this sound is coming from the caffeine molecules whitewater rafting down my capillaries. They're even wearing little yellow helmets and calling out rowing commands to each other. I know this isn't how the body works, and I'm not completely sure what capillaries even are, but how cute would that be?

I should get up and walk around to dispel some of this misplaced energy. It's time for the final phase of killing time, anyway: call best friend to complain while roaming around the fluorescent-lit hallways.

"Why don't you just leave?" Rett asks. "Alexis will never know."

"Trust me. She'll detect my departure from the salon where she's getting her hair done right now." I wouldn't put it past her to install invisible trip wires at all the exits, with alarms set to wail if I try to escape early.

"At least you didn't drive her this time. I still can't believe you took her to that weird spa last month."

Alexis saw a viral video about a place that does LED light therapy facials, but they tie you down with lavender-infused straps and play wind chime simulations through a VR headset the entire time. She was so excited to book a coveted appointment, how could I refuse to take her? Her car was in the shop, and she needed to stimulate her collagen production.

"The waiting list for that place is insane. She would have had to wait five months if she missed it."

"That is not your problem. That woman stresses you out so much it sounds like you're having a hard time even talking right now."

I don't mention that this doesn't really have anything to do with an overbearing boss and is instead due to my bodily functions competing in rapid river races as we speak. I veer into the big conference room on this floor and sit down at the head of the giant glass-topped table.

"What are you doing this weekend?" she asks.

I turn my chair so I can look outside the floor-to-ceiling windows. Our office building is in a corporate park, so there's a small courtyard area with a few benches and tables set up between the buildings. I wonder who else is out there looking out the window waiting for their weekend to begin.

"Not sure. I'll probably work on the quarterly marketing deck." Alexis has a big presentation on Tuesday that she'll want to run through Monday afternoon. Sure, I could have been working on that for the past two hours instead of dicking around an empty office building, but I do my best work during a nice Sunday night panic. "Oh, and Andrew is coming by at some point to pick up his suitcase for his trip."

The sigh she heaves could be heard from Mars. "I don't even know where to begin."

Rett has been out of town for the last few weeks helping with family stuff going on back home. She's basically my only friend so I've definitely missed her, but I'm selfishly relieved she's not here right now. I have no doubt that the interrogation I'm about to endure is better experienced over the phone rather than in person. Suddenly, I long for a leisurely afternoon spent color-coding Alexis's calendar.

"Why do you still have your ex-boyfriend's suitcase?"

"Well, I haven't unpacked it yet." I spin around a few times in the chair before realizing that I probably shouldn't add motion sickness to the mix.

"Okay." She clears her throat. Haughtily, somehow. "Follow up question. Why have you still not unpacked a suitcase when you've been in your new place for six months now?"

"I just haven't gotten around to it." Busy doing other things, like staring off into the abyss and contemplating a bleach job or cutting my own bangs.

Another sigh. "What are you doing that's not work or ex-boyfriend related?"

My only response is a shrug that she can't even hear through the phone.

"Faye." I know this tone. It's what I imagine a lecture from a parent about to give me a very important life lesson feels like. I wouldn't know, considering I spent most of my childhood being raised by a grandfather whose idea of parenting was limited to allowing me to watch horror movies I was way too young for and telling me that he didn't care what I did as long as I didn't get arrested. This is hilarious to me now, because the most criminal-like activity I engaged in was stealing a pack of Skittles from the North Carolina Zoo's gift shop on a school field trip in second grade.

"I haven't said anything yet because I've been giving you time, but I'm worried. You spend over forty hours a week working for a company that barely knows you exist. You are allowed to do something else for the measly forty-eight we're given on the weekend. I'm starting to think you like having to work late every day just so you won't have to think about your life."

"Wow. Give it to me gently."

"And one more thing. How are you going to move on if you're still talking to Andrew all the time?"

Yep, I could be pondering the merits of green or yellow in the calendar for client meetings right now.

"First of all, that's harsh. The company knows I exist." I work for a pretty big software tech company and I'm not delusional enough to think the CEO knows who I am. But at least the marketing team knows who takes the lunch orders and makes sure the conference room is set up for our Monday Morning Mind Merge. Yes, it's really called that. "Second of all, we don't *talk* all the time. We *text* maybe once a week, twice at the mo—"

"That's so weird," she interrupts.

"We're still friends, though." Kind of. It's not like we have deep heart-to-hearts or anything. Yesterday I asked him when he'd like to come by and get the suitcase. Last week I had to let him know that I saw the lemon biscotti out at Trader Joe's. He loves those.

"How? Even if you want to be friends still, I figured he'd have more self-respect than that."

"Jesus, Rett!"

"Sorry." Her voice softens a little. "But it feels like a bit of a 'having your cake and eating it too' situation. I know you want to stay friends with him, but do you worry he might have an inkling of hope that you'll want to get back together?"

On some level I know she's right, because she's very succinctly verbalized what might be causing the incessant gnawing I've had in my gut ever since he asked me the single question that I had been mortifyingly unprepared to hear. The question that most people would be waiting in blissful anticipation to be asked after being in a committed relationship for six years. It's a burning guilt that no number of Tums will fix that propels me to keep reaching out to him, like I need some kind of reassurance that he doesn't hate me.

But what if he is holding out hope that we'll get back together? I don't want to be someone who keeps that hope alive, no matter how awful it feels to disappoint him. That damage has been done already.

I get up and draw a doodle of a big red heart on the dry erase board behind me. "Yeah, I don't want him to think that."

"It's good he's going out of town. In fact, I'd like to not so humbly suggest you *don't* reach out to him while he's gone."

I've practically been walking on eggshells in my own life since the breakup. It's especially hard because I'm the bad guy in this scenario. I've been nonstop plagued with visions of Andrew standing in front of a roaring fire, tossing our mementos into the flames, camera zooming in to show a slow motion shot of a single tear gliding down his angular cheek.

She continues, breaking me out of my reverie, "And you need to climb out of your hermit hole and have some fun."

"Hermit hole is a little dramatic." So what if I have a bundle of blankets and pillows arranged on my couch that I affectionately refer to as my nest? "It's called being cozy."

"Whatever. Want some help unpacking tonight?"

"Sure, are you coming back today? What about your grandma?"

"I'm almost to her house now. She's got something she wants to talk to me about before she *makes her exit*. I told her she's just moving to a nursing home, not stepping one foot in the grave."

It makes me think of my own grandpa still living at

home alone. I visit him every Sunday and he has a nurse that comes by a couple of times a week to check in on him, but I wonder how sustainable that really is. I've never even thought about broaching the subject of him moving out. It's got to be difficult to leave the place you've called home for over half your life.

"If there's anything I can do to help just let me know."

I hear a car door slam through the phone. "I'll text you when I'm on the way over tonight. Please go home now."

It's 3:45, so I think I can safely make my escape. "Yes, ma'am. Tell Grandma Minnie I said hello."

I make my way back to my desk, check my email one more time, and head for the elevator. After stepping inside, I lean my head against the back wall and close my eyes, letting the hum of the cables soothe me.

My phone buzzes with a text.

Andrew: Sorry I've had something come up tomorrow afternoon. Can I come by in the morning instead? Maybe around 10?

I don't answer yet, choosing to continue my elevator meditation session for another moment. I feel the first twinges of a caffeine-comedown headache and want nothing more than to crawl into my definitely-not-a-hermit-hole and take a nap.

A small part of me wonders if Rett is right, and I use work as an excuse to avoid thinking about things. Sure, I'm tired and want to go home, but what's waiting for me there? At least she's coming over later and I won't be spending yet another Friday night alone.

The elevator jerks to a stop on the third floor, or what everyone here refers to as "no man's land" because it's where the accounting and human resources offices are located. I've never had a reason to go there, but I've always imagined a completely windowless space with a single, flickering light bulb dangling from a wire in the ceiling. I bet some hapless accountant has spent the entire day sweating over the single spreadsheet keeping this company running, also not allowed to leave because of a boss that guilt trips them into working outside of usual hours.

I step aside to allow them to enter.

And when my brain catches up to my eyes and I see who is getting into the elevator with me, I become seriously worried that I might be hallucinating.

Because why else would Andrew's college roommate and oldest friend, who lives in New York City, be casually entering the elevator of the company I work for in Raleigh, North Carolina?

His golden-brown eyes light up, crinkling with a grin. "Faye, hey! I was wondering when I was going to run into you."

2

FAYE

I BLINK, thinking he'll go away. Nope, still there.

"Eli? What are you doing here?" And why was he clearly expecting to see me?

"I just started working here this week," he says, in a tone that insinuates I should know this bit of information. Why didn't Andrew mention that not only had Eli moved back, but that he got a job where I work? That news seems way more important than what's currently stocked at Trader Joe's.

"I had no idea. When did you get back?"

"About four months ago. Maybe five?" He reaches up to scratch the underside of his jaw. "Time flies."

The last time I saw him was graduation night five years ago. Andrew, Eli, and I had gone out to celebrate and I stayed over at their place like I always did after a night out. I woke up in the middle of the night dying of thirst and stumbled down the stairs to find Eli sitting alone at the kitchen table eating Oreos.

I wonder if he's also remembering that night spent talking about our plans. I was starting an internship at the very same company I'm currently working at. He was off to New York City the next day with no job or permanent place to live lined up. His leaving felt a little sudden, even for him, but I chalked it up to Eli being Eli.

He asked me if I would come visit him and I was taken aback, not because of the question, but the way he asked it. Like he was holding his breath for my answer. It hit me then, that he was really leaving. It wasn't some kind of whim, and these late-night conversations that had become commonplace for us were never going to happen again.

Then he hugged me in a way that felt like goodbye, and our three-person unit was down to two. We were moving on and transitioning into the next phase of our lives. Andrew visited him several times, but I never did. I'm not sure why, other than this instinctive need I have to protect myself from some future disappointment. Eventually, we'd probably all stop visiting each other altogether, so why prolong the inevitable?

"It really does," I say, looking up to watch the floor numbers tick down as we descend.

At first, I think he looks exactly the way he did that night. He still has the same tall, athletic build. The same light brown hair curling over his ears, like he's always in need of a haircut. An ease of movement, like there's no place he doesn't belong, whether he's leaned back in a rickety dining chair eating cookies at four a.m. or waltzing into this elevator and completely throwing everything off balance.

Do I look the same to him too? Or is he also realizing, like me, that so much has changed since then. I see now that the boyish charm he always had in college has been replaced with something more mature, almost rugged. His skin is tan—like he's spent the whole summer outside—

and what was formerly a baby face now has a bearded jawline.

And when he reaches up to adjust the strap of his backpack, I notice his right arm is sprinkled with tattoos down to his wrist. Those are new.

"How have you been?" he asks.

Now there's a loaded question. "I've been good. Are you happy to be back?"

"Yeah, it's good to be home. I've missed everyone." He smiles then, and as if recalling a fond memory. "I've missed the food, mostly. First thing I did when I landed was go to Bojangles for a chicken biscuit."

The elevator dings our arrival on the ground floor, and we step out to walk toward the exit to see the security guard, Tom, always sitting sentry at the building's entrance. Tom has been the security guard in this building for over twenty years. He has one of the most impressive thick white mustaches I've ever seen, and he eats a ham and cheese sandwich for lunch every single day. "Miss Faye, what are you still doing here?" he asks as we approach.

"You know the hustle never sleeps, Tom."

He gives a good-natured chuckle. "Well, since you are here, FedEx just dropped this off for Alexis. He holds up a small rectangular box. "Should I keep it locked up this weekend for her to collect on Monday?"

I can't help but smile at his diplomatic way of asking me to please take the cursed package off his hands, so he doesn't have to deal with Alexis on Monday.

"No, don't worry about it. She asked me to grab it for her."

He looks relieved as he hands it to me. "Have a good weekend and try to stay out of trouble."

I place the package in my tote bag. "You know I can't

make any promises." Tom and I do this same song and dance every week, where he makes a joke about being on my best behavior during the weekend, and then I come in on Monday morning and say I did something super wild like try a new coffee creamer. I notice that Eli is watching our exchange with amusement. "Tom, this is Eli."

Eli reaches out to shake his hand. "Nice to meet you, Tom. I hope you're able to get out of here soon, too?"

"I've got about an hour left on the clock. Then I'm going fishing with my granddaughter this evening."

"It's a perfect day for it. Where do you fish?" Eli asks.

I guess Eli's gift of gab is something that hasn't gone away. They go back and forth for a few minutes until I decide to put an end to the bonding session when they start talking about whether nightcrawlers or something called a Texas rig makes the best bait.

"Alright Tom, we'll let you back to it." I start walking to the exit door and Eli follows me. "See you on Monday!"

We walk in silence for a few seconds as we make our way across the breezeway that leads to the parking deck. The sun feels good on my skin, thawing me out after freezing inside all day.

Eli playfully elbows my arm. "What kind of trouble are you getting into this weekend?"

"Let's see. I'm currently in the middle of a very riveting *Survivor* re-watch."

We reach the parking deck's elevator and step inside. "What floor?" he asks.

I rack my brain trying to remember where I parked that morning. "Um, five."

He reaches across to press the five button, and the sleeve of his white T-shirt moves up so that I can see where his tattoos continue up his arm. There doesn't seem to be a particular pattern or theme to them, more like random images scattered across his skin in simple black line work. The look suits him, and I wonder if they extend up to his shoulders and back.

"What season are you on?"

"Hmm?" My face heats, realizing I've just been staring at his arm.

"Your re-watch. What season?"

"Oh. Twenty, I think?" Saying it out loud makes that too real. Twenty seasons of *Survivor* watched in a six-month period has surely landed me on some kind of watchlist.

He smiles down at me, bright and genuine, and things go topsy turvy. "That's a lot of tribal councils."

Eli has smiled at me countless times before and I never reacted this way. Between that, the tattoos, and this new facial hair he's sporting, I suddenly feel unsettled.

When did Eli get so hot?

I'm so relieved when we arrive on the fifth floor that I scramble out of the confined space so fast that my bag slides off my shoulder and hits the concrete with a thunk.

And then it begins to vibrate.

I look at Eli as if he can provide some explanation, but all he does is raise his eyebrows.

The bag starts to pulse, like a steady heartbeat beneath the canvas cloth. I rush to pick it up and feel that the vibrating is coming from Alexis's package.

"Have you ever shopped at a Sharper Image?" I ask him, trying to remember the last time I even saw a Sharper Image store. But I think I know what this is, and I really want to be wrong.

"Isn't it an electronics store?"

I hold it up and let the *bzzt-bzzt-bzzt* fill the silence.

He bounces his head to the beat. "It's got a nice rhythm to it."

We look at each other for a couple of seconds, both on the verge of laughter. "What do I do?"

"Let's open it," he says, like it's a treasure we've found that he can't wait to get his hands on.

A silver ring on his right index finger catches the afternoon light as I hand him the package. Our fingers briefly brush against each other before he pulls his keys out of his pocket and uses one of them to cut the tape along the top of the box.

"Please tell me it's not what I think it is," I say.

He peeks inside and says in an impersonation of a QVC salesperson, "Today, we've got a lovely personal massager for you folks at home." He places the box up on his palm, on full display, eyes glowing with playful mischief. "Boasting dual motors and a waterproof silicone design."

I snatch the box out of his hands. "Please stop." The packaging has a clear plastic front, so the vibrator is clearly visible, hot pink silicone resting snugly against its black velvet backing. "My boss really just gave me a vibrator to test over the weekend." I didn't realize I'd said this out loud until he laughs.

"What do you mean you're testing it?"

At this rate, I will never have to purchase blush ever again. "Sometimes she gets me to test things for company gift ideas."

"Is she planning on handing out vibrators like other companies give out water bottles? Will they be company branded?"

"This isn't funny." It's extremely funny, and I can't help

but smile up at him. "I should pretend I didn't get this, right?"

He tsks and shakes his head. "I don't know . . . Tom and I are witnesses."

"I know Tom would vouch for me. You wouldn't keep a secret for me?"

"Faye, you know I'd take a *bullet* for you." He pauses to allow the vibrator joke to land. "But as a new member of the HR team, I don't know if I could be involved in your deception." He grabs the box back out of my hand. "In fact, I think I need to take this as evidence."

I reach for the box, and he dangles it out of my reach. We're both fully cracking up now, because the way I'm flailing to take it back from him is hysterical. I stop trying when his words register. "Wait, you work in HR?" I don't see him as the kind of guy who enforces company policies. If anything, he'd break them.

"Well, technically recruiting, but it's under that umbrella."

I nod, impressed. "That's great." The box is still buzzing away in his hand. "We need to turn that thing off."

"Oh yeah, wouldn't want it to run out of juice. Although . . ." He stops to read the back of the box. "It does operate up to four hours on a full charge."

"Stop making me laugh about this. It's mortifying."

He hands it back to me. "Look on the bright side. Your weekend just got more interesting."

I wedge my fingers into the package and feel for the off switch, refusing to pull the vibrator out right here in front of him.

It's now that I notice the only car parked on this level is my lone Honda Accord, and his car is nowhere to be seen. "Where is your car?"

"Oh, I parked on the fourth floor."

"Why didn't you get off there?"

"Because we were talking." He says this as if it's obvious, like we were chatting about the most important thing in the world and not my pathetic weekend plans. "And then I couldn't leave a lady distressed over her vibrating box."

I bite my lip to keep him from getting the satisfaction of getting another laugh out of me. "It isn't *my* box."

"Mm-hmm." He walks with me to my car. "Why didn't you leave early like everyone else?"

I nod down to my bag in answer.

"That's why you were working so late?"

That, and avoiding my life, apparently. "It's complicated, but yes. What were you still doing here?"

"Trying to get a jump on things. Had a riveting orientation video about workplace safety to watch."

I open my car door and toss my tote bag into the passenger seat. "Just wait until you get to the data security portion."

He gives me another smile that makes my breathing do a weird thing that has nothing with coffee overconsumption, and everything to do with something surprising sparking in my chest. "It's good to see you, Faye." He turns to walk toward the stairs and waves to me. "Good luck on your testing!"

I wave back and get into my car, immediately resting my forehead against the steering wheel. My heart is pounding, mind racing to process the last thirty minutes. Was he just flirting with me? Was I flirting back? I attempt to ignore the butterflies emerging from dormancy in my stomach.

Really? You wake up for the first time in months, and it's for Andrew's best friend?

Almost as if I've summoned him with my traitorous thoughts, my phone buzzes with a text from Andrew.

I can come by later if that's too early.

In all the commotion, I forgot he had even texted me.

I text back, 10 works. See you then.

3

———

ELI

FRIDAY NIGHT DINNERS have been a staple in the Miller household ever since I can remember.

I've always looked forward to them, even though I did go through the usual teenage phase of wanting to be anywhere other than the dinner table on Friday night. It was the only thing my parents ever required of us. I could go hog wild, as long as I had my ass in the chair at seven o'clock every Friday.

Even though we've all aged out of the attendance requirement, we never really stopped having the dinners. There were several times I would FaceTime in back when I lived in New York.

Tonight, we have one addition joining us at the big round table in the dining room. My older brother Emmett's daughter, Florence, is sitting between me and my younger sister, Evie. She looks down at the green beans on her plate, scrunching up her freckled nose, like they're a big pile of worms she's being forced to eat.

"You've had green beans before, Flo," Emmett says. He looks tired. But then again, he always looks tired, like he came right out of the womb with his pointer finger and thumb pinched above his nose.

"But these look different," she says, poking at them with her fork. "They're not soft like those."

"Probably because they didn't come from a can," Evie chimes in. If Emmett always looks tired, Evie is whatever the exact opposite of that is. She's a walking ball of energy, like she was born with Red Bull running through her veins.

Emmett glowers at her. "Canned vegetables are better than no vegetables."

"You don't have to eat them, honey," my mom says from her spot at the head of the table.

"Two bites," Emmett says by way of attempting to compromise with a four-year-old.

She points to my plate. "Eli isn't eating any." She's right, I hate green beans. But I know when I need to take one for the team.

"I'm saving the best for last," I say, scooping some green beans onto my plate and stabbing my fork into one. I nod to her plate, encouraging her to do the same.

"Okay," she says solemnly, like eating this green bean is her final gauntlet.

We take a synchronized bite. I still hate them, but I pull a dramatic face. "Mmm, delicious."

She giggles and then takes another bite before looking at her dad like, *Are you happy now?*

Dinner continues as it always does. Evie and I dominate the conversation while Emmett frowns down at his phone. He's currently renovating a house, and he seems to be in a constant state of frustration about it. We've been calling it his "divorce project" since he bought the house shortly after separating from his wife, Mara, last year. No one, not even Mom, knows what happened with them. It's kind of an unspoken agreement we've all made with each other to not bring it up.

Dad methodically eats everything on his plate, one food at a time, while Mom nods and laughs along to whatever we want to talk about.

Evie has now steered us in the direction of my parents' upcoming thirtieth anniversary. "You have to have a party," she says.

"We'll have a party for our fortieth," my mom says, attempting to brush off the suggestion.

"What if you die before that?" Evie asks.

"What if we all die tomorrow?" my dad asks, saying the first words he's uttered in about fifteen minutes.

"No one is dying," my mom says, nodding deliberately toward Florence.

Emmett covers Flo's ears. "We're all technically dying."

Mom tosses her napkin onto the table. "Good Lord, enough about dying."

"So, it's settled then," Evie says with a pleased grin. "We'll have a party."

"I like parties," I say.

"I love parties!" Florence shouts.

I can see my mom's resistance waning in the face of her children and grandchild's enthusiasm. We're all well versed in how to wear Mom down. "Fine, but nothing crazy, Evie. Just a few people."

Evie picks up her phone. "Let's make a plan. First, we'll need a caterer."

"I can cook," Dad says, getting up to grab our empty plates to take into the kitchen.

"You can't cook for your own party," Evie objects.

"Let me rephrase. I don't want to pay for a caterer."

Evie shrugs. "Fine. No catering. Music?"

"How about that band that played at Emmett's high school reunion?" I ask. "What were they called again?"

Emmett leans back in his chair and crosses his arms over his chest. "Wet Blankets?"

"Or was it Dirty Blankets?"

"*Something* Blankets," Evie says, typing it in her phone.

"No bands!" Dad shouts over the running water in the kitchen sink.

"Why not? Live music is fun!" Evie yells back.

"It is fun," Mom says. "But having a party at all is going to cause noise and I don't want the whole neighborhood in a tizzy."

"By neighborhood, you mean Mrs. Webber?" I ask. Mrs. Webber is a woman in her mid-sixties who takes her position as a member of Poplar Street very seriously, like it's her sworn duty to protect her neighbors from the dangers of a single out-of-place blade of grass. "She'll be in bed watching *Forensic Files* by then, anyway."

"Still, I don't want a big thing," Mom says. "It's a lot to clean up and there's always someone who ends up drinking too much and causing a scene."

"We just won't invite Uncle Tony," Evie says.

"Isn't he in Arizona? Or was it Vegas?" I ask.

"He's in Myrtle Beach, working as an Elvis impersonator," Mom says, shaking her head.

"Too bad we can't have him perform at the party. I'm sure Mom and Dad would love to re-enact their first dance to Tony's rendition of 'Can't Help Falling in Love.'"

Evie springs up from the table and goes into the kitchen. "Someone will need to give a toast."

"Not it," Emmett replies.

She grabs a bottle of Gatorade from the fridge and gestures to me with it. "Eli can do it."

"This is your thing. Why can't you do it?"

"Because I don't want to," she says simply.

I turn to Emmett. "Why can't you do it?"

Evie says in a loud whisper, "Because of the d-i-v-o-r-c-e."

"Evie . . ." Mom chastises.

"What?" she asks innocently.

"Sorry," I say to Emmett. Why would he want to stand up in front of people talking about the beauty of love and marriage?

Emmett just shrugs and says, "I also have to fight the urge to puke every time I have to talk in front of a group of people."

I turn back to Evie. "Okay, he gets a pass. I still think you should do it."

"Tennis match for it?" she asks. "Whoever loses has to give a speech."

"That's not fair and you know it." She's really fucking good at tennis. And I haven't picked up a racket since high school, when I was on the tennis team for a season my junior year.

She shrugs. "Take it or leave it."

My odds aren't the best, but they aren't zero. "Okay, deal."

"Meet me at the park courts tomorrow morning at ten?"

"Sure, sounds good."

She grabs her keys from the kitchen island. "I'm out. Got to meet Daniel for a workout."

"Tell him I said hello," Mom says.

Emmett stretches with a yawn. "We need to head out too. Ready to go, Flo?"

"I guess." Flo reluctantly gets out of her chair. She's been quiet, but you can still feel her excitement from being around everyone. Even if she's not part of the conversation, she likes feeling included. I remember feeling that way too, as a kid.

Fifteen minutes of goodbyes and hugs ensue, until it's only me and my parents left at the table. I feel a little left out, with everyone else off to continue their Friday night plans, and here I am at home with Mom and Dad. Andrew is packing for his trip, so I'd be in his way if I went over there. I guess I can call some other friends to see what they're up to, but I don't really feel like doing that either.

I think about Faye and our conversation earlier, wondering if she's at home watching *Survivor* right now. I pick up my phone and scroll to her contact. It's been so long since we've texted, I don't know if she has the same number.

I thought about reaching out to her when I got the job at her company, but since we haven't seen each other in years and after the breakup with Andrew, it didn't seem like something I should do.

Part of me was hoping I'd see her again and would only feel excited to reconnect with an old friend. But when those elevator doors opened and I saw her big, blue eyes shocked to see me standing there, I felt the swirl in my stomach I'd been fearing.

Because the thing is, I've had a tiny crush on my best friend's girlfriend since I first met her. And as it turns out, five years apart didn't eradicate it as much as I hoped. She's still so pretty, with her curly dark hair wrangled into a bun on top of her head. The peachy-pink glow of her skin, and that little gap between her two front teeth you can only catch a glimpse of when she laughs.

I forgot how much I like to make her laugh.

I open a new text thread and my fingers float over the keys, trying to think of something to say to her.

What are you up to?

How's the show?

Used that vibrator yet?

I set my phone down on the table and move to get up. Maybe I'll go for a run or for a drive—anything other than thinking about Faye's shiny new toy.

"Just a second, Eli. There's something your dad and I want to talk to you about." Mom's voice is serious, and Mom isn't ever this serious about anything. I run through possible scenarios. Cancer. Death. Food Lion was out of stock on the slightly salted cashews she eats like candy.

"We are so proud of you for getting this new job at such a good company. You've not had an easy time of it lately, and we are so happy for you."

"Is there a 'but' coming next?" I ask.

"We just wanted to check in to see how the search for a place to live was going."

Oh yeah, did I mention that I'm twenty-seven years old, and have been living with my parents for the past five months? Or that I've been sleeping on a fold-out couch in the basement next to a treadmill that hasn't run in over a decade because my old bedroom has been converted into a home office?

"But you said I could stay however long I needed," I say.

Mom sighs, but she has a soft smile on her face. "You will always have a place to stay here. But we need our basement back."

Realistically, I know I can't live with my parents forever. And I do miss having my own space. The time has gotten away from me and I haven't gotten around to apartment hunting.

"But I just got a job this week. I can't pay for rent yet." I sound like a whiny, privileged asshole, and I know it. Asking

Mommy and Daddy for help they can barely afford to give. I depleted my entire savings after losing my job, before returning to North Carolina with my tail tucked between my legs and nothing but fifty dollars to my name.

"You don't have to move out tonight. I just want this to be something you're keeping top of mind if any opportunities come up." She places a reassuring hand on my forearm. "You're smart and resourceful. You will always have our support. But you need to try a little harder."

"She's right, son." Dad returns to the table and gives my hair a playful ruffle. "You'll figure something out. You always do."

4

———

FAYE

ONE GOOD THING about Friday nights is the undeniable bliss of having an entire weekend ahead of you to do whatever you want.

Tonight, it's just me, my couch, and the reliable presence of Jeff Probst in his little khaki shorts on my television. When I hear him say the words, "Last time on Survivor," all my worries fall away. I'm watching him explain the rules of tonight's immunity challenge when Rett breezes into my apartment in swirl of copper hair, black skirts, jangling bottles, and a waft of that mysterious perfume she refuses to name.

Her freckled face flushes from the effort it takes to haul her giant black leather purse onto my kitchen counter. She then proceeds to pull things out of the bag like some kind of fairy goth-mother. Two bottles of red wine, a bag of salt and vinegar chips, red nail polish, and what looks to be some sort of knife sheathed in leather. I don't even want to know *that's* intended purpose.

Then she takes out a lighter and a small bundle of herbs with tiny branches wrapped in twine.

"Are you about to sage my apartment?"

"Grandma told me to do this. She said it'll help rid your spirit of bad vibes or . . . w."

Honestly, I'll take all the help I can get. "Alright, go for it." I rummage around my kitchen drawers to find a corkscrew.

"I got the twist-top kind," Rett says over her shoulder. "Assumed you didn't have an opener."

"Hey, I could have one." I close the drawer I was sifting through. "Theoretically."

I grab a couple of jam jars I use for water glasses and pour some wine for us. I watch Rett glide along the perimeter of my apartment and hand her a glass.

"I've been thinking," she says after taking a sip.

I flop on the couch. "Oh no."

"It's time for you start dating again."

I turn the volume up. "Is it?"

She waves her hand in a circular motion over me. "This *ennui* thing you have going on is getting old."

"I don't have ennui."

"Really? Because it doesn't look like you've cleaned this place in weeks and earlier, I caught you staring off into the distance for five minutes, looking like you were in the middle of a factory reset."

I look around my apartment. The pile of cereal bowls stacked in the sink need to be washed. The dust bunnies that have become my quiet companions in the corner of the living room beneath my front window. Maybe I don't keep it as clean as I should, but it's not *that* bad. It's hard to feel motivated to pick up after myself when it's just me having to answer for my own filth. I wouldn't call it ennui, though. I think it's just that part of me wants to live amongst the rubble for a bit to make up for hurting Andrew the way I did.

"You're doing it again."

"It's just—I think I might be a terrible person. Do you think he hates me?" She doesn't have to ask who I'm talking about.

"Terrible people don't worry about being terrible people. Relationships end every day, and you did nothing wrong."

I appreciate the loyalty that only a best friend can provide, but she kind of has to say that, doesn't she?

"What if my decision was wrong?" There are worse things in life than marrying someone you aren't in love with anymore. Like death. Or being yelled at by a TSA agent.

"You and Andrew didn't have a real relationship. What you had was a safety net." She polishes off her wine and pours more into the jar. "Didn't you say y'all were barely having sex?"

I lay back on the couch and cover my face with a pillow, vowing to never tell her anything about my sex life, or lack thereof, ever again.

"Don't lie to yourself and pretend you had something with him that you didn't."

Is that what I'm doing—lying to myself? Hating to come home to this empty apartment, more specifically my empty bed, every night is not a lie. That's a truth I avoid by sleeping on the couch. If I pretend hard enough, the back cushions feel a lot like a supportive chest at my back. It's hard not to miss having someone there next to you, even if you don't touch anymore. Even if they roll over before you have a chance to touch them.

She continues, "He's off on his healing journey to do

drugs and go to sex clubs. Let him be free. And you're free, too!"

I sit back up and finish my glass. "You know Andrew would never go to sex clubs. He's way too worried about disease."

She refills my wine. "Still, you get what I'm saying. You deserve some good old-fashioned debauchery."

"I just don't know how."

"How to what?"

"How to be fun!" I point to a beautiful woman in a commercial for some kind of heart medication. She is laughing on top of a mountain with her hands placed triumphantly on her hips. "Like her. I bet she's fun."

"I'm sure she is, but so are you. You just need to get out of whatever funk you're in right now."

"And you think that starts with dating someone new?"

"Among other things," she says.

"What other things?"

"I see it kind of like this." She goes over to her bag and pulls out a notebook and pen. I watch her draw a pyramid divided into five sections. She writes the word *social* in one of the sections.

"Are you doing like a hierarchy of needs thing?" I briefly majored in psychology in college, so this is something I vaguely remember.

"Exactly. Except more like a *Hierarchy of Fun*. This can be your guide." She fills in the rest of the sections. I see the words *sex* and *career* and I'm already regretting asking for Rett's help with this. She's drunk on more than the bottle of wine we've downed. I've made her way too powerful.

"Does that say 'environmental?' What does that even mean?"

"It means your apartment. Your car. It means you need

to stop living like you don't understand the concept of a nightstand." She holds her arms out wide. "You have your own place, which is fucking amazing. You can do whatever you want with it."

She writes *hobby*, and I really start to squirm.

"It seems like a lot, though."

"This is just my suggestion. You can change these if you want, but I think you should try to do *something* to get out of your comfort zone a little."

I look at the pyramid, and part of me knows she's right. I can't wallow forever. "Let's say I agree, where do I begin?"

"I think you should start with this one." She points to the sex section. "Let's go out next weekend."

I groan.

"It's that, or I make you join a dating app."

"You wouldn't."

"You need to stop punishing yourself and go home with a guy with stick-and-poke tattoos who you meet in a shitty bar with cheap well drinks and a questionable sanitation score."

"And that's fun?"

"If they know what they're doing, it is."

Drunken sex with a stranger you meet in a bar does seem like a post-breakup rite of passage, but how cliché can I be? I haven't slept with anyone new in six years. Am I really going to waltz into a bar with the sole purpose of finding someone to go home with?

"I feel like I'm too old for that kind of thing."

"You're twenty-six, not ninety."

"Okay, but you'll have to help me. I haven't had to make come-hither eyes at someone from across the bar since . . . well, ever."

I met Andrew when I was twenty years old. He was my

first real relationship, unless you count my two-month-long courtship with Tanner Davis in tenth grade. I have no idea how to even begin seducing someone.

"Saying 'come-hither eyes' does make you sound elderly."

"Fine, we'll go out next weekend. But I'm making no promises."

"I told Minnie about your breakup, and she said that you've already been in—" She holds up air quotes. "—good vibration with another man." She shakes her head. "Although, she told me I was going to marry my high school boyfriend's older brother, which is *definitely* not happening, so take it for what it's worth."

Her Grandma Minnie's mild clairvoyance has always been one of those things Rett and I joke about—but nine times out of ten, she's been spot on. Last year, she told Rett that she was going to come into an influx of cash, and two weeks later, Rett found an old wallet that had a twenty-dollar bill in it.

She opens the bag of chips and grabs a handful. "Had any *good vibrations* with anyone lately?"

My eyes automatically move to my tote bag hanging on the back of a dining chair. I can almost see the vibrator through the package in glowing neon x-ray vision. "Well, technically. . ."

She sits up. "Okay. Spill."

I tell her about my conversation with Eli after running into him in the elevator. And then about the whole vibrator situation.

"You've been sitting on this information all night?"

I swat her away. "It's not really anything. He's Andrew's best friend."

"Is he hot?"

"He's Andrew's best friend," I repeat.

"So, he is hot."

I roll my eyes and refuse to neither confirm nor deny Eli's attractiveness. I've been willing my own brain to stop thinking about him since I drove home earlier.

"Maybe Minnie's right. Seems like you've been given a gift from the fun gods." She wiggles her eyebrows suggestively. "Why squander their blessing?"

———

I'VE BEEN HAVING a face-off with the vibrator on my coffee table since Rett left.

What could it hurt, really? Sure, it was given to me by my boss, but I'm still not convinced it wasn't all some big mistake. But what if Alexis asks me to report on it on Monday?

I try to get my wine-fogged brain to rationalize the wild idea that Alexis will ask me to give her my opinion on how this product might be good for our employees. I need to be able to be honest about its capabilities, right?

I tear it from the plastic packaging and hold it in my hand. It looks a little bigger than it did before when Eli was holding it. This is easily the nicest one I've ever owned. My last one sputtered out its last dying buzz over a year ago.

I lay back on my couch, settling a pillow comfortably behind my back. Phone in one hand and vibrator in the other, I pull up Pornhub. An alert pops up asking for my name and address because of some law that requires that information to enter the site.

There's no way I'm putting my information in there, so I decide to do this the old-fashioned way. Surely, I can conjure up a good fantasy all on my own.

I close my eyes and try to think of something that turns me on. But my mind is blank, nothing but pure static.

Come on, Faye.

What do I like? Why is my brain not allowing this to happen easily? My god, I've had so much wine, this should be easy.

Oh, hands! I really like hands.

But then all I manage to come up with are some detached hands floating in a blank space. That's horrifying.

The hands need to be connected to a body. But who? I need a fantasy man.

I settle into the cushions as I expand the image, adding a nice pair of forearms with a sprinkling of hair. This fantasy man is pretty tall, probably at least six feet, and when I reach up to touch his shoulders, I discover that they are wide and strong. I move my hands up to his neck and can feel his pulse beneath my fingertips.

"Can I touch you?" he asks. Nice voice. The kind of voice you'd want giving you directions on Google maps, or to reading you a bedtime story. It's warm, a little raspy, and vaguely familiar.

Since things are getting good now, I place the vibrator against me and put it on the lowest setting.

"Yes," I whisper, adding a background to the fantasy. Looks like I've placed us in . . . a barn? There's hay beneath us, but it isn't itchy at all. It's soft as linen, smelling of lavender and sunshine. I look down to see I'm wearing a purple plaid dress with ruffled sleeves.

He lifts the hem of my dress and runs his hand up my calf to the back of my thigh. His palms are rough and calloused, and I like the sensation of them brushing up against my soft skin. My skin is always soft here in this fantasy land. I wake up every morning glowing, radiant, and velvety smooth.

"You're so soft," he says. "But I bet you never even have to moisturize."

"I do wear lotion," I tell him. "But it's from our magical goats with magical goat milk that leaves your skin glowing for years on end."

He moves his hand up higher. "Can I touch you here?" he asks.

"Yes," I say, moving the vibrator up a level.

His fingers are deft, and I imagine he is one of those men who can effortlessly hop a fence or chop wood blindfolded. "I could touch you for hours," he whispers into my ear.

I hear a rooster crow in the distance. "We have to leave soon," I say. "No one can catch us up here."

"A man can dream," he says, adjusting the pressure of his fingers and leaning down to kiss my neck.

"I'm so close," I moan.

"You can do this, you've got it," he encourages.

I come with a gasp as I finally look to see the face of this fantasy wild west man I've created.

And there are Eli's pretty, smiling eyes looking down at me.

5

———

FAYE

MY ALARM WAKES me up at 9:30, and in those first few moments of being awake I feel that deep sense of regret that can only be felt when you're half asleep and questioning the life choices you made the night before. The wine, the fun list, the accidental Eli fantasy.

Oh, and telling Andrew that of course ten o'clock on a Saturday morning is a perfectly fine time to swing by.

I force myself to sit up, and then force myself to change clothes and put on a little makeup before he arrives. I'm nervous about seeing him again, and what memories might stir up because of it.

Andrew and I met our junior year in an Intro to Statistics class.

It was the first day of spring semester and I was uncharacteristically late—thanks to covering someone's shift at my hostess job the night before. I barely woke up in time to throw on a pair of sweatpants and rush out the door.

I spotted a single seat available on the front row of the auditorium, which I hated because I preferred to sit in the middle with a full wall of students surrounding me. After wrangling out of my puffy winter coat while questioning my sanity for signing up for an eight a.m. class, I wedged myself in between a pale, dark-haired guy with glasses and a middle-aged woman knitting a chunky green scarf.

I took out my notebook and wrote the date at the top of the page.

"Do you need to borrow a pencil?"

It was the glasses guy.

"I'm sorry?"

He nodded toward the ballpoint pen poised in my hand and held his own pencil up in the air. It was a fancy silver mechanical one that probably cost more than I made in tips the night before. "Pretty brave to use a pen in this class."

"Why do you say that?" I wasn't too concerned because the first day of class was always general stuff, and I was lucky I had anything to write with at all. Did he think we were going to be diving into equations right away?

"What if you make a mistake?"

That was why I hated sitting in the front, because you were inevitably next to someone who probably *chose* to sit in the front and had weirdly strong opinions on the right and wrong writing implements to use. I wanted to insinuate that it wasn't any of his business what I was writing with, but there wasn't any malice coming from his heavily-browed, dark eyes. I couldn't see much emotion at all, as if he were just stating a known fact that using a pen in a Stats class was entirely incorrect.

"I'll just have to be extra careful, I guess."

He nodded at this and turned back to look at his own notebook, almost like he regretted saying anything about it. I found myself noticing that he was attractive in the way a guy can be when they're sort of nerdy and likely missed the memo that they're actually hot.

At the end of class, he set his pencil down on top of my desk. "Just in case you want to be less careful," he said, with a ghost of a smile. I'd later learn that this barely-there quirk of his lips was the equivalent to him doing a mating dance right there in SAS Hall.

We sat together the rest of the semester, and I didn't even care that we were so close to the front that I could see the spit flying from the professor's mouth as he droned on about standard deviation.

Andrew asked me out on our first date the day after finals. I thought he'd never do it.

He asked me to marry him six years later. I wished he'd never done that.

He hasn't seen my new place yet, and knowing he'll be here any minute, I do a quick scan of the space. The apartments were built in the 1930s, with all the quirks that come with a building that's seen so many years. The windows are painted shut, but they have their original wavy glass. None of the kitchen cabinets close all the way. And the thing that made me fall in love as soon as I saw it, the bathroom tile is seafoam green.

This morning, with Rett's words echoing in my head about my messy apartment, I spent some time cleaning up. But there are some things I can't pick up because there's nowhere for them to go. I have a huge stack of moving boxes still sitting in my entry way that he'll for sure notice. We got some of them from the liquor store, so I like to pretend I'm gearing up for a party and not putting off the prospect of unpacking stuff I don't have a place for yet.

While I wait for him, I peek inside the Jim Beam box on top of the stack. I see a sweatshirt I bought on a trip we took to Colorado a couple of years ago, a half-empty bottle of perfume, an old eyeshadow palette, and a phone charger.

The eyeshadow must have cracked because there's shimmery bronze powder all over everything.

A knock at the door interrupts my rummaging.

For some reason, I have a thought that I won't recognize him when I see him. Maybe because eight months has felt like years. But when he steps inside, I see that he's the same Andrew. He's the poster boy for perfect posture and practiced movements. I've never seen the man with so much as a thread hanging from his shirtsleeve.

"Hey," he says, shutting the door behind him.

"Hey! How are you?" This comes out way too bright because I'm so nervous.

"I'm good." He puts his hands in his pockets and rocks back on his heels. "How was your week?"

"It was okay. Nothing crazy."

He looks around and I watch his eyes snag on all the things I love about the only place I've ever been able to call my own. The quirks that I know he dislikes on sight because his interior design tastes are more "Scandinavian minimalism" and less, "Did that come from the set of *The Twilight Zone*?"

Somewhere in these unpacked boxes is a framed poster of a lipstick ad from the 1960s that I never had a spot for in his apartment.

"I could always see you living somewhere that might be haunted," he jokes with his polite smile. While he may not like something, he'd never let you know it.

I could take offense at this comment, and to some it might come across as judgmental. But he doesn't mean any offense. I play if off with a joke, too. "Yeah, the rental agreement had a paranormal activity clause."

At this, he meets my eyes for the first time since setting foot inside and things almost feel normal again. But that gaze, hard as granite, has always been a barrier to his thoughts. You'll get glimpses here and there, though. Like, when you say something interesting, he squints just a little. When he's annoyed, he blinks super slow.

I do know what I'm thinking, seeing him again, even if the conversation feels forced. And I can't help but want him to feel it too, as unfair as it is for me to wish for it. We were a part of each other's lives for so long, and even though I broke his heart, I have a selfish thought.

I miss my friend, and I want him to miss me too. But can I really ask for that?

He's the first to look away as a silence descends that I'm able to stand for about three seconds. "So how is work?" I ask.

He adjusts his glasses. "Good, I got a promotion last month. It's more responsibility, but it's going well so far." I don't think I ever fully grasped what he does for a living, but he's some type of risk assessment analyst for the city.

"Wow, that's great. I know you were looking for something higher-level."

He nods his head, chewing on the inside of his cheek. That's another Andrew tell. He's also nervous. "How's work going for you? Alexis still as great as ever?"

"She might be worse," I say, willing myself not to look over at the couch where I shoved the vibrator under a couch cushion. I really don't want to bring any thoughts of Eli up while I'm standing in front of Andrew, but I can't help but be curious as to why he didn't tell me Eli was back. "Speaking of work, I saw Eli at the office yesterday. I had no idea he was back and working there now."

"Didn't I tell you?"

I shake my head.

"Sorry, I thought I mentioned it." Did he purposely not

mention it? Have I been forcing this "staying friends" thing? Come to think of it, I am always the one to text him first. He always texts back, but am I bothering him?

"Have you two hung out a lot since he's been back?"

He shrugs. "A few times. We both have a lot going on and I've been gearing up for my trip."

"Speaking of,"—I roll his suitcase around from behind my couch—"it's all yours."

"Thanks. Sorry if you were still needing it."

"No, I'm sorry. I should have gotten it back to you months ago."

As he pulls it closer to him, I notice that it still has the airline tag from a trip we took to Chicago last March because the flight was so cheap. A trip that ended with us not being an "us" anymore.

Pretty sure he notices it, too.

"You have any plans coming up or been anywhere recently?" he asks, chewing some more on his cheek. He's going to break skin soon. I can't tell if he's curious or just trying to make small talk.

"No. Not really." I cross my arms, wishing I could burrow inside that glitter-covered sweatshirt right now. It's all catching up to me now.

Why *don't* I have plans?

Why am I *not* having fun?

Why *couldn't* I just say yes?

I lied about never being able to get a read on those mysterious eyes of his. The night I told him I wasn't going to marry him, I watched them fill with the dawning realization that he'd done something he avoided at all costs. Something so deeply instilled in him that he couldn't help but worry about keeping my statistics notes pristine the first day I met him.

He'd made a mistake.

It wasn't the first time I'd felt like a mistake to someone, but I needed it to be my last.

"Well. . ." He rolls the suitcase back and forth a few times. "I should probably get going."

I wonder if he resents me. If, when he sees my texts appear on his phone with some stupid reference to our shared past, he wishes I'd just leave him alone. Was he driving over here this morning telling himself this is the last thing he must do, the last item he needs to check off before he can be done with me?

I spent most of my late teen years watching my mom's exes leave with the last of their belongings. She'd sigh and light her cigarette, not even bothering to watch them pull out of the driveway. I'd always watch them, though. And even then, I kind of understood they were better off leaving.

I need to let him go.

I give him a strained smile. "Have fun in Amsterdam and be sure to eat a stroopwafel for me."

He nods. "I will." And with an awkward wave, he's gone.

The click of the lock echoes through my apartment. Now the boxes filling my hallway feel less like a task I've been too lazy to complete and more like a reminder of the self-imposed pause I've put on my life.

Captain Morgan mocks me from his perch, so sure of himself and his place. *You'll never unpack me*, he sneers and gestures to my pathetic lack of furniture. *You have no storage options.*

I turn him around so he's facing the wall.

I dig through the Grey Goose box until I find the hammer and nails my grandpa gave me when I first moved to Raleigh for school.

"Make sure you find a stud first," he'd said. "You don't want a paintin' to come crashing down on your head in the middle of the night. See this knot?" He pointed to a spot just above his brow. "The dogs decided to play poker on my forehead."

I smile at the memory.

I find the lipstick ad in another box and hang it prominently by the front door. Now, this blonde model with beehive hair and bubblegum pink lips will greet me every day when I get home. She looks good, like she belongs there.

And I belong here, too.

6

———

ELI

"IT'S A BEAUTIFUL MORNING."

"Perfect conditions for me to wipe the court with you," Evie says, plucking the strings of her tennis racket.

I do a few stretches and warm up exercises in an effort to make this as painless as possible. "That's a little brutal for ten o'clock in the morning, even for you. This is already unfair enough."

"You didn't have to agree to this."

"Is it true you made your own teammate cry?" She played on the club tennis team at UNC, and I'd never tell her, but I'm a little scared I'll be reduced to tears after this.

She tightens her ponytail and adjusts her visor. "How about we also make a bet on whether I can make *you* cry today, old man?"

"I'm only four years older than you," I point out.

She serves the ball, and it flies past my face before I even register that she's hit it.

"Could've fooled me. You've got the reflexes of a slug."

I bounce up and down on the balls of my feet. "Maybe if you'd give me some time to warm up first."

I'm pretty sure I hear her mutter the words, "an elderly slug," under her breath. To be fair, when I hit the ball back to her, I think my shoulder joint actually creaks.

"I thought you were supposed to be the athletic one in the family," she says as she serves again, only slightly less aggressively.

I still don't hit it.

It stings a little, even though I know she's joking. Because she's right. I played every sport I possibly could growing up and it always came easily to me. I just haven't felt like doing much since I've been back. Although, I think I accidentally joined a local rec softball league last week when I was walking our dog Pebbles at the park. I saw some people playing, started talking to the guy on the first base, and suddenly I'm on the team.

"I like to play sports because they're fun, not because I want to see if I can give my opponent irreparable emotional trauma."

She rolls her eyes and serves an ace. "Why can't you do both?"

We play a couple of sets, and I somehow manage to win a few games, which momentarily gets my hopes up. Turns out, she was only taking pity on me, and it wasn't anything to do with my own stroke of luck.

Eventually, she serves for match point and when I barely shuffle over to make contact with the ball it bounces off the side of my racket into the bushes behind the fence.

"That's one way to put yourself out of your misery," she says.

"You're a humble winner, as always," I say as I walk over to the bushes where the ball landed. I see that I'm not the only one who's met this fate. "It's like a tennis ball burial ground over here. How do I know which one is yours?"

"It has my initials on it." Of course it does, because Evie would never want to risk someone else taking her stuff.

"Do you really need this tennis ball?" I ask, narrowly avoiding taking a branch to the eye as I dig around.

"Tennis balls don't grow on trees. I'm a poor college grad, remember?"

After digging around for a few seconds, I finally spot it and toss it to her.

"This isn't mine," she sniffs.

"It says 'E.M.' on it."

"Must be someone else with my initials." She throws it back to me. "Check again."

"You better not be fucking with me," I shout over my shoulder as I go back to sift through the balls again.

She doesn't answer and when I look over, I see that she's sitting down on the court next to a jug of orange juice and a thermos.

"What are you doing?"

She pours a splash of orange juice into the thermos. "You were taking so long I decided to go ahead and make refreshments."

"I really hate you sometimes." I hold up the ball I found initially. "This is your ball, isn't it?"

"You should learn not to be so gullible."

"You should learn not to be the worst."

She takes a couple of red solo cups out of her bag. "Want a mimosa?"

I sit down to join her, taking the cup from her hand. "All's forgiven if you have food in that bag, too."

She looks at me like she's wondering how I could doubt her, and hands me a sausage biscuit. "You find a place to live yet?"

"I just found out last night that I have to move out. And

how do you even know about them talking to me about that?"

"Mom told me. And I thought that would have been obvious since you moved back. Were you going to live in our parents' basement forever?"

"No, it's just not that easy. And it's fucking expensive. Maybe once I have a few paychecks under my belt."

"How is the new job going, by the way?"

"Good so far. You know how the first week is, just meeting everyone and doing orientation stuff."

"You're doing recruiting still?"

"Yeah, basically just phone screening job applicants and setting them up with interviews if I think they're a good fit."

"So, you get to talk all day? You probably love that."

Theoretically, I should love that. But calling people and going through the motions of asking the same questions over and over gets old. And I hate sitting at a desk for hours. But I'm anxious to do well in this role after losing my last job. I can't let myself fall into the bad habits I did before. Apparently, companies don't like it when you show up to work late multiple times a week, and also fail to meet any of your performance goals. "Everyone has been pretty cool so far. Someone I know from college works there, too."

"Oh yeah?"

"Andrew's girlfr—ex-girlfriend." I'm still working through the fact that they aren't together anymore. The only thing Andrew really told me about their breakup was that it just didn't work out. Leave it to him to be extremely vague and pragmatic about something that would devastate most people.

She visibly perks up. "Andrew's single? Interesting."

"Don't even start," I warn her. Ever since Andrew came

along with us on a family beach trip ten years ago, Evie has had heart eyes for him. If a fourteen-year-old Evie terrified him as much as she did, I don't even want to know what twenty-three-year-old Evie would do to him.

She shrugs and refills our cups. "Okay, let's talk about the party."

"Why is this party such a big deal to you?"

Evie has always loved a project, but she seems to be a little *too* into this party for some reason.

"It just is. Last week I was going through old photo albums and found a picture taken of them after dad proposed. I think we should re-enact that moment by having a sunset ceremony that you'll officiate just as the sun makes its descent below the horizon. Then, we'll have a—"

"Officiating? I thought I just had to give a toast."

"Yeah, basically the same thing." She brushes me off. "I'm working on the final guest list. I'm assuming you won't be bringing anyone?"

"Why do you assume that?"

"Name one time you've been serious enough with someone to bring them home to meet the family."

"What about Hannah? We were together for six months." I didn't bring her home to meet the family because . . . well, she might have a point there.

"Six months is nothing."

"Half a year is not nothing." It was long enough for it to sting when I saw her cuddled up to another guy at our favorite cocktail spot. I stood there in shock watching them before they noticed me. He was twirling his hand in her hair mindlessly, like it was something they did every day.

After I confronted her, she said she was sorry, but she'd been trying to find a way to end things with me because she didn't think I was serious about her. Or about anything, really.

"You have no goals," she'd said. "I need to be with someone who is driven and wants the same things I do."

"I have goals," I protested. "I want the things you want."

She just shook her head as if she pitied me. "You have a terrible way of showing it then."

It felt awful that she saw me that way, but did I do anything to disprove what she said? I don't want to be the kind of guy who comes across that way to the person he's with.

Maybe I should start dating seriously again. I had a brief fling with someone right when I got back, but it's been months since I've gone on a date.

The thought of meeting someone new used to excite me. I'd live for those initial moments of learning and discovering, finding what they like or don't. But I can't help but feel a little exhausted at the prospect of another night spent swiping left or right, coming up with a clever opening line. If I meet someone now, I want it to be organic. Two hands accidentally brushing against each other as we both reach for the same avocado at the grocery store.

Or as I'm handed a vibrating box.

I wonder if Faye is single.

It's a thought I've had several times since I saw her yesterday. A thought I need to stop having. I think I'd rather get back on Hinge than get back to nurturing a crush on someone I shouldn't.

"Well, give me a plus one. I'm bringing someone."

Surely, I can find someone that I'd like to bring to the party in the next month.

She raises her eyebrows. "Okay. What about Andrew?"

"What about him?"

"You think he would come? I'd love to catch up with him."

"Aren't you already dating someone? Dylan? David?"

"You know his name is Daniel," she says, making herself another mimosa. "We broke up last night." She says this so casually that it takes me a second to register it.

"Fuck, Eves. I'm so sorry. Are you okay?"

She sniffs. "I'm fine." She puts on a tough face, but she was with him for a few years so there's no way she feels as casual about it as she sounds.

"Do you want to talk about it?"

She balls up the biscuit wrapper and shoves it in the paper bag. "Let's see. Do you want to hear about how I saw him texting another girl while we were at the gym last night? Or how he had the nerve to break up with me because he said I'm *just not meeting him where he's at right now?*"

"What does that even mean?"

"Fuck if I know."

"I'm sorry. Maybe it's for the best, though."

"Of course it's for the best. But I should have been the one to end things with him. The fucking nerve of this guy."

I want to laugh, but am smart enough to hold it in, at her only being upset about the breakup because she wasn't in control of it.

At least that explains her above-average aggression during the tennis game.

"So, back to the party. I'll send Andrew an invite just in case."

"I think he'll still be on his trip." Which reminds me, I'm supposed to meet him in—"What time is it?"

She checks her phone. "Noon. Why?"

I hop up to grab my stuff. "I was supposed to be at

Andrew's place thirty minutes ago." I'm taking care of his plants while he's gone, and he wants to walk me through everything I need to do to keep them alive.

"Tell him I'll send him an invite just in case!" Evie shouts as I jog to my car.

7
———

ELI

"THIS IS A TYPE OF SUCCULENT. You shouldn't need to water it too much, if at all." Andrew nods to the binder in my hands. "You can reference page 15a for more details."

I open the binder that contains instructions for each plant he owns. It includes diagrams, watering schedules, and even a frequently asked questions section for each plant. "15a. Got it."

He moves the pot about a millimeter to the left and I start to sweat. Andrew cares about his plants like they're his own flesh and blood. I know if I so much as let a single dead leaf appear on one of them that I might not only lose his friendship, but maybe my own life.

This binder needs to become my Bible, basically.

"If you have any questions, just message me. I've got international texting."

"We should be fine," I say, pretending to hug the giant—I flip through the binder to find which plant this is—fiddle leaf fig. I see the word *temperamental* bolded in red and almost regret offering to do this. But it will be fine. All part of the new responsible me. I've turned over a new leaf. Literally.

Andrew finishes his plant tour, and we make our way to his kitchen.

"I like your place," I tell him. His apartment is one of those buildings that used to be a factory or something, so it has brick walls and tall ceilings with giant windows. "I bet your plants love all this natural light."

It's a real grown-up apartment, nothing like the places I've lived in the past few years. I guess this is the kind of place you can live when you have your shit together.

"Thanks. I like it here." He opens the fridge and takes out a jug of almond milk and pours some into a glass. "Feel free to eat or drink whatever is in here whenever you stop by."

I take a seat at one of the stools by his kitchen counter. "When you do you get back?"

I've sort of been hoping he'd ask if I wanted to stay here while he's gone. That would temporarily solve my current problem of finding a place to live. It feels like too much to ask, and I'd just be freeloading on someone else again.

He takes a tub of protein powder out of a cabinet and spoons some into the cup. "About a month-ish."

I've known Andrew for ten years now and if there's one thing I know for a fact it's that he doesn't ever put "ish" at the end of anything.

Andrew and I met in eleventh grade, when I convinced a group of people to climb onto the roof of our high school one night after basketball practice. He was new on the team, having just moved to Raleigh that school year. There was a formality to him that was so out of place in a sixteen-year-old that I think a lot of the guys on the team didn't really know what to do with him. He spent the entire first practice worrying over which play was which and where he was supposed to be on the court. I later found out that he hated playing, but his dad made him do it.

I remember thinking he seemed nice enough and always welcomed the challenge of corrupting someone like him in a harmless way. In a way that seemed harmless to me, anyway. I had a fearlessness that came with being young and stupid, operating under the belief that nothing bad could ever happen to me. I was always getting into some kind of trouble. Nothing major, but little infractions enough to annoy my parents, but not enough that I'd land myself in a serious situation.

Case in point, I had the bright idea that we should all climb onto the roof of our school. Why? Because, why not? I told him it was all part of the basketball team's initiation.

"What if we get caught?" Andrew asked, stiffly clinging to the bottom of the ladder behind the utility room at the back of the school.

"We won't," I reassured him.

"I can't believe I'm doing this," he said before slowly following me up.

He echoes those words, standing frozen in the middle of his kitchen.

"Why do you look like you're about to throw up that protein shake?"

He looks down at the drink in his hand, like he forgot he'd even made it. "Just nervous about my trip."

"You seemed excited before. Why are you so nervous?" He's always been so hyper-focused on work and moving up the corporate ladder that he's probably on edge because he doesn't know how to take a vacation.

"Yeah, but something's changed," he mumbles.

"What do you mean?"

He sighs and looks out the window above his sink. "You'll question my sanity if I tell you."

I lean forward, eager now to hear what's going on. "Well now you have to tell me."

"I don't want to be late for my flight," he says as he dumps the protein shake down the drain.

I check the time on my phone. "Your flight isn't for five hours. What's going on?"

"I'm meeting someone."

"In Amsterdam?"

He nods his head. "Yeah, she's from a town just outside of there."

"Who is *she*?" This is even more exciting than I thought. A secret girlfriend. I didn't know he had it him.

"Her name is Emma."

"How did you meet her?"

He shakes his head and adjusts his glasses. "You're going to laugh."

"Let me guess. You accidentally ordered the wrong tulip bulbs, and she was the customer service rep you reached out to online, but now you're scared because you're going to get there and find out you've fallen in love with a chat bot."

"How do you come up with this stuff? No, I didn't fall in love with a chat bot." He taps his fingertips on the countertop. "We met on the houseplants subreddit."

"Wooing the ladies with your knowledge of rare moss varieties."

He snorts. "Something like that."

"I think that's cool. Getting back on the horse. Taking

the bull by the horns. Other animal-related motivational stuff."

"Please, shut up."

"Do you know what she looks like?" Not that looks are super important, but I'm sort of curious about this woman because since I've known him he's only ever dated Faye. I wonder if she looks like Faye.

"Yeah, we've FaceTimed each other."

"So, she's pretty?"

"Yes, she's pretty," he says, exasperated.

"And she has a good personality?"

"Yes, she's really smart and we have a lot in common."

"So, if she's pretty and cool, then why are you acting like you're being forced to visit her against your will?"

"Because I feel ridiculous. Flying to a foreign country for someone I've only been talking to for a few months."

"I think it sounds romantic, like something out of a movie." Maybe I should take a page out of his book and forget the dating apps and scout out *r/bakedgoods* instead.

"So, you agree that I am trying to live out some cliché fantasy?"

"That's not what I mean. What's the worst that could happen?" When Andrew is spiraling like this, you have to talk him through a worst-case scenario.

"She murders me."

Maybe that wasn't the best line of questioning. "She won't murder you. Just don't touch any mysterious ferns or whatever you two are probably into."

"I guess if it's too awkward, I can just come back home."

I already see him forming an escape plan. "Don't talk yourself out of a potential great time before you even get there. If you've gotten good vibes from her so far, you should have nothing to worry about."

"I guess you're right. I need to stop overthinking it."

"Does Faye know?" I blurt out the question before I even have a chance to think that it might a weird thing to ask.

"About?"

"About plant girl. Emma."

"No. Do you think I should have told her?"

If I were Faye, would I want to know my ex was off to frolic in a field of tulips with his cute new Dutch girlfriend?

"I guess not. Are you two on good terms?"

"We still text sometimes. I saw her yesterday for the first time in a while. We didn't talk too long, but we're on as good of terms as we're going to be, I think."

On Friday afternoon she seemed a little tired, almost sad, to me. I think that's why I wanted to make her laugh so badly and experience the satisfaction of distracting her for a few seconds.

"Just asking, since she and I are working together now. Don't want to break some kind of code by talking to her."

"There's no code. I mean, it's fine if you talk to her."

"Do you think you two would ever work things out?" I've been wondering this ever since he told me they broke up. This is one detail I can't stand not knowing anymore. Is this trip just his way of going off and experiencing something new, before he comes back and realizes what he needed was back here all along?

"No." He pauses for a few seconds. "Or . . . I don't know. Seeing her again . . . brought back some feelings. We'll see how this trip goes."

If he's saying maybe, that means he might be keeping that option open. And that's answer enough for me. I need to get my mind out of the Faye gutter.

My cap feels tight suddenly. I take it off to adjust it. "You're good with me being friends with her?"

"Of course. She could probably use a friend. She doesn't put herself out there much, you know?"

That's what we'll be, then. Friends.

I stand up, eager to get up and do something. "Ready to go?" I ask.

8

———

FAYE

I WALK into Alexis's office on Monday morning to discover that something isn't right.

Alexis is in her late thirties—fairly young for a VP of Marketing—but she has the soul of an eccentric villain, with a girlboss twist. She follows *Lean In* like a playbook, her platinum blonde bob is somehow always the perfect length, and she wears nothing but monochromatic pant suits. She's assertive, and hates clutter, small talk, and children. I've never seen her laugh at a joke or cry or do anything that isn't proper and above board.

Which is why I almost don't compute what I'm seeing because I have no context for it.

You know those massage areas in airports, where you're sort of sitting but sort of leaning down in those weird little chairs? Well, Alexis is face down in one of those right in the middle of her office. Today's pant suit is navy blue and behind her is a very tall middle-aged man with slicked back salt-and-pepper hair, wearing a white linen lounge set and a very determined expression. He's entirely focused on the massage he's currently providing Alexis's shoulders.

"Oop, so sorry!"

She keeps her head down in the face hole. "Faye? I'm glad you've finally made it in."

It's 8:30, and the office opens at nine.

But I know I need to apologize anyway because it just makes her easier to deal with. I perk up into my "work voice," cheery enough that people like to work with me, but not so cheery that my coworkers think I'm some kind of corporate robot that cannot be trusted. "Sorry, you know how crazy Monday morning traffic is."

She lifts her head up, piercing blue eyes communicating that no, she does not understand why I'm unable to wield traffic to my commands. She probably operates motor vehicles like she's Moses parting the sea of cars in her BMW.

"Come on in. I want you to meet Conrad."

I walk into her office and sit in one of the faux leather chairs in front of her desk, wondering why I need to meet this man. Wondering why she had her door wide open for just anyone to walk in on this scene.

"Nice to meet you, I'm Faye." The chair squeaks as I cross my legs. I've always hated these chairs because they're the color of a sinus infection and are super uncomfortable.

He grunts out a barely audible, "I'm Conrad," but doesn't look over at me.

"You two are going to be working together on the initiative I told you about on Friday."

I don't tell her that she didn't give me any details on this initiative, but I've learned it's best to never accuse her of not doing something. "Can you remind what the objectives are for that? I'd like to make sure I understand the outcomes you'd like to achieve." Alexis loves words like "objectives" and "outcomes."

"Our quarterly employee survey results were awful,

with responses indicating that stress levels are high. I'm heading up a new self-care initiative." She nods up. "So, we're bringing in Conrad."

"To do . . . massages?"

The man in question grunts again, never once taking his eyes off Alexis's shoulders.

"I'm doing a trial run this morning. You can work with Conrad on scheduling a day for him to come in and give a tutorial on the massage thing I had you test over the weekend."

"He's going to do tutorials . . . on the . . . massager?"

"Yes, I was thinking we could do ten-minute individual massage slots and then do a group class on the massager."

"A group . . ."

At this point I'm wondering about her mental health because she seems to have taken the words self-care to a whole new level. Why can't we do what every other company would do and just give everyone a ten percent off voucher to a local med spa or something? Now I have to put together a plan for an actual masseuse to come into a professional office environment and touch all my coworkers. And guide us along in a group session for how to use the massagers?

"Are you sure that's a good idea?" I don't really know how else to confirm this is what she wants without coming out and saying that the company would likely be sued for even giving *me* that massager, much less handing them out to my coworkers and encouraging them to practice a little self-care with them . . . at the office.

She ignores my question and asks, "Did you test it over the weekend?"

"Did I—" I cough.

"What did you think? I thought it seemed like a great

model and not too expensive. We're not made of money here, you know."

"It was . . . well, I guess it—"

"Did it help with your relaxation at all? I've heard some friends of mine say after they use them they feel much more limber. Slept better, too."

Come to think of it, I did sleep like a baby Friday night. "It—yeah, I mean it seemed like a well-made . . . device."

"Good, because this is very important for employee morale. We need everyone happy and relaxed."

Kill me.

"To confirm, you want me to order the massagers for everyone?"

"Yes." She holds her phone out where she can see it through the little face hole in the chair. "Let me forward you my original order email so you can be sure to get the same model."

"Should I use my company card?"

Or should I head back down the elevator, get in my car, drive to the airport, buy a ticket to Nevada, shave my head, and assume my new life as a mystical desert woman, world renowned for my glass sculpture garden?

Maybe I'm already dead, and this is some kind of purgatory I've found myself in.

"Yes, and rush the shipping. I'd like to get this started ASAP."

I head back to my desk, bewildered at the direction the morning has taken, and see that I have a Slack notification. Normally a message from a coworker first thing on Monday morning would be annoying, but right now it's such a normal occurrence that I welcome the distraction from this bizarre day. I'm banking on the message being one of two things: someone making three times my salary needs to know why a calendar invite isn't opening, or someone making twice my salary needs to talk through something out loud before their client meeting.

But it's neither. I see Eli's name and feel a fresh new bit of jitters.

Eli: SOS

Faye: What's wrong?

Eli: Why is the coffee machine mad at me?

Faye: I'm not sure. It's usually very kind to me.

Eli: It beeped at me and won't give me coffee.

I spent the drive to work this morning telling myself I could avoid him for a few days, just to give myself time to forget the fact that I accidentally fantasized about him feeling me up in barn while using a company-bought vibrator. Telling myself that the only reason my mind placed him there was because Rett and I were just talking about him.

But there's no way I can make it through this morning without coffee, so maybe I should go ahead and face the music.

———

I WALK into the breakroom to see a very confused Eli standing in front of the coffee machine. He's wearing the exact same outfit that he wore on Friday: plain white T-shirt and a pair of tan utility pants.

He turns around when he hears me enter. "I'm used to an old Mr. Coffee that only works if you hold your mouth just right. This is way too fancy for me."

I walk over to stand next to him, willing myself not to look at his hands. Specifically, the way he's rapidly pressing the *on* button with the tip of his middle finger.

"Not sure the, um, tapping technique will work for this particular model."

He smirks and takes his hand away from the machine. "What technique have you found to work best?"

"Maybe, um, unplugging it and plugging it back in?"

He looks down at me and grins. "Didn't think of that one."

I reach behind and remove the plug from the socket. "It's a tried-and-true method." I plug it back in and the machine lights up.

"Well, look at that. I'm glad you came."

Oh, you have no idea. I cough and grab a mug from the shelf. "You want regular drip coffee?"

"Yeah, that'd be great." He crosses his arms and leans against the counter. "Are you okay? You seem a little flustered."

The machine buzzes as the coffee fills the cup. "I'm fine. Just had a weird morning."

"Why has it been weird?"

I peek around to make sure no one else is in earshot. "Remember the . . . package from Friday?"

"Yes. Why are you whispering?"

"Because," I whisper louder. "It's much worse than I thought."

"The vibrator? Seemed like a nice one to me."

My face heats and I wish I hadn't even brought this up to him, considering my whole plan to avoid seeing him at all. I think I just couldn't keep this information to myself and there's no one else in the office for me vent to. "She wants me to order one for everyone in the company. Because we need *self-care*, apparently."

He barks out an amused laugh. "I'm relieved to know this company really values my self-care."

I take a fortifying breath. "I think I need to find a way to make sure she doesn't give these out to everyone." I can just see the look on Tina, our sweet receptionist's face. I don't want to judge based on appearances, but she wears pineapple-yellow cardigans and calls everyone "sweetie." I can't let this happen to Tina.

"Shouldn't your boss be the one worried about potential backlash of this thing?"

"You haven't met Alexis. She operates in a universe that we'll never begin to understand."

I pull up my work email on my phone to see if she's sent me the last order yet. And I can't believe what I'm seeing. "Oh my god." I could cry from happiness.

"What?"

"Look!" I show him that the original order was for a massage gun. "It was a mistake. Oh, thank God, I won't have corrupt Tina."

He pulls a sad face. "Dang. That's not as fun."

I wonder if I need to tell Alexis I was sent the wrong thing. What if she asks me to return it. I can't return a used vibrator, can I? No, I need to pretend that I got the massage gun.

He looks at me over the rim of his cup. "Did you test it?"

"I—" I should have stayed at my desk. I should have let him figure out the coffee machine himself. I should have kept the vibrator tucked away, safe and warm inside my tote bag. "That doesn't matter."

"So, you *did* use it." He leans over and places his hand in front of his mouth as if hiding what's he's going to say, even though we're completely alone in here. "Your secret's safe with me."

I bat him away. "There's no secret." I busy myself by making my own drink.

"You're right. It's none of my business." I glimpse his smile before he takes a casual sip of his coffee.

I avoid looking at him by checking my phone and see that I have a text from Rett.

Rett: I'm thinking Low's for Friday night. Thoughts?

I flip my phone over, not wanting to think about what Friday night's potential activities.

"Something wrong?"

I show him the text. "My friend Rett is forcing me to go out and be fun again."

"Are you not fun now?"

I'm not sure how to answer this, because I doubt my ex-boyfriend's best friend really wants to know the truth about how I've been coping (or not) with a breakup. Eli is the type of person who is nice to everyone, even someone who broke their friend's heart. He'd have the most hateful DMV employee baking him brownies within ten minutes.

"I guess you could say I haven't really been getting an—I mean—having any. Fun, that is."

Heat engulfs my face so fast you'd think the flames of Hades were reaching up to lick my neck. *Do not think of neck licking right now.*

"Ah, I see." He smiles in a way that tells me he definitely noticed.

I hide in my coffee mug for a couple seconds to take a sip. "I haven't been out in a while."

"Yeah, me neither, actually."

I'm shocked. "Really?"

"Really." He shakes his head. "I probably need to go out more and meet people, because I just told my sister I'm going to bring a date to my parents' anniversary party in a month."

"Well, if you decide you want to venture out, you know

where to find me," I say without thinking. "Or, you know what I mean, find . . . other women. Dates. Potential dates."

He laughs. "Yeah, maybe I'll see you there." He holds up his coffee. "Thanks for your help. I should probably get back to my desk."

"No problem."

I text Rett back: Low's sounds good.

9

FAYE

ANOTHER DAY, another regrettable beverage choice.

The tequila fights a path down my throat, into the pit of my empty stomach. I wonder how my capillary friends are faring in these conditions. I bet they're hanging over the side of the raft, helmets askew, wondering why I thought it was a good idea to eat nothing but Cheez-Its for dinner.

"I'm going to hate myself for this later," I say, willing myself not to gag. I hate myself for this *now*.

Rett slams her shot glass down on the bar with dramatic flourish. "It's all part of the process." Then, to the bartender, "Two more, please."

"Oh no," I grumble.

I'm a lightweight on a good day, and it's been a very long time since I've had a night out drinking. At this rate, my head will be in the toilet in less than two hours. "Living on a Prayer" is blasting so loud I can't even hear myself think. Poetic.

"I just smell it in the air. It's going to be a great night for us."

The only thing I smell in the air is professional-grade

disinfectant with a faint hint of urine. The bartender sets the shots down in front of us and Rett raises her glass. "To Fun Faye!"

This shot goes down a little easier, meaning I don't heave this time.

"How about Fatigued Faye?"

"This isn't going to work if you resist. What's wrong?"

I spread my arms wide to gesture at our surroundings. "There's a man humping a pinball machine over there. Something is *very* wrong."

"Nope. Talk to me."

My instinct is to do anything but talk about the thoughts swirling around my brain. Thoughts that I'd much prefer to have alone in the comfort of my own home that I can easily push aside, because no one is sitting in front of me, bluntly asking the question: *What's wrong?*

But when I look at Rett, sitting there so strong and sure of herself, despite the bit of swaying she's doing on her stool, I think that maybe I do want to tell her what's on my mind.

"I used the vibrator," I blurt out.

"Good!" she says, excited. Then she must register that I don't look excited. "I mean . . . bad?"

"No, it wasn't bad. In fact, it was good. It was really good."

"What's the problem, then?"

"I sort of fantasized about someone . . . unexpected."

She shrugs. "That's totally normal. Was it an older man?"

I shake my head.

"Older woman?"

I shake my head.

"Was it an—" she mouths the word, "Alien?"

"It was Eli."

"Who?"

"Andrew's best friend. The new coworker?" I take a sip of water, and its gross and warm, not refreshing at all. "The *hot* new coworker," I clarify.

"Ohhhh." She looks thoughtful. "Maybe you should sleep with him, then."

I shake my head vehemently.

"So, avoid him."

I hiccup. "I might have invited him. Here." I tap the top of the bar with my fingertip. "He might come here." I've been surreptitiously looking around the bar ever since we arrived, seeing if I could spot him. But it's so crowded and dark he could be any one of these undulating blobs of people.

"Sounds like you might want to do something with him, then."

"No, I think he was just there, and he mentioned he hadn't been out in a while and I asked before thinking about it."

She looks like she wants to discuss this more, but decides not to push it. "Don't worry about it." She looks around the bar. "You can find someone else here."

"I don't want to have sex with someone in this bar tonight."

"You don't have to do anything you don't want to do, obviously." She swivels toward me on her stool. "But, like I said before, you need to expand that zone of comfort at least a little."

I must be looking at her like I don't know what she could mean because she adds, "Maybe you kiss someone?"

"There's no one here—" I burp. "I want near my mouth."

"Come on. Won't know for sure until we scope out the

entire place. At the very least you need to talk to someone." She stands up from her stool, gripping the side of the bar to remain upright. "Let's mingle."

The bar is very narrow and so full that we have to elbow our way to the back. This place is so old, I don't think they've changed the décor in decades. The lights hanging over the pool tables probably haven't been dusted since the Reagan administration, and there's decades of cigarette smoke baked into the green felt.

Rett suddenly grabs my arm in a tight grip. "I see potential. Those two." She nods to a couple of guys leaned against the wood paneled walls. They look perfectly fine, I guess, but I don't feel any kind of invisible tug drawing me to them.

I groan. "I don't want to." I'm drunk and sleepy and fighting the urge to stomp my feet like a toddler. "I want to go home."

She grabs me by the shoulders. "You can do this. You can try."

She's right. I'm never going to move on if I don't try. Hierarchy of Fun and all. "Fine. But I'm gonna go pee first."

I navigate my way through the crowd and luckily the bathroom is available. As I wash my hands, I take a look at myself in the mirror.

Do I want to kiss someone tonight?

I touch up my lipstick. Kissing might be nice. Kissing might be very nice. I look deeply into my dazed eyes. "If kissing is meant to happen, it will happen," I say out loud to myself. The universe will send me a sign.

I come out of the bathroom to find the door has been barricaded by a couple making out in front of it.

There is my sign, I guess.

"Excuse me," I say, trying to gently nudge them out of

my way. But they just push toward me. I may die of suffocation via the mass of dark hair currently shoved in my face. Her hair smells good, though. Like coconut. I wonder what kind of shampoo she uses.

I give them another push, a little less gentle this time. But they seem to take this as invitation because the next thing I know the guy has raised his head from the woman's face and he smiles at me.

The woman looks back at me and her face lights up. "Oh my god, you're so pretty." She says reaching out to touch my forearm. "I love your hair." She twirls a lock of my hair around her finger.

"Thank you," I say. "I like yours too. It's smells amazing. What kind of sham—"

"Faye?"

I look over to see Eli standing next to me with an amused grin on his face.

The couple realizes I won't be joining in, so they get back to making out. I turn to Eli and I mean to give him a side hug, but it's so crowded and I'm so wobbly that it ends up being what can best be described as a drunken pat down of his abdominal region. "Hey, you came!"

He nods to the interlocked couple. "You having a good time?"

"I think I was in the early stages of joining a threesome."

He laughs. "Sorry to interrupt. Should I make myself scarce, then?"

"No, not sure I'm ready for that stage in my fun journey." I gaze wistfully back at them. "Although I really wanted to know her haircare routine."

I look around, wondering where Rett is. She's probably worried I've made my escape. I spot her talking to the two guys she pointed out, and she makes eye contact with me. I give her a questioning look and we do a pantomime to each other in which I tell her I'm coming over there and she shakes her head and points to Eli.

That's right, she doesn't know who Eli is, thinking he's some random guy I've met in line for the bathroom. This gives me an idea. The sooner I complete this mission, the sooner I can go home. And if he's anything like he used to be, he'll be game for the shenanigans and will probably think my idea is funny.

I turn to him. "I could use a favor."

He looks down at the hand I didn't even notice I'd placed on his forearm. "Sure, what's up?"

His skin is warm and taut, covered in hair that I can feel beneath my fingertips. I'm suddenly on the verge of throwing up, not from alcohol, but from a rush of nerves. What am I thinking? I was just having a crisis about the very fact that I can't do those kinds of things with him. I remove my hand finger by finger. "Actually, never mind."

"What is it? How can I help?"

His eyes are so kind, full of concern and a hint of curiosity.

It makes what I'm about to say all the sillier. I take a deep breath, and my words come out in a rush. "I need you to pretend to flirt with me so I can pretend to flirt with you so I can go home to my nest."

I don't mention the kissing part, hoping Rett will be satisfied with just the flirting.

He arches a brow. "Okay . . ."

I look over to where Rett is standing, and she gives me an encouraging nod. "See that redhead over there?" I point to Rett's direction and then move so that we're turned away from her. "She told me I can't go home until I . . . ki—flirt with someone. And I'm tired and don't feel like having to talk to someone new."

He has an intrigued expression. "Alright. What specifically did you have in mind?"

"Just . . ." I look around. "Oh! I know." I sway a little and catch my balance on the wall. I gesture to an empty pool table. "You can show me how to play pool. In a . . . flirty manner."

He reaches a hand out, cupping my elbow to steady me. "A flirty manner?"

"Yeah, like in the movies where you stand behind me and teach me how to line up a shot. And say things like . . . 'Wow, Heaven must be missing an angel tonight,' or whatever."

He brings his head down to my left ear so I can hear him better. "Is that how you like to be flirted with?"

The deep rasp of his voice sends sparks straight to my belly button, obliterating all feelings of drunkenness and replacing them with other feelings. Like, I haven't had sex or even kissed someone in—I'm too drunk to do the actual math—way too long, feelings.

I brush the thought away. Flirting is one thing, but to kiss him would be crossing some kind of line I don't have the brainpower to think about right now. It's just the tequila talking.

I already forgot what he asked me. Oh yeah, do I like to be flirted with like that? "Um, I think so?"

"If memory serves, you already know how to play pool. I remember you kicking my ass once or twice."

Thanks to my pool shark of a grandpa, I've been playing since I was tall enough to see over the table. I'm surprised he remembers us playing. "That's all part of the pretending, I guess."

"Then let the pretending begin." His thumb grazes the inside of my shoulder blade for the few seconds it takes to guide us over to the table.

He hands me a stick before racking the balls. "You want to break?"

"No, you go ahead."

I watch him bend down to line up his shot, forearms flexing as he glides the stick over his hand. With a crack, the balls scatter on the table. "Should we play nine ball?"

"Sure. Sounds good."

I bend down to line up my shot, and feel him move to stand behind me.

"May I?" he asks.

I nod and feel the heat of his chest at my back. He places a hand over mine so that he can guide me where I need to aim. My hair stirs against my cheek as he asks, "Is this how they do it in the movies?"

"Yep, that's . . . exactly it," I squeak.

"What usually happens next?" I can hear the smile in his voice without even having to look.

I can't help but look anyway, and sure enough I see a grin that I know means he's having fun with this. I knew he'd be a good partner in crime for this faux-flirting game.

"I think I should hit the ball now. With your guidance."

"Like this?" He guides my hand back and forth a few times to line up the shot before giving a final, forceful jab that knocks the number one ball into the pocket.

He doesn't move away, though. "Nice shot. Now what?"

I swallow. "Since I made the shot, I get to shoot again."

I feel his chuckle against my back. "I know that. I mean, what's next for the flirting?"

"Oh, um, I think you're supposed to whisper something romantic in my ear."

He leans further in, so close I can feel his lips move against my cheek. "You smell so good, it's distracting."

I don't move a muscle. "What do I smell like?"

He guides my hand for another shot, but it doesn't go in. Standing up straight, he says, "Like warm blueberry Pop-Tarts straight from the toaster."

I snort and bat him away. "Blueberry Pop-Tarts? You can do better than that."

He steps over to take his own shot. I'm momentarily mesmerized by the strong, yet gentle, motion of his arms. The stick strikes the cue ball, sending the two ball into the pocket. "What? I'm flirting."

"No one likes blueberry Pop-Tarts, though. Strawberry? Acceptable. S'mores? God-tier."

He misses his next shot. "Well, I like blueberry."

"Fine. I'll accept blueberry." I take my turn again, and the act of play returns so naturally, I make four more shots.

While I try to determine my next move, he moves next to me, propping one arm on the table. "I think something is missing from our little charade."

"What is that?" I feel his eyes on me, watching me continue to play.

"It's just that I'm doing a lot of the heavy lifting here. You're not pretending to flirt with me, too."

I move to stand closer to him. "How do you like to be flirted with?"

He pauses, as if thinking of the perfect response. "You could compliment me. That's always nice."

I roll my eyes. "Fishing for compliments?"

He grins. "Always."

My eyes glide up and down his arm, so close to mine

that I can feel his body heat against my own skin. "I like your tattoos. How long have you had them?"

"Thank you. Most of them are a few years old. This one is my oldest." He points to a heart on his bicep. "Got this right after I moved."

"Do they mean anything?"

"Most were spur-of-the-moment, no huge meaning behind them other than I just felt like getting one." I like this about him. He felt like doing a thing, so he did it.

"Did you know I have a tattoo?" It's a tiny daisy just below my left hip bone. I got it in a brief moment of rebellion when I was seventeen.

He raises his eyebrows. "Oh yeah? What is it?"

"A daisy."

"*Where* is it?"

I put on my best sassy flirty voice. "Wouldn't you like to know?"

He barks out a laugh. "Now she's pulling her weight, ladies and gentlemen."

He makes it so easy. I think I could pretend to flirt with him all night and it wouldn't even feel taxing at all. He looks at me for a second that stretches like molasses.

I look away first, and take my next shot. It's not long before I win the game.

"Look at you, hustling me."

"Not true. You knew I could play."

"I thought we were playing pretend."

It felt real. I've been having genuine fun with him and that sends a crashing realization through me. This can't be real.

I glance over to Rett and she's watching us like a hawk. She gives me a look that asks if I'm okay. I smile and give her a little *Ok* hand sign. She mouths the word *kiss* to me and I shake my head and look away.

Eli looks down at me with a quirk of his brow. "What was that about?"

Maybe it's the tequila, or the burst of confidence I feel from the pool game, but I suddenly don't want the night to end. "I may not have mentioned everything I need to accomplish tonight before I can go home."

"Something else I can help with?"

What could it hurt if it's just pretend? The flirting went well, so might as well finish what I've started. "Any chance you'd be down to pretend to kiss me, too?"

10

———

ELI

IT TAKES me a couple of long, but pulse-quickening seconds to register that she didn't just say the words "kiss me," but "pretend to kiss me."

Which is somehow even more interesting. "What does pretend kissing involve?"

She looks anywhere but at me and crosses her arms over her chest. The motion draws my eyes to her cleavage, and I force my eyes up. "We would just need to make it look like we're kissing when we're really not."

This sends my brain into overdrive, thinking of all the ways I can pretend to kiss her. Pretend to kiss her on top of the pool table. Pretend to kiss her against the wall. Pretend to kiss her while she's hoisted up on the bar, trapping me between her thighs.

She continues, "Forget it. Pretend kissing. So dumb."

She's embarrassed that she's asked me to do this, and I don't want that. "Not dumb at all. I have an idea."

"Eli—"

I point to the corner next to the TouchTunes. "We can

go over there, and I'll block you so all anyone will be able to see is my back. What do you think?"

She looks over to where I've pointed and chews on her bottom lip. I watch her think for a few seconds and then she nods decisively. "Okay."

I grab her hand and lead her over to the corner. Her palm is warm, a little sweaty, and I wonder if she's nervous. I move so that she's wedged in the small space. From an outside perspective it would just look like a couple making out. "How's this?"

She crosses, then uncrosses her arms, like she's unsure what to do with them. "What should we do now?" She laughs the tiniest bit in a nervous way. "Does it look like you're just some creep trapping me in the corner?"

The last thing I want is her to feel uncomfortable or that I'm hovering over her in a creepy way. "Sorry, I don't want you to feel like that." I straighten a little so I'm not as close to her.

"No, I'm okay. I'm glad it's you—I mean that you're here. That I don't have to—" She takes a shuddering breath. "I *need* to do this. Even if it isn't real."

"If you want something to do with your hands, you could put them on the back of my neck? Like you're going to pull me in."

She nods. "Right, yeah that's a good idea."

"Then I can move my face down next to yours and it'll look like we're kissing from her point of view." I'm hoping if I spell everything out then she'll feel more comfortable.

"But you won't actually kiss me?" She says this in a way that I can't read. I can't tell if she's ensuring I won't or if she's hoping I will.

"No. We won't actually kiss."

She brings her hands up to the back of my neck and

rests them against my nape before sliding her fingers into my hair. It feels so good, a pleasant shiver rolls down my spine.

"You could put your hands somewhere on me," she suggests.

I was so busy focusing on where she'd need to put her hands to make this convincing that I didn't allow myself to think about getting to touch her. Back when we were playing pool and I stood behind her and placed my hand over hers, it felt so right, so good to be near her like that. "Where?" I ask, voice cracking.

Her hands twitch in my hair. "On my waist?"

I rest my hands along the waistband of her jeans. The bottom of her tank top lifts and I can feel her skin, soft and warm against my hands. This is a terrible idea. An excellent, terrible idea.

"This okay?" I ask.

"Mm-hmm."

"Sorry if I'm a little scruffy," I say, bringing my face down by her right cheek. "Haven't shaved in a while."

"It's okay. I like it. I mean—" She shifts slightly, and I slide my hands around to clasp my palms against her lower back. "It suits you. The beard."

I'll never go clean-shaven again. "Thank you." I move my head to the other side, mimicking the act of kissing by her left ear. "You still good?"

"Yeah," she says, sounding a little breathless.

"Why do you have to kiss someone before you can leave?"

"It's part of my hierarchy of fun."

"That sounds very serious."

She huffs a laugh and the way her breath feels against my neck makes me feel like I've reverted to being a teenager again, when the slightest touch from a girl would send me into a horny tailspin. "It's something Rett and I put together as a guide."

"And kissing is part of that?"

"Among other things," she says, and I glance over to see a flush of peach move up her neck into her jawline. I'm curious about these other things, too, but push that aside for now.

"Kissing is fun," I say, unable to keep myself from looking at her mouth.

"Yeah, it can be."

"So why aren't you really flirting with someone tonight?" I move back down to nuzzle by her neck. "Really kissing them?"

She glides her hands to rest on top of my shoulders. "Because I don't feel like it?" I lift my head to see that she's grinning up at me, like she knows she's not being completely honest, but maybe it doesn't matter anyway.

It's always been like this with her, like she doesn't want to share anything of herself—even what I'd consider small things. I remember asking her where she was from when she and Andrew first started hanging out, and she responded, "Somewhere you've never heard of, probably." And then it became a game for me to try to guess the town she grew up in. Come to think of it, she never ended up telling me.

Naturally, I push a little on this too. "Why don't you feel like it?"

She sighs and tucks a piece of hair behind her ear before placing her hand back on my shoulder. "I don't feel like having to do the whole song and dance. I'm bad at it."

"I disagree." The piece of hair she tried to tuck behind her ear falls back down and I fight the urge to tuck it back in for her. "Start with the secret tattoo, and you're totally in."

She laughs and it turns into a hiccup. It's adorable and I want to make her do it again. "I should have never told you about that."

She's right. Ever since she mentioned it, I've been wondering where it could be. We used to go to Andrew's family's lake house all the time, so I've seen her in a swimsuit. I know it's somewhere, hidden from just anyone's view. Maybe low on her hip? Or just below her lower back? Maybe she got it recently and it could be anywhere my eyes can't see right now.

No, I can't go there. "Point is, you could be really kissing someone right now if you wanted to be."

A full blush blooms up her cheeks, like a signal that I'm getting close to something. But where am I trying to get? Shyness has always drawn me in, something I can't help but want to explore. What is she thinking? What does she want? I've been surprised by her tonight, and I don't know what to do about it.

There's nothing I *should* do about it.

"We can probably end this soon," she says, almost as if she could read my thoughts.

"Am I not meeting your pretend kissing standards?"

"It's not that. I haven't given you a chance to meet anyone tonight. Sorry for hogging all your time."

In all honesty, I forgot that the whole reason I came out tonight was so I could meet someone new. But I don't want to talk to anyone else tonight. I want to stay in this corner of the bar talking to her until they kick us out. Which is why she's right. This should end soon.

"Thank you. For helping me." At this, she removes her hands from my shoulders.

I step back. "Glad I could be of service."

"Want to meet the friend responsible for this farce?"

"Absolutely."

I follow her up to the bar where the tall redhead Faye pointed out earlier turns to greet us as we squeeze through the crowd of people. She doesn't smile at me in greeting and simply looks at me the way a scientist would look at a specimen under a microscope. Neutral, but curious.

Faye gestures to her. "Rett, this is Eli. Eli this is Rett."

"That's a cool name," I say, feeling a need to warm her to me somehow. "Is it short for something?"

"I could tell you, but then I'd have to kill you," Rett says, and I think she might be serious.

Faye stands on her toes and says in an overdramatic whisper, "It's short for Loretta."

Rett glares at Faye, but I can tell she's not actually mad at her. Faye looks up at me, conspiratorial.

"My lips are sealed," I say to Rett.

"Wait a minute, did you say your name was Eli?"

"Yes, why?"

She looks at Faye in a suspicious way and Faye returns her look with an innocent widening of her eyes. They go back and forth with the kind of silent communication that only best friends have.

Rett turns back to me and smiles at me. "No reason."

"Should we get the Uber now?" Faye asks.

"I can give you a ride if you need one," I offer.

"No, I don't want you to have to leave too. You should continue your night," she says.

"I'm kind of tired, honestly." Maybe the biggest lie I've ever told. I've never been so keyed up in my life. I don't want to stay here, and I don't want to go home, either.

"Are you good to drive?" Rett asks me.

"Been drinking water all night." Since I have a thirty-minute drive back to my parents' house after this, I didn't want to drink too much. Turns out, I haven't even wanted to drink at all.

Rett leads Faye over to the side to have a private conversation, but I hear bits here and there.

"Is *that* Eli?"

"Shhh, you're yelling!"

"Should *I* get the Uber and leave you two?"

". . . just friends . . . helping me . . ."

Does that mean Faye had already told Rett about me? I wonder what she said to her. They turn back to me, and I pretend I wasn't listening.

Rett loops her arm through Faye's. "Off to her murder-apartment it is, then."

———

"YOU'RE A MCANGEL."

Faye is nestled in the passenger seat of my truck, McDonald's bag snuggled up to her chest. We're parked on the street in front of where she lives, an old brick building that looks one development deal away from demolition. I think I know what Rett meant earlier with the murder-apartment comment.

Rett pipes in from the back seat, "A guardian McAngel."

I pop a chicken nugget into my mouth. "Yeah, I come to earth once a year to bring the McRib back."

Faye giggles through a mouthful of fries. "The McRib Messiah."

"Do not say McRib to me right now unless you want me to throw up inside of this hat." Rett holds up a cap I got at a charity basketball game I played in a couple of years ago.

It's a wonder there's even room for her to sit. "Sorry for the mess back there."

She removes the Red Bull can she's sitting on. "I'd say this the perfect ambience for post-drinking fast food."

Faye leans around to hand Rett a burger, pausing midway to turn to me. A piece of her hair falls down to tickle my arm. "It's okay if we eat in here, right?"

"Yeah, that's fine." The idea of going back to the pull-out couch in the basement is something I wanted to put off as long as possible, so I was eager for the detour we took before heading to Faye's place.

"So Rett, did *your* fun needs get met tonight?" I ask her.

"You told him!" Rett screams, grabbing Faye's shoulder.

Faye gently removes Rett's hand. "Please calm down."

"Was I not supposed to know?" I ask.

"I'm just surprised," Rett says. Surprised Faye told me, or surprised Faye "kissed" me?

"So, what are the other fun needs?" I ask.

"You really don't need to know," Faye says, unwrapping her burger.

"You tell him about the needs, but you won't show him the full list?"

I turn to Rett. "Exactly. What if there are other things I can help with?"

"Nooo," Faye says, covering her face. "You've helped enough."

"Maybe Rett will tell me."

"Well first," Rett says, ignoring Faye's objection. "I told her we needed to go out so she could meet someone and then go home with them and—"

"Rett, I swear to God," Faye interrupts her. "Don't

finish that sentence." She reaches into her purse and pulls out a lipstick, her phone, and crumpled piece of paper. "You might as well see the whole thing, I guess."

I unfold the paper and see "Faye's Hierarchy of Fun" written at the top with a scribble of a pyramid below it.

Faye's Hierarchy of Fun
Hobby – find one
Social – have a ~~party~~ *small get-together*
Sex – have some
Career – new job
Environmental – apartment feels like home

"So the pretend kissing was supposed to lead to . . . pretend sex?" I can't help but tease her, it's a disease.

She covers her face again. "I'm sobering up way too fast for where this conversation is going."

"Pretend?!" Rett screeches.

Faye gives me a shy smile, like we were both in on a big secret. "We weren't really flirting," she explains. "Or . . . kissing."

The flirting was very real on my end, and the pretend kissing was almost better than the real thing, as far as I'm concerned.

Rett sighs dramatically. "Well, you two should take up acting."

Faye gives me a quick look before doing the most obviously fake yawn I've ever seen. "Time to go to sleep, I think."

"Do you guys need help getting to your apartment?"

"No, I think we're good. Thank you again for giving us a ride."

"No problem. I'll see you on Monday."

They both get out and hook their arms together as they make their way up the sidewalk.

"Nice to meet you, Loretta!" I shout out the window.

Rett gives me her middle finger in answer.

This makes Faye laugh in a way that goes straight to my bones—and other areas—saying, *That right there* and *How can I make you do that again?*

11

FAYE

I PULL into my grandpa's driveway and attempt to dodge a giant hole where the gravel needs to be filled in. I mentally add that to the list of things I need to do this week as I head inside. He's lived in this brick ranch house forever, and nothing has changed at all. I don't think the two white plastic lawn chairs sitting in the front yard have moved in twenty years.

I guess I consider this my childhood home, but I think I've always just thought of it as a place I lived for a short time. If thirteen years could be considered a short time.

The screen door slams shut with a whack as I walk in.

"It's me!" I shout, otherwise he won't hear me over the television he's always blasting.

I dump the grocery bags on the yellow linoleum kitchen counter next to a pile of mail, and peek into the living room to see that he's in his usual spot—in his brown recliner watching *The Walking Dead* at full volume. I can see the top of his Teamsters trucker hat over the back of the chair.

"Can you turn that down?" I yell over the sound of a zombie getting its head chopped off. It's a small house, and I don't want the sound of zombie brain splatter as my background while I unload the chili I brought.

The volume lowers slightly. "You got the goods?" he asks.

"Yes, but Donna tells me you aren't taking your blood pressure meds." Donna is an in-home nurse who comes by twice a week to check in on him. She gives me updates since I'm the one who hired her.

"She narc'd on me, huh?"

I unload a few pre-made salads he may or may not actually eat. "She's trying to take care of you."

"Hate those damn pills. Make me have to take a piss every two seconds."

"I know, but you've got to take it. Otherwise, you can't have these." I hold up a bag of Reese's cups. I'm hoping he won't notice they're sugar free.

"Alright, alright."

"I made you some chili to eat this week. I'll put it in the fridge."

The older he's gotten, the more he doesn't want to cook for himself. I try to make it as easy as possible for him, but he's stubborn about accepting the food I bring him for some reason.

"I've been eating down at Roy's."

Roy's Restaurant, known for healthy fare such as the Big Belly Burger and something called "Fried Gravy." I don't ask because I don't want to know. "Well, if you want to give Roy a break, you can heat this up." I place the chili container in the fridge and toss out some expired milk and the container of soup I brought him last week.

"You didn't like the soup?" I ask, as I sort through the mail stack.

"Hmm? Oh, I forgot it was in there."

His mail is mostly junk, from real estate agents or lawn care companies. But then, I come across something that gives me pause. The envelope has already been opened, so I take out the wedding invitation, its swirling embossed calligraphy inviting my grandpa to a celebration of love between Marsha Lee Clifton and Michael Bowers at a church in Charlotte on September 28th.

That would be my mom and her latest.

I slide the invitation back into the envelope and head into the living room to take my usual spot on the love seat adjacent to his recliner.

He glances at me through the aviator glasses he's always worn. "You're looking a little green in the gills there, Bambi."

He's called me Bambi ever since I was a toddler because he said I walked like a baby deer.

"I'm fine," I say, although I feel a little unsteady today. "Met some tequila the other night that didn't like me very much."

"Could never stand the stuff. If you want a little hair of the dog, I've got some Jim Beam in there somewhere."

My stomach lurches. "I'm good. Played some pool though, which was fun. It's been forever."

"Oh yeah?" He sits up, interested in where I've taken the conversation. "You still any good?"

"I was surprised how fast it came back to me."

"Who'd you play with?"

"My friend Eli."

"Eli, huh?"

I curl my legs up under me. "Yep." I keep my voice distracted, wishing I hadn't brought up the pool game. I wonder if it's one of those things where you secretly want someone to ask you about something, but you don't want to make it obvious.

"Were you on a date?"

"No!"

"I hope he's not like Andrew."

"I thought you liked Andrew."

He shrugs. "He was a good guy. Not for you."

"So, he was too good for me?" I say this in a joking way, but I'm curious because we've never really talked about Andrew. He's always been tight-lipped about his opinions on my love life. And if he doesn't ask, I don't tell.

He makes a brushing off motion. "No one is. He was too . . . preppy."

"Preppy?" I hear the word preppy and think of polo shirts and mint juleps. Andrew's parents are preppy, but he's not. I think this word is my grandpa's shorthand for saying that Andrew was a little too formal for him.

We watch the show for a couple of minutes and when it goes to a commercial break, I finally get up the nerve to ask what I've wanted to ask since I saw that invitation.

"She's living in Charlotte now?"

He hums in assent. "Moved out there last year, I think."

"Are you going to the wedding?"

"Yeah, guess I'll go."

"Why?"

"Because she's my daughter."

Is it that simple? If I was engaged to Andrew right now and sent my mom an invite, would she come to the wedding simply because I'm her daughter? Good thing I won't have to find out the answer to that one.

"You could come with me," he says. "She told me she sent you one, too."

"I haven't gotten anything." She probably doesn't even

know I moved or that Andrew and I broke up. We don't exactly talk that much. She sends me a *Happy Birthday, honey* text every year and occasionally, she'll call me to ask how things are going. Superficial conversations that are easy and don't involve getting into anything that might stir up unwanted memories or feelings.

"I didn't go to the last two. Why would I go to this one?" I hate the way my voice wavers a little bit when say this. I'm being stubborn and more than a little resentful. Is it completely her fault we have a strained relationship?

Or if I hate that I felt myself falling into the same pattern she fell into? She's always been so afraid of being alone that she'd marry any man who asked her. And I felt the draw of that when Andrew asked me.

But Andrew didn't deserve a proposal acceptance brought on by platonic feelings of love or, even worse, avoiding loneliness. Neither did Alan or Steve. I always felt sorry for them. But the more I've thought about this since my own breakup, I realized that I really felt sorry for *her*, because for the first time in my life I think I finally understood her decisions.

"I brought an activity for us to do today," I say, swiftly changing the subject.

"I just want to watch my show."

I pull out the two paint by numbers I bought at the grocery store on the way here. Maybe painting can be my new hobby. "You want the sunflower or the city skyline?"

"I want to catch up on my show," he repeats.

"Sunflower it is."

I set up our painting stations on the TV trays he keeps by his recliner.

"What's with the arts and crafts?"

"We need to broaden our horizons. Try new hobbies."

"I'm too old for new hobbies."

"It'll be good for you. Keep the mind sharp."

He just sits there and doesn't move to paint at all.

"Fine, we can have the show on in the background."

By the end of the episode, I've almost finished my painting, although the city skyline ends up looking more like a city oil spill because I barely pay attention to the where the numbers are telling me the paint should go. I'm distracted, thinking about my mom. Thinking about Andrew.

Thinking about Eli.

My phone lights up with a text.

Eli: How you feeling today?

I guess he has the same phone number he had in school. This makes me happy for some reason, knowing I could text him if I wanted to.

I snap a photo of the murky brown paint water and send it to him.

Faye: Like this. Safe to say my liver and I would like to forget Friday night ever happened.

Eli: That hurts. My heart and I thought our pretend flirting meant more to you than that.

I snort and it startles my grandpa awake. He fell asleep somewhere between zombie attacks.

"Did they kill him?" he asks.

"Yeah, they got him with the barbed wire baseball bat thingy." I have no idea what he's talking about, but he seems to take this as a good thing.

Faye: Tell your heart I'm so sorry. I'll be better next time.

I catch myself smiling at my phone and put a stop to any giddy feelings this might be stirring up. I turn my phone over to keep myself from watching it for his response.

We watch another episode together before I do my usual weekly cleaning routine for him. This week it's a quick vacuum and hitting the high spots in the bathroom and kitchen before I decide I need to head home and nap away the afternoon.

I give my grandpa a hug. "I'll talk to you later this week. Don't forget your chili."

"Have a good week," he tells me before switching over to watch something else. I hear the *X-Files* theme song start to play as I leave his house.

When I get inside my car, I finally allow myself to look at my phone to see if Eli texted me back.

Eli: My heart says thanks and it's looking forward to it.

12

———

FAYE

WHILE I MAKE my way into the office on Monday morning, I have the naive hope that it will be a quiet day with no weird requests or strange deliveries. That I can leisurely sip my coffee while checking emails. Laura from sales will come by my desk to tell me about her kid's ballet recital over the weekend. A normal, boring Monday.

Then I walk into the lobby to find that the worst possible event that could be occurring is happening today.

The annual blood drive.

I'm not opposed to giving blood, in fact I love that the company sponsors this event every year. But considering that I'm somehow still so hungover that I can barely blink my eyes without feeling like my very existence is wobbling, I think giving blood is the last thing I should do today.

Before I even make it to my desk, I'm intercepted by Alexis at the elevator.

"I told Richard you'd help with the blood drive this morning. Tina was going to do it, but she's out sick. Several people are out today with some kind of flu that's been going around. We need someone to guide employees where they need to go."

I guess the giant banners I just walked past don't communicate that loud and clear.

Richard is Alexis's manager, and he's the only person that I've ever seen Alexis show any signs of insecurity around. She probably jumped at the chance to tell him that her assistant would be happy to help in this emergency just so she could feel like she's saving the day.

"Okay, yeah. No problem."

"Great, you can set up at Tina's desk in reception."

I try to see the silver lining: at least in the reception area, my pounding headache and queasy stomach I'm battling won't be made worse by coworkers having loud conversations in our open office space. Maybe I can get some work done.

Three hours later, I'm sending a friendly reminder to the marketing team to let me know their lunch order for this week's lunch and learn, "Making EQ Work for You," when an Eli-shaped shadow appears in front of me.

We didn't text any more yesterday, but I have found myself thinking about Friday night too often. The tequila shots. Our pool game. The edge of Eli's mouth tickling the edge of my ear. Our pretend kissing. Wanting the kissing to be real?

I feel flustered, seeing him standing there. He looks the opposite of hungover, all bright-eyed and brimming with his usual charm.

He takes a bite of the cookie I just watched him sweet-talk from the blood drive volunteer.

"I see you've been doing some more pretend flirting this morning." I nod to the cookie table. I shake my head and tsk. "Just for more snickerdoodles."

It was hard not to watch him talking and laughing with the volunteers, seeing them respond to his playful flirtations with sweet smiles and batting eyelashes. How does he always know what to say? It's almost like the act of breathing is harder for him than talking.

He snaps the cookie in half and hands part of it to me before tossing the other half into his mouth with a self-satisfied grin. "You mean Edith? Who said that was pretend?"

I force the bite down, wondering if cinnamon and sugar will help or hurt right now. As the morning has gone on, I've somehow managed to get much worse. How long should a hangover last? I feel like I've been hit by a truck. I remember Alexis mentioning a flu going around, and I wonder if what I'm battling right now is more than just Jose Cuervo-related.

He leans in, conspiratorial. "Don't worry, though. You're the only woman I've ever pretended to kiss."

I look up at him and our bodies are positioned in much the same way they were the other night, and I'm reminded of the fact that I know what it feels like to have his full attention on me. That, much like the women handing out cookies, I'm not immune to his charms. My stomach bounces and lurches in a weird dance between nervous giddiness and nausea.

I shiver, suddenly very cold, and tighten my sweater around me. "I'm honored, but can we forget about that, too?"

Eli's face turns serious, and he holds his water bottle out to me. It's gigantic and navy blue with stickers all over it. "You okay? Do you want some of my water?"

I wave the water away. "No, I'm good."

He nods outside to the blood drive van. "Have you ever given blood before?"

"I didn't even give blood today. I think I'm still just feeling off from drinking." If I tell myself that enough, it might make it true. Because I can't be sick. I have way too much work to get done. I need to call Conrad to book the massage sessions. I need to get weekly metrics to Alexis. I need to . . . do a lot of other things I'm having a hard time remembering at the moment.

"Maybe you should go home."

"Can't. I'm supposed to sit here for another hour and make sure everyone is able to read that sign." I point to the banner with a drawing of a drop of blood with vampire teeth and a speech bubble that says, "I want to take your blood!"

"Says who?"

As if on cue, Alexis emerges from the elevator. "Looks like it's thinned out. Faye, you can head back upstairs."

I stand up way too fast, and have to brace myself on the desk. "Okay, sounds great!"

Alexis turns to me and gives me a suspicious look. "Are you feeling well? If you don't feel well, you shouldn't be here spreading germs. I have a gala this weekend that I cannot miss."

How bad do I look? They're both acting like I'm about to drop dead in the lobby.

"I'm fine. Just didn't sleep well last night."

She doesn't look so sure, but doesn't say anything else before floating out with the same confident ease she moves through every area of her life.

"Faye," Eli says.

"Hmm?"

"Why don't you want to go home? You clearly feel bad."

I grab my things and head for the elevators. "Too much to do. And like I said, I feel fine."

Also, the thought of going home sick to my sad apartment feels worse than pushing through the rest of the day at the office.

The elevator arrives and we both step inside. As soon as it starts its ascension up to the sixth floor, I know I can't keep lying to Eli—or myself—anymore.

I feel like shit.

———

I WAKE up in an unfamiliar bed.

It's pitch-dark, and all I can see is the outline of streetlights through the blinds. I panic, rolling over quickly to try to get up, but I'm wrapped in a blanket that I've managed to twist around myself in a tight burrito.

The blanket is familiar, though. It may be dark, but I know that it's plaid and fleece and one I've owned for over ten years. And the bed I'm in is only unfamiliar because it's located in the bedroom I never sleep in. I feel around to see if I can find my phone, but it's too dark to see. I don't have a bedside lamp, and I guess Rett was right about needing that nightstand.

The last thing I remember is Eli giving me a ride home from work because he wouldn't allow me to drive. In hindsight, I'm glad he did. But how did I get in the bedroom? I would have gone straight to the couch.

I hobble out into the living room where a lamp has been left on. There's a sticky note taped to the lampshade.

Why is this your only light?

Below it is a very bad doodle of a vampire.

"Someone's never heard of mood lighting," I grumble.

Just the act of taking the ten steps from the bedroom to the living room has exhausted me, so I sit on the couch and look around for my phone. Not on my coffee table. Not under the couch cushions.

There are two sticky notes on the arm of the couch.

Heading back to office.
Text when you wake up?

I wonder what time it is. If it's this dark, it has to be pretty late. I get up and flick the light on in the kitchen. See? I have other light sources. I see my phone charging on the counter and see that it's 9:13 p.m.

I unlock it to text Eli when my eye catches on something else on the linoleum. My "Faye's Hierarchy of Fun" list. He's seen it, but it's one thing to talk about something while you're tipsy and another to see physical evidence of this silly thing I might be doing.

I thought about throwing it away, but something held me back from getting rid of it. At the very least, it's a funny keepsake. It's still incredibly embarrassing that he's seen it, though.

I text him: Thank you for giving me a ride home!

Eli: Of course. How are you feeling?

Faye: Better. Question though. How did I get in the bed?

Eli: You don't remember? I tried to carry you, but you kept squirming around. We ended up sort of hobbling together up the stairs and I helped you into bed.

I have vague memories of this, but that must have been

some fever I had. This is so embarrassing. He was trying to help me, and I was fighting him all the way?

Faye: I'm so so sorry.

Eli: For what?

Faye: That you had to bring me home and then wrangle me into my apartment.

Eli: No big deal. It was my lunch break.

Eli: I tried to find sheets to make your bed.

Faye: I don't actually own any sheets yet.

Seeing those words typed out really does something to me. How did I let things get so bad? Who doesn't own sheets? And why did I just tell him I don't own sheets?

Dots pop up to indicate he's typing. They go away and come back a few times.

Eli: Might wanna get sheets for some of those fun activities you want to do.

Faye: Ughhhhh

Eli: I'm 100% in support of this fun journey of yours by the way.

My stomach growls, which I'm taking as a good sign that I'm on the mend. I check my cabinets, hoping that some chicken noodle soup will magically appear. I see another sticky note placed on the shelf next to a box of Frosted Flakes.

Check your door.

Intrigued, I open the door, having no idea what I expect to find, but it definitely isn't two grocery bags full of stuff. I glimpse a box of Saltines and a huge bottle of blue Gatorade. My stomach twists again in a very new way that I don't feel like analyzing at the moment.

Faye: You did not get me groceries.

Eli: Technically Monica, a lovely Instacart employee, got you groceries.

I unload the bags, finding a variety of soups, some bananas, a loaf of bread, and a Vogue magazine.

Faye: The Vogue is a nice touch.

Eli: You seem fashion-y so thought you might like it.

Eli: Is fashion-y a word?

Faye: This is too much. What's your Venmo? I will pay you back.

Eli: We need you healthy again so you can get back to your fun needs.

Faye: I think I've had enough fun for awhile.

Eli: You're not giving up yet are you?

I pour the can of chicken noodle into a bowl and place it in the microwave.

Faye: It feels silly

Eli: Not owning sheets is silly

Faye: Rude

The microwave beeps and I use the blanket wrapped around me as an oven mitt to remove it.

Eli: I think you need a coach.

Faye: I think I need new friends who don't pressure me.

Faye: p.s. the soup is a lifesaver

I precariously set my soup down on the coffee table and get settled in on the couch.

Eli: It's not pressure. It's encouragement.

Eli: I hate soup, but it seemed like the right thing to get.

Faye: You hate soup??? It's the best food.

Eli: No way.

Faye: I could eat nothing but soup for the rest of my life.

Eli: Gross

Eli: p.s. you can't change the subject. What's next on the list?

I get up to grab the list from my counter and bring it back over to the couch, smoothing out the wrinkled paper.

Faye: New job is a pretty high priority.

Eli: Good idea. Maybe something with better pay so you can afford a set of sheets.

Faye: GOODNIGHT

Faye: And thank you again.

Eli: You're welcome. Goodnight.

I finish my soup and curl up in my couch nest, feeling much better.

13

———

ELI

"I THINK you're ready for your first role assignment."

I'm in my first one-on-one meeting with my manager, Melissa. She's not much older than me, but she carries herself in a way that makes me a little terrified of her. Sitting here in her office, I feel like a little kid being sent off to spend the day with their scary great aunt who thinks sorting coins is a fun activity.

I sit up in my seat. "Awesome, that sounds great."

"There's an opening for a project manager role in the operations department. The last person in this role was let go for insubordination."

"Wow, what happened?"

She puts her glasses on, like she needs to get a better look at me, and I feel a little uncertain. I'm not someone who hates attention by any means, but the way she's looking at me feels like I'm under a microscope and she's searching for something that I will never be able to understand. "Does that matter?"

"I guess not. Just . . ." I shift uncomfortably in my seat and wipe my palms against my pants. "Curious, that's all."

She continues, "Looking for someone with a background in tech, preferably. You'll find details on pay and benefits in the portal." She pauses, glaring at my hands that I'm way too slow to realize are empty when they should probably be writing this down.

"Sorry, can you give me just a second? Forgot my notepad at my desk."

"Hurry back," she says while turning her chair to face her computer screen.

I jog out to my cubicle and grab the neon blue Millionfish branded notebook sitting on my desk. I got it in a welcome package on my first day, along with a water bottle and a sweatshirt with Guppie, the company mascot, on the front.

Melissa is talking on the phone when I step back in her office. "Mm-hmm, yeah, mm-hmm, got it. Okay, mm-hmm, perfect."

"Everything okay?" I ask after she hangs up.

She sighs. "Look, I'm going to give it to you straight. We are embarking on a rapid growth initiative and need more bodies."

"More. Bodies." I nod along and write the words in bold in my notebook.

"The problem is that we're struggling to be competitive with other big companies in a similar space to us. Employee retention is at an all-time low and management is scrambling to not only hold onto the talent we have, but hire more people to align with where the company wants to be."

I remember Faye mentioning that her boss said something about this to her, too. "I see. So is the company making changes to their offerings?"

"How so?" she asks.

"Well, benefits or other perks?"

"Oh, well, that's the other thing. We don't really have the revenue right now to offer better health benefits or anything like that. But we do have our annual company party coming up that usually provides a little boost."

"But nothing long-term?"

Her eyes harden and I remember that I'm scared of her. "Eli. You have a job, and I have a job, and we know what we have to do. Right?"

"Right. Sorry, just anticipating potential questions a candidate might ask."

She seems to like this answer, and I relax a little. "That's good thinking. Just stick to the talking points. You're just doing intro calls, so there shouldn't be too much detail given."

I resist the urge to mention that health benefits would be the first thing most people ask about during these intro calls. I guess I'll figure out how to navigate that when the time comes.

"What is the timeline for when they're looking to have someone in place?"

"Ideally within a month," she says.

That's soon, considering how long these things usually take between working with schedules and finding candidates that are a good fit for the role.

"Okay, no problem." I can do this. I can make this happen. No need to stress about a repeat of my last performance review at my previous job.

Unreliable. . . No growth mindset. . .

"I think you'll be a great fit here, Eli. You should have access to the applicant portal so you can begin screening. I look forward to hearing about your progress."

This bolsters me up a little, and I feel more confident. "I'll get started this afternoon."

I MAKE about ten phone calls before I start to feel like I'm going to lose my mind if I have to leave another voicemail. Two people have called back so far, and both said they weren't interested when they found out the pay for the role. One woman was so shocked, she said she thought I was joking when I told her the salary.

Focusing on a single task like this goes against every fiber of my being. I feel so full of pent-up energy, I could sprint laps around the office. I think a little afternoon exploration break is needed, so I send a Slack message to Faye.

Eli: What are you doing?

Faye: Working?

Eli: Come with me to the duck pond.

Faye: Can't. I'm swamped.

Eli: Are you making a pond joke?

Faye: Not intentionally, but that was pretty good though.

Faye: We have a duck pond?

Eli: I heard there might be baby ducks.

Tom told me about a small pond located on the property that may or may not have a family of ducks living in it. And I know I'm curious about it. Who can resist the pull of potentially seeing some baby ducks? I see dots pop up and go away a few times before she responds.

Faye: I guess I could use a break too.

We meet in the lobby five minutes later. This is the first time I've seen her today. She looks pretty in a flowy skirt with flowers all over it and a white T-shirt.

We head outside and I lead us toward the path Tom told me about.

"Are you sure this is even on company property? I feel

like an old man is going to come out of the trees any minute screaming for us to get off his land."

"According to Tom, it is. I'm surprised you don't know about it, since you've been here so long."

She shrugs. "As you can tell, I very much stay in my cubicle-shaped bubble."

"Well, I'm glad you broke out today. Although, it's fucking hot out here." It's stifling, like the air itself is as bored as I was.

"Summer's last, dying, humid breath," she says, puffing the collar of her shirt up and down. I tear my eyes away from the little bits of skin that are revealed each time she lifts the fabric.

The tall grass brushes against our legs as we keep walking along the overgrown path. We finally reach a point where I can see water sparkling through the trees. "There it is."

"This is actually really nice," she says. "I wonder why they never told us about this place."

There's an old picnic table by the water that we precariously sit on. No sign of the ducks yet, but it's still a relief to be out of the office for a bit.

"How are things going so far?" she asks.

"I actually got my first role assignment today."

"That's awesome. Hitting the ground running."

"Yeah, I only have a month to get it filled. And based on the calls I made today, I've got my work cut out for me."

"What's the role?"

I tell her about it, and I watch her visibly perk up. She doesn't say she's interested, but I can tell she's intrigued by it.

"You interested?" I ask.

"In what?"

"The job. I can send you the posting if you want to take a look."

"Oh my god," she says, frantically pointing at the water. "Babies!"

A duck swims into view, and sure enough, there are about eight or nine baby ducks swimming along behind it.

"I thought Tom was messing with me when he told me there were baby ducks."

She smiles. "There's even a little straggler falling behind. This is so cute, I can't stand it." The ducks swim by us, and we watch as they make their way to the other side of the pond where a tree has fallen into the water.

In my periphery, I spot two swans along the edge of the water by the trees. "Holy shit, look over there."

"This is crazy," she says in awe. "Where am I right now?"

The swans move slowly, gracefully, through the water. "Did you know swans mate for life?" I ask.

Do her cheeks flush or is it just the heat? "Oh yeah?"

"Saw in on *Planet Earth*, I think."

"That's sweet. And surprising."

"Why is it surprising?"

"I don't know. I wonder why they only have one mate. Like, evolutionarily it doesn't make sense."

"Maybe they're in love," I say.

She snorts and almost smiles. Almost.

The swans do this push and pull sort of thing, dancing around each other in the water.

"It's kind of mesmerizing," I say.

"Yeah, it is," she says.

They continue their dance until finally wrapping their necks around each other. I look over at Faye to see if she sees this too, hardly able to believe I'm witnessing this at all.

I expect to see the wonder that I'm currently feeling. But she looks almost sad when she says, "I feel like we're watching something not meant for our unworthy human eyes."

I look back at the swans, still wrapped up in each other, completely unaware that we're even watching them. "Maybe they aren't real, and are just some kind of mirage."

"Maybe they're an omen or warning," she says in a doom-filled voice.

"Maybe they're casting a spell on us," I say.

She looks at me, then, her blue eyes big and serious. "Maybe we're cursed."

"Oh no," I say, not breaking eye contact. "How do you think we break it?"

She shifts her focus back to the water. "I'm thinking blood sacrifice."

"Or a nice, high-quality baguette."

She laughs, the sweetest sound I've ever heard, and I add it to my mental tally.

"We should probably head back," she says, hopping off the bench and brushing the backs of her legs off.

I take one last look at the swans before following her back up the path.

14

—

ELI

MY DAD STARES at the giant old oak tree in my parents' backyard like it's an enemy he's been trying for years to defeat. He slowly marches around the trunk, scratching at his beard in deep thought. He's always had that beard, although now it's completely gray.

He's been at it for twenty minutes. "Do I need to leave you two alone for a bit?"

He jabs a finger at the tree. "Today is the day." He bends down to pick up a squiggly flower thing, and tosses it at me. "I can't keep scooping these things out of the pool."

"You're not cutting the whole thing down, are you?" This tree and I have shared some great memories together. Like in third grade, when I tried to climb it and broke my arm falling from the big branch that hangs out over the yard.

"No, this tree is older than God. I'd never cut it down." He looks up and points. "Just that branch hanging over the pool."

The pool is a newly installed gift he got my mom for their big anniversary. He pretends it was something he did for her begrudgingly, but we all know he secretly loves having something to tinker with. I haven't even had a chance to swim in it because he's convinced the chemicals aren't quite right yet.

"Shouldn't you get a professional to cut it down?" Normally I'm all for trying something new, but I'm not sure I'm ready to venture into the tree-trimming business. "Or at the very least, Emmett might be a better help than me. He's at least used a power tool before."

"Nah, I watched a few YouTube videos." My dad goes by the "why pay someone to do it when you can do it yourself" way of living. "And Emmett was busy today," he adds.

He moves the ladder next to the base of the tree closest to where the branch hangs over. "You get up on the ladder and I'll hand you the trimmer."

I climb up the ladder, and he hands me the tool he's rigged with some kind of extension that allows for further reach. I see another broken arm in my future. "Do I just start chopping at the branch? What if it falls on my head?"

"Oh shit, hang on. I've got a hard hat here somewhere."

He disappears by the side of the house, but I hear him rummaging around in the garage. He comes back with a purple bicycle helmet.

"Thought I had one, but I think I let your brother borrow it for his kitchen demo." He tosses the helmet up to me. It's covered in sparkly star stickers and has Evie's name written in Sharpie marker on the inside of it. "This'll do just fine."

"You sure about that?" I put the helmet on my head, but since it's obviously not made for a grown adult, it just perches on top. I can buckle the straps, but barely. "I think OSHA might think otherwise."

"The branch won't fall on you. It'll go into the pool."

From this angle, the branch looks even more large and

menacing. I have flashbacks to when I fell from it. "And we meet again." I look back down at the ground and try to imagine what a professional would do in this situation. "How heavy do you think this thing is? Won't it just crash into the water and make a big mess?"

Dad snaps his fingers in the air. "Ah, good thinking. Let me find the pool cover."

I hear the sounds of more digging in the garage. This time, he comes out dragging a big blue tarp behind him.

"Forgot we hadn't bought the cover yet, but this will work." He spreads the tarp over the top of the pool. "Alright, give her a good chop, son."

I turn the trimmer on and start by cutting a tiny off-shoot from the main branch to see what happens. It floats down, and lands quietly onto the tarp.

"See? This'll be easy," he encourages.

Feeling more confident now, I drive the trimmer into the base of the branch. Since it's pretty thick, this might take a while. My shoulders are already starting to burn, but I power through. I pause to take a look at how far I've gotten, because it feels like it could fall at any minute.

But I've only cut about an inch into it.

"What on earth are you two doing?"

I lower the trimmer slowly and rest it on top of the ladder. "I thought you said she was out running errands," I whisper down to my dad.

He shrugs apologetically. "You know I can't keep up with her."

"Hey, Mom. How are you today?" I smile down at her in the way that usually gets me out of trouble.

She pulls her sunglasses on top of head and glares at me. "Eli Thomas Miller, get down from that ladder."

The smile has never worked on her.

My dad turns to her. "Patti, you said that you wished there was a way to keep the pool from getting so dirty."

She gives him an exasperated look. "So, you've got our son up on a ladder risking life and limb?"

"He's doing a great job. Look, he's almost done." My head darts back and forth between the two of them like I'm watching a verbal tennis match. I decide it's best not to interject that I'm not even close to being done. Right now, the branch looks like it's been poked at a few times by the world's tiniest axe.

I feel my phone vibrate in my pocket.

"We can call somebody to do this. It's dangerous," she says.

"Mom, it's fine. See?" I knock my knuckles against the side of the helmet. "Safety first."

She shakes her head, and I vaguely hear them talking in the background while I check to see who has texted me.

Faye: Hey coach, you busy this weekend?

I take a selfie and send it to her.

"We need to take a break anyway," my dad says. This is definitely his way of admitting defeat without actually admitting defeat.

I climb down from the ladder, careful not to accidentally trim one of my own limbs off.

"Are you hungry?" Mom holds up a white paper bag. "I have hot dogs."

We head inside and she lays the food out on the kitchen island. I grab a hot dog and some fries and head into the dining room but stop short when I see a bunch of stuff piled up on the dining table. "Why does it look like Party City threw up in here?"

"Evie," she says bluntly. "She's getting a little carried away with this party planning."

"Sounds like typical Evie to me."

Her brows furrow in concern. "Maybe, she seems . . . off."

"Breakups are tough," I say, taking a bite of the hot dog.

"Breakup? I didn't know about a breakup." Oh no. I mentally prepare for Evie's wrath when she finds out I broke this news to Mom. "Steve, did you know about Evie's breakup?"

Dad mumbles through a mouthful of food, "Never liked the kid."

"Still, poor Evie-bear." She takes her phone out of her purse. "I should call her."

"She seemed okay about it when we played tennis the other day," I say, hoping to hold her off for now.

"You're right, she's resilient. I'm sure she's fine." She pats my arm. "And how are things with you?"

I tell her about how the job has been going, about Andrew jetting off to the Netherlands.

"How's the apartment hunt going?"

So far, I've looked at two places in my price range where I'd have to either live with five other people or become well-acquainted with a colony of mold spores. "Not great. Unless you want me to contract a permanent respiratory illness in exchange for having your basement back."

"You'll find something," she says for what feels like the millionth time. "Any other news?" my mom asks nonchalantly, while she dips a fry in ketchup.

"Like what?"

"Evie told me you aren't dating."

There are no secrets in this family. Now I don't feel as bad about spilling the news about her breakup. "Is that a concern?"

"Well, honey, you're about to turn twenty-seven."

"And?"

"You just seem lost. Now that you're back home, I'd like to see you settled."

Settling down and doing the whole marriage and two-point-three kids or whatever has always been some vague idea of my future that I've never spent much time considering.

But she's right that I'm not getting any younger.

The pressure hits me suddenly. Where am I going to live? Say I meet someone tomorrow that brings this fuzzy future into focus. What are they going to think when I tell them I live at home with my parents, or that I've never been in a serious relationship before?

"One thing at a time, Mom." My mom means well, but I don't know how to tell her that all of the things she's suggesting I do feel impossible when your track record isn't the best. It would come out sounding like an excuse.

"Do you remember Claudia, my friend from book club?"

"Is she single?"

She continues without acknowledging I said anything. "She and I were talking the other night. Her daughter, Dani, just moved back from spending time with their family in Mexico. She is *so* smart and *so* gorgeous. Claudia gave me her number so you can call her."

A blind date doesn't exactly sound fun to me, but this isn't a battle I feel like fighting now. So, I do what I always do: agree and change the subject. "Sure, sounds great. Do I need to get a license or anything for the party?"

"For what?"

"To do the wedding officiating. Am I like a priest now? Can I wear an outfit?"

She shakes her head. "No, we're not doing a ceremony,

although this will be news to your sister. You just need to say a few words and that's it."

I'm honestly a little nervous about this speech. What do I know about marriage? What do I know about love? Specifically, about a love like the one my parents have. They communicate telepathically, that's how in sync they are. In fact, right now I watch them ask each other from opposite sides of the kitchen, *Will we regret asking Eli to speak at this party?* with nothing but two blinks. They're probably worried I'll say something inappropriate in front of my ninety-year-old grandma.

"Just be yourself. Everyone loves you and you'll know what to say. Just keep it classy and sincere."

I take my phone out of my pocket to check the time before heading over to Andrew's place to check on the plants. I see that Faye's responded to my text.

Faye: I see you're very busy . . . riding your Huffy bike?

Eli: Got my training wheels off and everything.

Faye: Wow big day for you.

Eli: Helping my dad with some yard work. Long story. What's up?

Faye: I was hoping to chat more about that project manager job.

Faye: I don't even know if I have the experience for it.

Eli: Yeah, we can def talk about it. Do you have a resume?

Faye: I'm sure I can dig one up, but I'm sure it needs work.

Eli: Do you want to meet up and look at it together? Might be easier to talk through in person.

Or am I just looking for a reason to see her? I could easily look at her resume and give her comments and suggestions over a phone call.

Faye: How about I buy you a coffee in exchange for the help?

"What are you smiling at?" Mom asks.

"Was I smiling?"

"You still are. Who are you texting?"

"Do you remember Faye, Andrew's girlfriend from school?" Faye practically lived at our apartment so I know they met a few times when my parents would visit.

"Yes, I remember her! She seemed sweet. Kind of quiet."

"She works at Millionfish, too. She might be a good internal candidate for a job I'm on the hiring team for. I think we're going to grab a coffee to look over her resume and talk about the role."

"She isn't in Amsterdam with Andrew?"

"No, they broke up."

"Aw, that's too bad. I hope Andrew is okay. He never responds to my texts inviting him over for dinner."

"He's a workaholic. I can't believe he's even taking a vacation, honestly."

"I'm glad he's taking some time off." She takes another casual bite of a fry. "Based on the smiling I'm guessing you and Faye are . . . friendly?"

I don't roll my eyes even though I want to. "Yes, Mom, we are friends."

A friend I selfishly enjoy flirting with. A friend I selfishly enjoyed taking care of when they were sick, maybe going a little overkill with the groceries. But seeing her laying there and not feeling well, knowing she'd wake up to that empty apartment. No one wants to be sick and alone.

Eli: How about tomorrow morning? What's your favorite coffee spot?

We decide to meet at 10:30 at a café near her apartment.

"Well, tell your *friend* I say hello."

15

———

FAYE

ELI and I are crammed in the corner of the coffee shop by the window, sitting hip to hip and hovered over my laptop. I cross my legs under the table and accidentally kick him in the shin.

"Sorry," I say. "Didn't think about how crowded it would be on a Sunday morning."

He bumps me with his shoulder. "I don't mind."

"So, what's the verdict?" I ask, ignoring the little flit of jitters I get when I'm around him now.

He scratches his beard. I've noticed he does this when he's uncertain, like he's buying time to think of the best way to say something. "This font is an interesting choice."

"Is that your way of saying it's terrible?" I ask.

"It's not a bad font, but not the best for a resume. You may want to use something easier to read."

I was so bored putting my resume together that I had to trick myself into making it entertaining by playing with fonts and formatting. "I was just trying to add a little flair."

"Flair is nice, but I don't know that it would be properly appreciated for this role."

The role in question is something I think I'd be good at, even though project management is very different from what I do currently. Although, managing Alexis's requests and moods can feel like a project in and of itself. I think I'm so desperate for something else, I'd take anything at this point.

"Flair aside, do you think I'd be a good fit for it? I don't have a ton of experience with a lot of what they're looking for."

"Sometimes that doesn't matter, especially since you have so much company knowledge. It says you started there as an intern?"

I nod.

"That's good. It'll show them you're loyal. Committed to your career goals." He waves his hand around. "You know what they like to hear."

"Oh yeah, I know how to play the corporate lingo game."

"Then this will be a breeze. I'm going to tell them they should interview you."

"Just like that?"

He shrugs. "Sure, why not?"

I laugh. "You make everything sound so simple."

"It's not simple, but—" He gestures to my computer screen. "You're the best I've talked to so far."

Eli scrolls through the document, erasing some of what I have and replacing it with wording that makes more sense. I let him do his thing as I let my eyes wander around the busy shop.

I look up to the front, making brief eye contact with the barista. He's tall, with short, blonde hair and I've always thought he was kind of cute. The butterflies in my stomach bounce around a bit and I'm relieved this isn't a purely Eli phenomenon. I've thought about that pretend kissing last weekend way too much. So much I started dreaming up scenarios where the kissing wasn't pretend at all.

And being so close to him in a cozy coffee shop isn't helping matters. Our bodies have been pressed together the whole time we've been here. I don't know if I'm imagining it, but my skin hums against his, like a purring cat in a patch of sunlight.

I watch the barista brush a piece of hair out of his face before smiling at a customer and taking their order. Maybe the hot barista would be a good option to explore, but I have no idea what to do or say. And he's working, so I don't want to be the kind of person that bothers him while he's trying to do his job.

"Are you okay?" Eli asks.

I shrug out of my jean jacket, attempting—and failing—to avoid touching Eli's arm in the process. "Yeah, it's just kind of hot in here."

"What are you talking about? When we arrived you immediately put on your jacket and complained about how they're blasting the AC."

"Well, I got acclimated and now I'm hot."

He smirks and nods toward the front of the shop. "Why do you keep looking up at the counter?"

"I wasn't looking up there."

"Do you know him?"

"Not really. He's working sometimes when I come in."

"He seems cool. We talked for a few minutes when I was ordering. Found out we went to the same summer camp back in elementary school."

"That reminds me, I was supposed to be buying *you* coffee." I got here and he had already ordered our drinks. He got a large coffee for himself and a vanilla latte for me.

"I got here early and figured I'd just go ahead since they were so busy."

"So how did you even find that out? About the summer camp?"

"I commented on one of his tattoos and said it looked like the logo for a camp I went to as a kid. It's an outline of a mountain range. Turns out he went to the same camp. I asked him if he still hikes there, and he mentioned he's going next weekend." He takes a sip of his coffee. "Small world."

"Interesting. So he likes hiking?" I don't get hiker vibes from him. He looks like the kind of guy who sits on a park bench while pretending to read *The Bell Jar*, but he's cute so you kind of don't care.

"I guess so." He taps my foot with his. "Do you have a little crush?"

"On him? No."

He leans forward and places a hand under his chin. "You seem very interested in his hobbies."

"I'm interested in getting this resume done. We're supposed to be coming up with my top five skills."

I delete the *Communication* bullet point.

"You seem like you want to talk to him."

He's like a dog with a bone. I fiddle with my straw, squeaking it up and down in my plastic cup. "I can't."

"Why can't you?"

"I'll be weird about it. I don't know how to talk to people."

"You talk to me."

"That's because I know you."

"Let's practice. Pretend I'm him." He leans back in his chair. "Ask me out."

I shift in my seat. "I think you've done enough pretend

stuff for me. Plus, I literally don't know where to begin. I've been scrambling for a conversation starter and the only thing I can come up with is that I should ask him if he likes coffee."

He smiles. "He might find that charming."

I give him a skeptical look. "More like embarrassing."

I can tell I've given him some kind of quest he wishes to complete, but I stop him from saying anything else by asking, "Now, what do you think about collaborative and adaptable as potential skills?"

Thankfully, this gets us back to the task at hand and we spend the next ten minutes working through the rest of the document. I'm pleased with what we've put together and already feel more confident, like I might actually have a shot at this.

"How long have you been coming to this coffee shop?" Eli asks.

"A couple of years. Plus, I can walk here now since I moved, and the coffee is really good."

"Yeah, it's nice having a place that's convenient and has good coffee." He looks out the window. He's got a bit of sunburn on his nose, I guess from being outside helping his dad yesterday. "This is a cool neighborhood. Have you ever been to that bar across the street?"

"Yes, I love that place. It's very cozy and dark."

"Maybe we could go there sometime. We can get espresso martinis to satisfy our caffeine fix."

"Yeah, maybe we can—" I stop, realizing what's he's doing. That was good. *Too* good. I sniff. "That proves nothing."

He smiles, eyes twinkling with triumph. "It proves that it's not that hard."

"But it's easy for you. You always know what to say, and . . ." I gesture to him. "You know . . ."

"What?"

"Your face . . ." I take a sip of my drink, wishing I'd never even said anything. "It's a . . . good one."

He seems baffled by this. "Thank you. But Faye, *you* are attractive. And he keeps looking back at you, too. All you have to do is bat those big blue eyes at him and he'll do anything you like." He sighs before continuing, "Trust me."

"You can't be serious." It can't really be that easy.

"Only one way to find out. It's slowed down, so you won't feel like you're in his way."

He's right, so I can't use the excuse that I'd be bothering him while he's busy. "Fine, but you can't watch."

The idea of him watching me fumble through a conversation with someone is too much. This is already strange enough, going from pretend flirting to pretend kissing the other night. Before, I could use being drunk as an excuse, but it's a bright, sober morning. I can't pretend this isn't weird.

"What if I close my eyes?" he asks, placing his hands over his face.

I take my hair down so I can re-do my bun. I'm stalling.

He peeks through his fingers and his eyes track the movement as I put my hair back up. "Stop stalling."

"Okay, I'll go talk to him."

Eli stands up so that I can get squeeze past him, whispering, "Go get 'em tiger," to me as I pass.

I make my way up to the counter and tell myself this is going to be fine. He's looking down at his phone. What if I'm interrupting an important text conversation, like maybe his great aunt needs a kidney transplant and if he doesn't respond within ten seconds she will die, and he'll have that on his conscience for the rest of his life because he had to be polite to a customer.

"What can I do for you?" he asks.

I smile in a way that I hope is warm and friendly and not like an alien who is mimicking human emotion. "Thought I might want to consume something besides caffeine this morning. These pastries look really good."

He moves to stand behind the pastry case. "Good call. What are you in the mood for?"

"What's your favorite?" This feels like something Eli would ask. I resist the urge to look back at where he's sitting to make sure he's keeping his promise of not watching us.

"The strawberry rhubarb danish is one of our seasonal pastries right now. It's a fan favorite."

"Okay, I'll try that one."

He moves to grab the pastry from the case.

"Actually, can I get a couple of those?" I ask.

"Sure thing." He wraps the pastries in some tissue paper and hands them to me. He punches the order in. "That'll be $8.50."

"Thank you." I swipe my card. "Um, I'm Faye, by the way. I come here so often, so I figured I should introduce myself."

He smiles at me. It's the kind of smile that doesn't quite reach his eyes, but still a pretty good one. "I'm Cameron."

"Nice to officially meet you," I say.

"It's nice to meet you too."

A woman comes up to counter. "Excuse me," she says. "Do you have any French loaves left today?"

Cameron nods to the pastries in my hand. "Hope you like it. I'll see you around?"

I nod emphatically. "Definitely."

When I turn around to head back to the table, I notice Eli was absolutely breaking his promise and was not only watching the entire thing, but sitting up biting his nails like he's trying to expend some kind of nervous energy.

"You said you wouldn't watch," I say, as he stands up to let me back to my seat.

"It looks like it went well?"

"I think so. I got his name."

"And?"

"That's it?"

His face changes and he now beams at me, like I've done something very impressive. "Well, that's a start. Maybe next time you can get his astrological sign."

I roll my eyes and hand him one of the pastries. "For your help today."

"Thank you," he says, smiling like I just gave him a gift he's always wanted.

I take a bite of the danish. It's good, but a little crumbly and some of it falls into my lap. I brush the crumbs off and in the process, they fall onto Eli's lap.

He looks at me and arches a brow. "Was that payback for forcing you talk to him?"

I cover my mouth to hide my smile. "No, I'm sorry." I almost reach down to brush them off his lap before catching myself. "I feel like I owe you more than a danish. Is there anything I can help you with, so I don't feel like such a leech?"

"You're not a leech." He shows me his phone screen. I see a string of texts from his mom. "Got any ideas for how to help with a meddling mother?"

One good thing about having a completely hands-off mother is that at least she's not a meddler.

"Who is Dani?"

"A woman she's trying to set me up with." He sighs and sets his phone down. "Apparently I have offered to take her to dinner this Saturday night."

The butterflies that belong to Eli sink down, like they're disappointed in this development. But this is good. Him encouraging me to talk to other guys and telling me about his dates with other women. I need the reminder that his help is strictly friendly.

"And you don't want to go?"

"For some reason a blind date seems so . . . I don't know. Bleak?"

"I get it. Kind of feels like the final dating frontier or something."

"Exactly. My mom just worries about me, I think. My parents have a big anniversary coming up, and she's got her mind on matrimonial bliss."

"How long have they been married?"

"Thirty years."

"Wow, that's . . . rare."

"Yeah, it is. And now they want me to give a speech." He shakes his head and puffs air out of his cheeks. "Not sure how I got roped into that."

I know exactly how he got roped into it. Because he's charming and handsome and exactly the kind of person you want giving a speech at your party.

"I'm sure you'll give a great speech."

"Everyone keeps saying that, but I'm a little nervous about it."

"Why?"

"Because . . ." He shifts in his seat and I'm seeing him express discomfort in a way I've never seen before. "I don't know what it feels like."

"What do you mean?"

"Being in love. I've never even been in a real relationship before."

I'm honestly not super surprised by this, considering Eli always had a steady but short-term sort of dating lifestyle from what I observed during college. Maybe that hasn't changed much. But I am surprised at how he seems to be disappointed by his lack of a serious dating history.

"I think you can still give a great speech about your parents without having experienced that yourself."

"Yeah, maybe." He looks down, almost like he's feeling shy about what he wants to say next. "I just feel like I *should* have experienced that by now."

"Have you . . ." I don't know how to ask this because it's none of my business. "Tried to be in one? A relationship, I mean."

"Kind of, but not really. I've been told I'm not serious enough."

Told by who? A previous girlfriend in New York? I want to ask more, but if he wants me to know more, he'll tell me.

He shakes his head. "I just haven't met the right person, I guess."

I ball up the tissue paper my danish was wrapped in. "You never know, maybe Dani will be the right person."

He chuckles. "I appreciate the optimism."

"I'm sure it'll be fun. You always make things fun."

He tilts his head, and I swear I almost see him blush a little. "Thanks." He leans back in his seat. "So, next time you come in you're going to get that date, right?"

"I thought I'd just pine over him for a few years before doing anything about it," I say.

He shakes his head at me, with a smile. It's a real one; the kind of smile that makes you feel like the only person who's ever been smiled at before. If he smiles at Dani like that, his mom will have nothing to worry about.

I shut down those thoughts along with my laptop and lift my empty coffee cup. "Cheers for good luck to both of us?"

His face is relaxed and earnest as he clicks his cup against mine and says, "Cheers to that."

16

———

FAYE

RETT and I are lying on my bed, newly clad in an overpriced striped linen duvet cover and sheet set I impulse-bought from an Instagram ad, staring up at my freshly-painted bedroom walls.

"What if I made the wrong choice?" I ask.

In the paint aisle of the hardware store, "Dark Burgundy Wine" felt very moody and relaxing. In reality, it's making me feel like I'm actually inside a glass of merlot.

"I don't really think there's a wrong choice. You like this color, don't you?"

"Do you think it's a little dungeon-esque?"

She shrugs. "Maybe this is just the right color for you right now. You can always change it."

The right color for me right now. That makes me feel better, like this doesn't have to be permanent. But it's a step in the right direction toward making some sort of change in my space and the *Environmental* part of my list feels less daunting.

But I really hope I end up liking this color once I live in it for a while. "I don't know if I can ever look at a paint roller again." It took us three coats before it stopped looking like a recent murder scene and the likelihood that I'll be able to lift my arms tomorrow is looking slim. "I just need to put together that dresser and I'll have a real, grown-up bedroom."

"You're on your own, there. I don't do furniture assembly." She rolls over onto her stomach and props her chin in her hands. "This is why you need to start dating."

"So I'll have my own personal Task Rabbit?"

"Exactly. Let's discuss prospects."

I dig my phone out from underneath the covers. "I'm starving. You want to order food?"

"Yes, please. Has anything more happened with barista guy yet?" I should have never told Rett about meeting Cameron, because now she won't leave me alone about pursuing something with him. She even said that Eli was her new favorite person for making me talk to him.

"Cameron? I don't think that's a good idea. Pizza or Thai?"

"Why not?"

"I don't know . . . don't shit where you eat. Or fuck where you drink coffee. Or something."

"Let's do pizza." She grabs her phone. "That's dumb. Give me two seconds." A few seconds later she shows me her screen. "Is this him?"

"Yep, that's him."

She presses play on his latest post, a video of him standing in a dark kitchen.

There are a few things I notice immediately about this video. First, he's wearing an apron and nothing else. Second, he's surrounded by white tapered candles that are dripping wax down onto the stainless-steel countertop. And third, he appears to be demonstrating how to create some kind of latte art.

"Well, I'm intrigued," Rett says.

The video goes on to show him pouring the hot milk into the cup. He begins to make a squiggly, sort of ruffled shape with the foam. At first, I think he's making a flower. But as he finishes the design, I think I must be mistaken, and this is some kind of inkblot test situation.

"Is that a . . . ?" I ask.

"A foamy vulva? Yeah, I think it is."

Then, it jumps to a close-up shot of his hand caressing the rim of the cup until he slowly runs his middle finger down the center of the design.

"Is he . . . ?"

"Stroking the foamy vulva? Yeah, I think he is."

"Please stop saying 'foamy vulva'."

But it's not over yet, because the video ends with a shot of him running his tongue across the surface to lick up the foam before looking up to smirk at the camera.

"Message him," Rett says.

"I'm sorry, did we not just watch the same thing?"

"I watched a very well-crafted video with some lovely cinematography."

It takes a single second of eye contract between us, and we both burst out laughing while we watch the video again. There's something weirdly fascinating about it, in a car crash kind of way. You can't seem to stop watching.

"I'm serious," she says. "Go out with him."

"I can't go out with a guy who makes latte art thirst traps. Now I'm going to have to find a new coffee shop to go to, as it is."

"He's perfect for your sex need!" She holds her phone up to show where she's paused the video, Cameron's face filling the frame as looks passionately down at his frothy creation.

I grab her phone to investigate his profile more. "I just want normal, run-of-the-mill sex. I feel like he would try to pour hot coffee on my body or something."

She shrugs. "You know what, that's fair. Food stuff isn't for everyone."

"Are you into that?" The closest I've ever come to anything like that was having sex on top of a pizza box once.

"No, but one time a guy did ask me if we could use local honey as lube."

"Sounds . . . sticky." I keep scrolling through Cameron's page. There are a few similar videos that I don't watch, along with quite a few mirror selfies and carefully crafted photos of coffee cups next to a journal that looks like it's never been opened. "Wait, did it have to be local honey?"

"He seemed to be very specific about it."

"Maybe he had bad allergies," I say, and we both start laughing again. "Did you do it?"

"For a ticket to the worst yeast infection of all time? God, no."

"See? This is the kind of thing I am severely unprepared for."

"He won't pour hot coffee on you. And doesn't he get points for creativity?"

Creativity is one thing, but that video was maybe the most cringe thing I've ever seen. But maybe she's right, though—someone like Cameron would be a low stakes start to my dating journey. "How would I even go about this?"

"First, follow him. Then, like a few of his posts. He'll come to you. I promise."

"Really?"

"Yes, I give it two minutes and he'll have already

followed you back and sent you a message saying something like, 'Hey! How's your day going?'"

I'm skeptical of this approach, but I find his profile on my phone and press "Follow." Then, I like the video we just watched along with a photo of a crushed Sprite can on a sidewalk with the caption, *"Find the beauty in the mundane."*

Sure enough, no sooner than I've placed the pizza order do I get a notification that he's followed me, and I get a message from him that says, "Faye! What's up?"

I show the message to Rett. "Guess I'll never doubt you again."

"Told you," she says, clearly pleased with herself.

"What do I do now?"

"Say nothing."

I toss my phone down and cover my face with my forearm. "I don't want to play this game anymore."

She gets up and picks up one of the drop cloths from the floor. "It's all part of the mystery. You leave a guy on read and they go feral for you."

"Maybe in your case." Rett has always been a free-spirited kind of person, drawn to people who are a challenge. Men and women fall at her feet, but the people she likes are usually terrible. "I don't want to be mysterious."

"You're the most mysterious person I know."

I pick up the paint rollers and try to avoid smearing red paint on myself. "What are you talking about?"

"You don't let anyone know anything about you. You float through the world like a mystifying little fairy."

"Let me see your eyes. I think the paint fumes might have gotten to you."

"I'm just saying, you need to use your mysterious ways

to your advantage. Don't respond to Cameron. If I'm wrong, I'll help you put that dresser together."

"Aren't you supposed to tell me I should be more open to people, and that it's okay to allow them to know me?"

"Sounds like you're aware of that already."

———

IT'S 11:22 p.m. and I'm determined to sleep in my bedroom tonight. I close my eyes and attempt to relish the quiet, savoring the ambient noise of the traffic on the street below. A car door slams in the distance.

I hate it. I check my phone and nearly jump for joy when I see I have a text to distract me.

Eli: You got that date yet?

Faye: No, but I did stalk him on Instagram.

Eli: Find anything interesting?

I send him a link to Cameron's video.

Eli: You think he ever burns his tongue?

Faye: 100%. Rett thinks I should still go out with him despite the cringey video.

Eli: What do you think?

Faye: I think I might die alone.

My phone rings and it's Eli. I hesitate before answering, but I'm admittedly eager to feel someone else's presence in the room with me. I pick up on the second ring.

"Don't say that," he says.

"I don't want to date. I want to magically be with someone and already know every single thing about them without even having to try."

"Unfortunately, I don't think it works that way."

"Bummer."

"How was your day?" he asks.

"I painted my bedroom," I say.

"Oh yeah? What color?"

"Dark Burgundy Wine." The dark red makes the room feel even more like a cave at night, like it sucks any hint of moonlight out.

"So you *are* a vampire."

"I can't sleep, so maybe that's true. A coffin would go well in here."

He chuckles and I hear a rustling of sheets. "Why can't you sleep?"

"Because I'm in my bed."

"Likely place for you to sleep."

I roll over and look longingly out my bedroom door. "I usually sleep on the couch. But I need to overcome my fear of this bed."

"Why are you afraid of your bed?"

"Never mind." I wish I hadn't steered the conversation to this. Afraid of a bed? I sound insane. "What are you up to?"

"Is this your first time living alone?"

Should have known he wouldn't drop it. "Yep. Clearly, I'm adjusting well," I joke.

"At least you have your own place. I'm currently curled up next to my family's Christmas decorations. Hang on." He sends me a selfie of him laying on a couch with a Santa statue hovering behind his head. He's got a sheet pulled up to his chest, but I can see he's not wearing a shirt. I now have confirmation that he has tattoos on his shoulder and chest too. "Imagine waking up to that staring down at your sleeping body. Don't recommend."

I laugh. "So you live with your parents?"

"Currently, but I'm trying to find a place."

"I got lucky when this apartment became available.

Even though I think something is living in my walls. The other day I heard what I'm pretty sure is a family of squirrels scurrying above my head while I was making dinner."

"See? You don't live alone." His voice is groggy, and I like to imagine he's got me on speakerphone, his phone resting on top of his chest while he's talking to me.

I don't say anything for a few seconds, and he doesn't either. "I think it's the sleeping alone part that's hardest," I finally say, voice barely above a whisper.

"Yeah, I get that."

"I've been eyeing this really nice sherpa body pillow for a while now."

"That's very sad, Faye." I like when he says my name, even when we're not talking about anything important.

"Or very comfy?"

He laughs. "You're right. I won't judge."

I feel my eyes starting to get tired. "I think I'm going to try to sleep now."

"See you in the break room for coffee in the morning?" he asks.

"Sounds good," I say before drifting off.

TWO WEEKS into being a plant dad and I've already encountered my first emergency.

One of the pothos has two dead leaves and I'm trying not to freak out. I've frantically flipped through the binder and don't see anything in the FAQ section related to this problem with this plant.

Wow, have I managed to create a never-before-seen plant ailment?

I even Googled it and that didn't help. Everything I read said things like, "This plant is impossible to kill!" or "If you manage to kill *this* plant, you might as well kill *yourself*!"

Obviously, the easiest route would be to text Andrew and tell him that we have our first casualty. But what if this is a special plant to him? And then he decides to cut his trip short just to fly back to deal with a problem I've created? No, I refuse to text Andrew about this because I don't want to admit that I couldn't handle this relatively simple task.

The only person I can think to ask for help from is Faye. It's shitty, but maybe she will know some sort of secret trick about this plant from living with Andrew for so long.

I dial her number, hoping she isn't still at work. It's 6:30, but she always stays later than I do so I wouldn't be surprised if she was still there.

She picks up on the third ring. "Hey," she says.

"Hey, are you busy?"

"I'm still at work. Everything okay?"

"Yeah. Everything is fine . . ."

"Why do you sound like someone is dead?"

I look down at the dry crackled edge of what was once a beautiful green leaf. "Well . . ."

"Oh my god, Eli. What happened?"

"No *person* is dead."

She sighs and waits for me to say something.

"I'm at Andrew's place and I think I killed one of his plants."

"That's even worse. I'll be there in thirty minutes."

———

"THIS IS BAD." Faye bends down so she's at eye-level with the dead leaf.

"I know."

"These are impossible to kill," we both say at the same time.

"Should I just pull the dead leaf off?" I ask, reaching out to touch it.

She grabs my wrist. "No!" She lets go and says, "That could make the plant freak out and decide to self-mutilate it's other leaves."

I widen my eyes. "Plants can self-mutilate?"

"Yes." She looks unsure. "I think."

"Is that why that one is called a monster?"

She looks to where I've pointed to a large plant in the

corner of Andrew's living area and giggles. "That's a *monstera*."

"Are there, like, plant doctors? Maybe someone in the agriculture department at State could help."

She rubs her hands up and down the tops of her bare arms. "That could be an option."

I walk over to the thermostat and turn it up a couple of degrees. Maybe I gave the plant hypothermia when I adjusted the room temperature last night? Andrew keeps his apartment at a sauna-like temperature, and I couldn't take it. "Maybe I should just hide it."

"Hide it?" She looks skeptical. "From the man who paid someone to create an app where he could track his plant inventory and health?"

"I'm so dead."

She walks around the small table. "When's the last time you watered it?"

"Um, two days ago." I know it wasn't yesterday because I had a softball game then crashed afterward. The day before that I was involved in a minor traffic incident that resulted in three-hour AutoZone visit. "Give or take."

"Let's give it a little water and see how it looks tomorrow. No reason to worry just yet."

"Good idea. Maybe it just senses that Andrew isn't around, and this is some type of plant separation anxiety or something?" How do these things survive in nature?

"Sure, or that." She looks around. I see her eye the empty pizza box sitting on the kitchen counter, and then the duffle bag sitting on the dining table. "Are you staying here?"

"Oh, uh, yeah. I figured the place was sitting empty and only a few nights. And . . . . the plants were lonely?"

Plus, it momentarily got me out of my parent's house. I

forgot how nice it is not to share your space with decades of family junk. I'm hoping Andrew won't mind. Again, I didn't want to bother him on his trip to ask. At least, that's what I keep telling myself.

"Andrew doesn't know you're sleeping here?" The way she asks this confirms that I am making a mistake by not asking him. But what's the harm, really? It's not like I'm using his toothbrush.

"He'll be back in a few weeks, so I figured it wouldn't hurt anything."

"It's your funeral," she says, grabbing her purse from where she'd placed it on the kitchen counter.

I don't want her to leave yet. "Let me buy you dinner. As a thank you for helping me."

"You don't have to do that," she says. "I didn't really help that much anyway."

"As a thank you for the emotional support, then. How about Mexican food?"

She tries not to grin. "I guess a burrito would be a fair exchange for talking you off the ledge."

———

WE GO to a local Mexican place that was a regular stop for us back in school. It's crowded, but we manage to get a booth in the back corner.

The waiter brings chips and salsa to the table and takes our order. Faye gets a chicken burrito, and I get beef enchiladas. We both get margaritas.

"So what should I expect from the town hall at work tomorrow?" I ask, loading up a chip with salsa. Apparently, the company has these meetings once a month where they make important announcements and introduce new employees.

"Nothing too crazy. Although, I happen to know that we're short on quarterly sales goals so they'll probably say something vaguely encouraging, but what they really mean to say is that no one will get their bonuses."

"Ah yeah. The good old 'maybe next quarter' pep talk."

"Exactly. Meanwhile, the CEO is off doing CEO things like renting out a villa in Italy."

"Or a submarine to explore the Titanic."

She snorts. "Do you know what you're going to say?"

"For what?"

She dips a chip into the salsa and takes a bite. "For your two truths and a lie."

"I have no idea what you're talking about."

She looks at me with concern. "Didn't they tell you?"

"Tell me what?"

"When you're introducing yourself to the company, you're supposed to show your personality by telling two truths and a lie. And then we try to guess what your lie is."

When my manager told me about having to introduce myself, I do vaguely remember her mentioning something like that. "I'll probably just see what I feel like saying in the moment."

She looks at me like I sprouted another head. "Couldn't be me. I agonized over what I was going to say for days."

"What were yours?"

"I don't remember," she says, busying herself with taking her silverware out of the napkin.

"After agonizing over it for days, you don't remember?"

"That was like five years ago."

She definitely remembers, but doesn't want to tell me for some reason. Which only intrigues me further. "I bet you don't want to tell me because you know I'd guess it too easily."

"There's no way you'd guess it. You're not familiar enough with my lore."

I'd like to be. "So you *do* remember what you said."

She almost smiles but runs her tongue along her teeth to keep from fully allowing one to form. "You need to stop doing that."

"Doing what?"

"Tricking me."

The waiter returns to the table with our food. We both thank him before digging in. "How am I tricking you?"

"You get me to say what I don't want to say."

"You mean the truth?"

She rolls her eyes. "Shut up."

"When have I ever tricked you before?" I know I push sometimes, but I don't want her to think I'm ever trying to embarrass her.

"At the coffee shop. Suggesting we have espresso martinis, but really you just wanted to prove a point."

Was she disappointed about that? I know I set myself up for frustration with that one, putting the thought of a cozy bar date with Faye into my brain. Snuggled up in a corner with our cocktails, talking and flirting with each other. Kind of like right now.

"Sorry if that came across . . . wrong. But I did prove that point, didn't I?"

"You sure did," she says with a smug expression. "I'll be having espresso martinis with Cameron this weekend actually."

"You're going to that bar with him this weekend?" I don't know why this would bother me. It's not like I staked some kind of claim on espresso martinis in that particular bar.

"Actually, I'm not sure where we're going. He said he likes to be spontaneous and doesn't want to plan it too far ahead."

That's obviously his way of giving himself an easy out if he needs one, but I don't say that to her. I also don't say that she can do better than this guy, especially after seeing the videos he posts. But based on some of the comments I read, some people seem to be *really* into these latte fondling videos. Is Faye into that, too? "That's great."

I guess it's good that I have the date with Dani this weekend. Maybe that will keep me from focusing too much on how Faye's date is going.

"We'll see how it goes," she says in a way that almost sounds like she isn't looking forward to it.

I hate that there's a part of me that wants her to bail on him. But that would be a shitty thing for a friend to be thinking. I should want her to have a good date. "I'm sure you'll have a great time."

My phone lights up with a text from my sister.

Evie: Dress code for party is backyard chic. Make sure you look presentable.

I sigh and send her a one-word reply: Unsubscribe

"Everything okay?"

"It's my sister texting about my parents' party. What in the world is backyard chic?"

"No idea. Is that the party's theme?"

"That's the dress code, apparently. And she thinks I won't follow it appropriately, I'm sure."

"What are you planning on wearing?"

"I don't know, probably something similar to what I have on."

Faye gestures to my outfit—a white T-shirt and a pair of black athletic shorts—and shakes her head. "I can see why she's worried, then." She has the tiniest teasing gleam in her eyes—almost gone as fast as it appeared, but I saw it.

"What is that supposed to mean?"

"Well, you are single-handedly keeping those Hanes white T-shirts in production."

I look down at my shirt. "What's wrong with that? You find something that works, and you stick with it."

"Okay, but this is a special occasion. You should try to dress up a little."

"It's being held in a backyard with plastic tables and chairs. How do I dress up for that?"

She takes a sip of her margarita. Her lips leave a pink impression on the rim of the cup where the salt used to be. "Maybe a linen shirt?"

"I don't think I own anything like that. Is linen stiff?" I hate wearing uncomfortable, itchy clothes.

She gives me a pitying look, like my lack of fashion knowledge is much worse than she thought. "What are you doing after work tomorrow? I was planning on shopping for something to wear on my date, if you want to come along."

I groan. "Does that mean we'd have to go to the mall?" *Does that also mean I have to watch you pick out a dress to wear for someone else?*

"Unfortunately, yes," she says sympathetically. "It'll be fun."

Not exactly my idea of fun, but since it means more hanging out with her, I'd be lying if I said I wasn't looking forward to it just a little.

18

———

ELI

DID I say I was looking forward to shopping? I take that back.

I haven't been to the mall in years because I usually order anything I need online, so I don't have to do exactly what we've been doing for the last thirty minutes. Has it only been thirty minutes? Feels like way longer.

Pretty sure we walked by an escape room on our way to Urban Outfitters, and I understand why they're here.

"Remind me why I agreed to this again?"

Faye is looking through a rack of shirts while I stand off to the side. It feels like I'm a kid again, back to school shopping for clothes with my mom. I battle a childlike, instinctive urge to hide inside the clothing racks and jump out to scare her.

"Because you want to look nice for the party and put some effort into your appearance."

I choose to ignore that this implies I don't usually put effort into my appearance and instead do what I do best. Distract myself by talking. "Did you guess my lie this morning?"

"Of course," she says, like it was too easy.

"How did you know it?"

She pauses her rapid swiping of hangers to turn toward me. "Because you are so not a *Star Wars* kind of guy."

My lie was that *The Empire Strikes Back* is my favorite movie.

"What kind of guy am I?"

She tilts her head to the side and bites her bottom lip. And I find that I'm the kind of guy who hasn't stopped thinking about what it'd be like to kiss that bottom lip ever since that night at the bar. The kind of guy who wants desperately to know what kind of guy she thinks I am.

"You're more of a *Lord of the Rings* kind of guy."

"Well, who doesn't like *Lord of the Rings?*"

"I bet I can even guess your favorite character." She moves to another rack and holds up a shirt in front of me before placing it back. "Legolas. For sure."

"Obviously. He's the best character."

She looks up, dreamy expression on her face. "I prefer Aragorn."

"You know, you kind of look like Arwen."

"I wish," she says, holding up a short-sleeved button down with a bunch of flowers on it. "Do you like this?"

"Too whimsical." I spot a gray shirt on the end of the rack that looks comfortable and hold it up. "How about this?"

"Are you allergic to patterns?"

"I'm allergic to uncomfortable clothes."

I follow her around the store for a few more minutes until she shoves the shirts she's been collecting into my chest.

"Let me grab a few things to try on. We'll meet in the dressing room area."

Ten minutes later I'm stepping out of the dressing room in a shirt that looks like it was pulled straight from my dad's closet in the nineties. "I don't think purple is my color," I say.

"It's not that bad. It's just not . . . you."

"It's *not* me, because I'm not allowed to wear any of my own clothes."

"No need to get grumpy. We'll find something new that's still you."

I'm not so sure about that, but I go back to try on the next thing, a blue and white striped button-down. It's as soft as a worn-in T-shirt and I still feel like myself in it. I step out of the room and do slow spin. "Survey says?"

She doesn't say anything and stares at me for a few seconds. I wonder if I completely misjudged, and the shirt looks terrible. But then I see her eyes do a slightly impercep-tible scan of my body and I wonder if she might actually be checking me out. I resist the urge to make a teasing comment about it for fear that she'll stop looking at me.

Her voice is a bit gravelly when she says, "I think that looks really good."

"Perfect," I say as I turn to head back inside the dressing room.

I reluctantly change back into my old shirt, not wanting to take off the new one if it means Faye looks at me the way she just looked at me.

When I come back out, we swap places so that I'm now sitting on the bench outside the dressing room.

"Thanks for your help," I say, in an attempt to drown out the sound of clothing falling off her body. I look up at the fluorescent lights to will myself not to think about the fact that I'm about three feet away from a half naked Faye. "Maybe I can wear this on my date this weekend."

"With the woman your mom is setting you up with?"

I watch her bare feet move around in the space between the bottom of the door and the floor. Her toenails are painted cherry red. "Yeah. We're going to a brewery downtown."

Her feet stop moving and she doesn't say anything for a few seconds. She clears her throat. "That should be fun," she says brightly.

"Yeah. It should be a good time." That's what I'm hoping, anyway.

She comes out in a green dress that flows down to her ankles. "How do we feel about this one?"

I already know I'm going to like anything she puts on, but in an effort to not sound like a dog salivating over a potential meal, I say, "It looks nice."

"I can't look nice. I need to look ravishing." She does a couple of turns in the mirror. "Too many ruffles." She goes back in, and I hear the rustle of fabric. "I think I may need your help with this one. I can't get the zipper up." She cracks the dressing room door open so I can step inside.

This dress is black with little white flowers all over it and it's much more form-fitting than the last one. The zipper starts at the base of her back and I drag it up, forcing my eyes not to snag on what I can see of her bra, pale pink with lace trim. Some pieces of hair have fallen out of her bun, and I brush them to the side so they don't get caught as I bring the zipper to the nape of her neck. "All set," I say, my own voice full of gravel now.

Our eyes meet in the mirror. One second. Two seconds. "Thank you," she says.

We step out of the dressing room, and she asks my opinion on this one. I try to form a sentence but the only words I can seem to form are, "It's . . . really pretty."

It's funny, because I always have something to say. But when met with Faye in this dress, I'm left without a single thought other than an embarrassingly caveman-like impulse to pull her close to me. This shopping trip has become the best and worst time I've ever spent with a woman.

"You're right, you're a terrible shopping buddy. Is it too revealing?" As she asks this, she adjusts the front of the dress, moving her boobs into a different position. My brain short-circuits.

"Um . . . you're wearing this for your date with Cameron?"

I think part of me is asking this to remind myself that this dress isn't for me. It's for fucking Cameron from the fucking coffee shop with the fucking Instagram videos.

"Yes." She turns to look at the back of the dress in the floor length mirror outside the dressing rooms. Do not look at her ass in the reflection. Do not look at her ass in the reflection.

"That's a good date dress."

Her shoulders droop and I worry that I'm going too far in a neutral direction with my comments and I've made her deflate like that. "I just want to get it over with."

"Are you dreading it?"

"It's not that. It's just—I haven't been with anyone since Andrew, and I want to get the whole sleeping with some part over with."

"Okay, so you're just wanting to have a casual hook up thing." This is more painful that the time the novocain wore off before my root canal was finished.

"Exactly. So do you think this dress will send that message to him?"

I bark out a laugh. Because if I don't laugh, I'll probably

do something super embarrassing like groan, because I'd consider that mission accomplished.

I've seriously got to get a grip. Faye and I have become really good friends again. And Andrew is my *best* friend. Can't forget that very important detail.

"You look great." Then, my mouth speeds ahead of my brain and I add, "But you don't need a dress to make someone want to be with you. You always look good."

This makes a tiny flush bloom on her cheeks, and she smiles fully, teeth and all. I take this as her being pleased with my compliment and, as always, I feel high from this reaction from her.

"Then I'd say we have a winner," she says.

I wish I had an industrial freezer I could sleep in tonight.

19

———

FAYE

WHEN THE UBER lets me out on a deserted street next to a warehouse on the outskirts of downtown, I'm convinced that instead of going on a date with a man who might be a little too into himself, I'm about to be murdered. The only movement I catch is some type of small-to-medium-sized animal rummaging around a tipped-over city trash can.

This is what happens when you start dating again. You end up so desperate to get laid that you find yourself standing alone, with nothing but you and the sickening realization that this is where your actions have led you.

I check my phone to see if Cameron has texted me and I see a message from Rett.

Rett: Where the fuck are you?

At least I had the good sense to share my location with her before leaving my apartment tonight.

Faye: Cameron said he knew some kind of exclusive chef's table they do here.

I'm now wondering if exclusive is a code for some type of weird cannibalism thing. Fresh, frightened flesh of a young, dumb woman coming right up.

Rett: You need to leave.

I see headlights in my periphery and decide to move so that I'm pressed against the building just in case it isn't Cameron. The car stops a few feet from where I'm standing, and he gets out of the car.

Faye: Cameron just got here.

"Faye? Is that you?" he asks, approaching where I'm standing.

I step out of the shadows. "Yes, it's me." I wave awkwardly. "Hi."

He gives me a hug, enveloping me in a waft of cologne. It smells good, maybe a little overpowering.

"Sorry I'm late. Had to cover someone's shift."

And he didn't think to let me know so I wouldn't be standing alone out here? "No worries." I gesture to the building. "Is this the right place?"

"Yep, it's just this way." He takes my hand and leads me to a door on the side of the building. He knocks and shortly after a man appears.

"Name?" he asks.

"Brooks," Cameron says.

"This way, please," the man responds.

Cameron gestures for me to step in ahead of him. We're led through a damp hallway and then down a pair of rickety metal stairs to another closed door.

The man unclips a ring of keys from his belt and flips to the key that unlocks the door. I hear chattering coming from inside and I feel relief that more people are on the other side.

"Right this way, Mr. Brooks."

Cameron places a hand against the small of my back as we follow him into a low-lit room with small tables scattered around, where other couples are eating dinner. He stops by a table and Cameron and I take our seats.

"Someone will be right with you," he says before disappearing through the door we entered through.

From what I can see of the space, it sort of looks like if you placed some tables inside an empty hardware store and shut off all the lights.

Cameron smiles at me from across the table, his perfect set of white teeth glowing in the dimness. He's good-looking in a very on-purpose kind of way. He's dressed in all black tonight. Black slacks, black button-down open halfway down his chest. He's wearing a necklace that has a delicate gold chain with a small pendant resting just between his pecs.

He must catch me looking because he holds the pendant up for me to view. "My family's crest," he says. "From our hometown in Ireland."

"Oh, are you Irish?" I've never caught the hint of an accent, but maybe he's been in the United States for a while.

"Two percent," he says proudly.

"Wow," I say, taking a sip of water. "That's cool."

"I'm glad I was able to snag us a spot here. Very hard to get in, but they had a cancellation."

"Luck of the Irish, I guess."

He leans forward. "What was that?"

"Luck of the Irish? Because you're . . . Irish?"

"Oh," he pauses for a second before smiling. "Good one."

How am I going to make it through this date if I have to explain every—admittedly stupid—joke all night?

A waiter saves us from the awkward silence when she approaches to tell us the menu this evening and moves to set a wine list down on the table for us to review. Cameron halts her before she can set the list down. "We'll just have whatever the chef recommends tonight."

"Absolutely, Mr. Brooks."

I get the sense that he's trying to show off for me and I wonder if this is his go-to first date spot. Everyone here seems to know him. Or maybe I'm just not used to eating at places where you're referred to by your surname.

Turns out, I don't really have anything to worry about on the awkward silence front because Cameron ends up talking enough for the both of us. I'm not a chatty person by any means, but I have said maybe ten words in the hour we've been here, and most of them were just "thank you" to the server.

I know all about Cameron, though. He's originally from just outside of Boston but moved to Raleigh for school, and decided to stay because he liked the "North Carolina vibes." I don't ask for details on that because I'm not sure I want to know what that might mean.

He loves working in the coffee shop but hopes he can get some brand deals from his latte art videos so he can be a full-time content creator. He has a "sick" vinyl collection that he's sure I'd love. How he'd know this, I have no clue since he hasn't asked me anything about myself.

This could be an ideal scenario, though. Maybe Rett is right, and I should lean into being mysterious. If I'm just looking for something casual, why would I want him to know anything personal about me? He doesn't need to know that I grew up about thirty minutes away in a town with no grocery stores, but three Dollar Generals. Or that I'm allergic to penicillin. I'll keep the focus on him.

"What's your favorite album you own on vinyl?"

He takes a thoughtful sip of his red wine. "They're kind

of out there and little experimental, but they're really fun live. You've probably never heard of them."

"Try me."

"Red Hot Chili Peppers?"

I think he's joking so I laugh, wondering if maybe I've just been misreading his personality and he's been doing some kind of bit this whole time. But then he looks at me expectantly and I see that he legitimately thinks I may not have heard of one of the most popular bands of the last forty years.

I decide to do a bit of my own. "No, never heard of them," I say, feigning ignorance.

"They're awesome. Super retro but not in a lame way, you know?"

I nod. "Mm-hmm."

"Seriously. This new stuff? Painful. There's no emotion behind it, you know?"

"Totally. I love music that you can just really *feel* in your soul."

"Exactly. I saw them last year at . . ." his voice fades into the background as I discreetly check my phone.

Rett: I'm assuming you're not strung up on a meat hook in that place.

Faye: Stop watching Peaky Blinders.

Rett: How's it going?

Faye: Fine?

Rett: Want me to come get you?

Faye: No, I think I'll stick it out.

I take a bite of my duck in some sort of red wine something or other. It's sad, but I've been more engrossed in the food than my date.

Faye: The food is amazing at least.

". . . a real spiritual experience."

"Wow, that sounds amazing. Are you just a music fan or do you play, too?"

"My band is actually playing a show this weekend. You should come."

"Oh yeah? What's your band called?"

I'm guessing a string of nonsensical words or a reference to a random historical figure.

"Lobotomy Beach."

Close enough. "Maybe I'll swing by if I'm not busy." It feels like the right thing to say, even if I have zero interest in finding out what his band sounds like.

We finish up our meal and he leads me back outside. It's a muggy night, but you almost feel the first whispers of fall in the air.

"Thank you again for coming tonight," he says, stepping so close to me that we're practically toe to toe. Is he going to try to kiss me?

Do I want him to kiss me?

"It was . . . interesting. Can't say I've ever eaten French food next to an auto body shop before."

"You're funny," he says, leaning down to tuck a strand of hair behind my ear. I resist the urge to shy away from his touch. "What are your plans for the rest of the night?"

"I should probably get home to my . . ." I scramble trying to think of an excuse to leave. I think I have an idea of where Cameron wants the night to go, but I've decided I don't want to go there with him. "Squirrels."

He, rightfully so, looks confused. "Your squirrels?"

I pull out my phone to request the Uber. My driver is five minutes away. "Yeah, they can't be left alone for too long." It's technically true. What if they finally manage to work their way through my ceiling? Someone should be there to monitor the situation.

"Okay . . ." He still seems uncertain, but accepts the answer. "Can I see you again?"

"Sure? I'd like that?" Am I asking him or me?

He pulls me in for a hug but doesn't let go as he looks down at me. Here it comes, the first kiss I've had since Andrew. I find myself bracing for impact as he brings his mouth down to mine. The kiss is fine, but I had hoped for something sweeter, the two of us in perfect sync.

Instead, it's clunky and I'm distracted trying not to think about how we're standing precariously next to a puddle of unknown substance. My thoughts wander to places anywhere but this kiss. Like, is Eli having a good date, and did he wear his new shirt? I didn't end up wearing my new dress. I put it on, and it felt wrong to wear it for this date, like it deserved something more special.

Cameron seems pleased when he pulls away. The Uber pulls up shortly after and I have never been so happy to see a silver Honda CR-V in my life.

"Have a good night," he says, licking his lips as he shuts my door for me.

I give him a small wave through the window, relieved that I can go home now. Even if I only have a family of potentially rabid squirrels for company.

I LOVE FIRST DATES. I'm good at first dates. I look forward to first dates.

That was my mantra as I brushed my teeth before heading out to meet up with Dani.

It was my mantra when I was waiting outside for her to arrive. I thought if I repeated those three things to myself enough, I'd start to feel excited about meeting her. I figured maybe my lack of enthusiasm was because it'd been a while since I'd gone on a first date. I was rusty, and that's why I was dreading it all day.

No matter what, though, I couldn't stop thinking about Faye and her date. Was she wearing that dress? Was Cameron making her laugh? Was she going to kiss Cameron in a not-pretend way?

I'm leaning against the wall next to the building's entrance, checking my phone yet again for any texts from Faye. I was sort of hoping she'd text me something funny about how awful the date is, and I would be able to make some kind of excuse to Dani to go meet up with Faye instead. I shake my head, trying to physically shed those thoughts because that's not exactly fair to the woman I'm about to be on a date with.

A woman approaches, and I know it's Dani based on my mom's description of her. "She's petite with beautiful brown eyes and the kind of curly dark hair I'd pay a fortune for," she had said.

And she wasn't wrong. She's very pretty, with a calm sort of confidence and a kind, smiling face.

"Eli?" she asks.

"Hey, Dani. How are you?"

"Nice to meet you," she says with a smile.

I open the door for her and follow her inside. We get in line to order our beers. "My mom told me you moved here recently from Mexico?"

"Yeah, I was living with my dad in Mexico City."

"I've always wanted to go there. It seems really cool. And beautiful."

"I loved it, but my mom wanted me closer to her. You were in New York, right? How have you been adjusting to being back to non-big-city life?"

"It's been mostly fine, but I definitely miss being able to walk to the store without having to cross a major highway."

She chuckles as she looks up at the chalkboard drink menu. "Seriously. I feel like I need to re-learn how to drive a car."

We get our beers and sit at the picnic tables outside in the back, making more small talk about what we do for work. She just started working at a law firm, and we bond over being newbies at our jobs. She seems funny and kind, but I'm forcing it. I sort of get the sense that she is too, though. About five minutes later, she puts me out of my own misery.

She places her palms down on the table. "Let's get

something out of the way. We'll tell our moms we had a great time tonight, but I'm so busy with my new job and you're focused on your—" She pauses and makes a vague gesture in my direction. "Something or other. We'll part amicably, knowing we've fulfilled our duties."

So she doesn't want to be here either, which piques my curiosity.

"Is it my hair cut? I just got it cut today and you know a hair cut kind of needs to settle in a couple of days before it looks good."

She looks confused. "No, your hair looks fine."

"Is it this shirt? My friend Faye told me I wear too many plain shirts. Is she right? Is this shirt too plain?"

She seems to pick up on my joking. "Yeah, I saw you standing there in that basic shirt and knew it was a no-go," she says with a grimace.

"I appreciate your honesty."

She takes a sip of her beer. "Actually, I'm already dating someone, but it's early days and my mom doesn't know yet."

"Ah, I see." Now, I feel more relaxed, pressure easing a bit. "So, tell me about them."

Her face lights up, like she can't wait to talk about this new relationship. "We work together and I kind of hated her at first. Attorneys are very competitive." She grins, like she's thinking of something amusing. "But then we started talking more, and the rest is history."

"That's awesome. Honestly, I'm kind of relieved."

"Are you already seeing someone too?"

"No, not seeing anybody." Again, my stupid brain goes to Faye. My stupid brain wants to date Faye. I want my face to light up, too. "Can I ask you for some advice?"

It sucks having the one person you normally go to for advice be the last one you should. I haven't heard from

Andrew since he left, and no news is usually good news with him. Maybe he's falling madly in love, and he won't care at all if I date Faye. This will be a funny story we talk about some day.

"Go for it."

"I'm sure you took all kinds of ethics classes in law school, right?"

"Oh yeah."

"On a scale of one to ten, how ethical is it to want to be with your best friend's ex?"

"I feel like I have to say that this is not legal advice, and all opinions are my own. But if one is murdering someone and ten is Mother Teresa, I'd say you're sitting at a solid seven to eight on the ethical scale."

"So it's not bad, then?"

"Not *bad* . . . necessarily, but it sounds messy. That's for sure."

"Yeah." I sigh. "It does."

Messy isn't really what I need right now, either. It may not be ethically wrong to date Faye, but it might create waves neither of us want to deal with.

"Ultimately, you have to follow your heart," she says and then shakes her head. "That was incredibly cheesy."

I laugh. "Cheesy, but true."

I wonder if my feelings for Faye are coming from the heart or just from my insatiable curiosity about her. Could those two things be one and the same?

"Speaking of cheesy—" She gestures to the grilled cheese food truck parked on the street. "Want to get some food?"

"Never been one to turn down a grilled cheese."

I end up having a good time hanging out with her, despite how much I didn't want to be there at first. She even mentioned she was looking for something active to do and I invited her to come check out the softball league this week.

After parting ways with Dani, I'm in pretty good spirits. But as I walk to my car, I can't stop thinking about how Faye and Cameron might be ending their date. Or if their date doesn't end at all, and they spend the entire night together.

I don't drive home yet. Instead, I spend about an hour driving around aimlessly before heading back to my parents' house.

———

A FEW HOURS LATER, I can't sleep and decide to call Faye.

I tell myself it's just to make sure she's home okay. We both have trouble sleeping, so I don't think she'll be in bed yet. The phone rings a few times.

What if she's still with Cameron? What is she's having sex with Cameron right this second? I pull the phone away from my ear to hang up when I hear her answer.

"Hey," she says, a little groggy.

I feel my stomach unclench. I sit up and prop my pillow behind me. "Hey." I'm suddenly at a loss for words.

She laughs out another, "Hey."

"Sorry, I don't know why I called. I—"

"I'm glad you called."

"Yeah?"

"I couldn't sleep anyway."

"How did it go tonight?"

She groans. "I don't know. I think my expectations were too high."

"So it was bad?"

"Not bad, just a little disappointing."

She tells me about how he took her to some kind of abandoned warehouse for a five-course dinner and that he was weirdly obsessed with the Red Hot Chili Peppers.

"How did you two leave things?" This is my very bad way of asking if anything happened.

"He offered to wait with me while the Uber arrived."

"Chivalry isn't dead," I say.

"Then he kissed me."

A hot wave jealousy hits me right in stomach. But for some reason I ask, "Was it a good kiss?" Why am I doing this to myself?

"I'm not sure."

I can't help but laugh. "I think you'd know if it was good."

"At first I thought it was bad, but I keep thinking about it." Her voice is muffled, like she's rolled over and she's partially speaking into her pillow. "I think maybe I forgot what a good kiss feels like."

If she's lying in bed, unable to stop thinking about the kiss, that means it was at least a little good. "Are you going to see him again?"

"I don't know. We'll see. How did it go with Dani?"

"She was nice. We had a good time." I don't tell her that Dani and I won't be more than friends. It's like I need to keep some kind of tether to something else right now.

"I would take someone nice at this point. Do you know any nice guys? That are kind and don't make the entire conversation about them?"

I think through the guys I know and selfishly don't want to introduce her to any of them. But that's unfair. I think I might know exactly this type of guy and he's on my softball team.

"Do you want to come to my softball game Tuesday?

There's a guy on my team, Chris, you might like." Chris reminds me a lot of Andrew, actually.

"I was joking, but . . . maybe?"

"Worst case scenario, you get to see my prowess on the field."

She giggles. "Be still my heart."

This has gotten so complicated. I can admit to myself that I want Faye but can't have her. But trying to set your best friend's ex up with someone else still feels wrong in some way, too. I can't think straight. It's like I'm caught in a current of shoulds and should nots with her.

Guess I'll just go along with it and see what happens.

THE PARK where Eli's softball game is taking place looks like it hasn't seen any upkeep in decades. Pretty sure I see what's left of a Snickers wrapper from 1995 stuck to the fence. To make matters worse, it's been raining all week and there's standing water everywhere, causing the mosquitoes to swarm.

"If I contract the latest mutation of the West Nile virus out here, I'm going to kill you." Rett gives her arm a smack. "Why are we here again?"

"Because Eli thinks I might hit it off with someone on his team and I didn't want to come by myself."

"Where is he?"

I point to where Eli is standing on the field. "Third base in the hat." He says something to the short brunette woman from the other team who made it to the base during the last hit. Whatever he said makes her giggle so loud it echoes through the park.

He's funny, but he's not *that* funny.

"No. I mean, where is the guy he's setting you up with?"

"I'm not sure. He didn't tell me much about him."

He didn't tell me much of anything, because Eli is notoriously bad with details.

"I still don't get why you don't just date Eli."

"Because I like having another friend besides you. And he's like a brother to Andrew. It would just feel wrong."

It sort of feels wrong to be getting closer to Eli even in a platonic way. Would Andrew see our friendship as a betrayal? I've kept my promise to myself and haven't reached out to Andrew at all while he's been gone. Being over at his place the other day when Eli had his plant debacle was a little weird. Not because I once lived there too, but because Eli's presence there was . . . loud.

"Do you at least know this mystery man's name?"

"The only things I know are that his name is Chris and that he works at an animal shelter. Or a cat café. Something with animals."

"Well, that's kind of cute." She yawns and I notice that her energy seems low.

"Are you okay? You seem a little down."

"Sorry, I've been trying to keep Minnie under control from two-hundred miles away. She's not adjusting well to nursing home life, and for her own cosmic reasons, she thinks I'm the only one who can take care of it."

I give her a side hug, even though she hates displays of affection. "I'm sorry. If you want to go home, just say the word. I don't want to make you be somewhere you don't want to be."

She shoves me away in a brushing off motion. "No, it's fine. This is a good distraction. I like watching people chase each other around in what amounts to an elaborate game of fetch."

Eli is still talking to the woman and now he's laughing at something she said. Why is the game not moving along?

Finally, the person at bat hits the ball and one of Eli's teammates catches it. That makes three outs, so the teams switch places. I make eye contact with Eli as he jogs to the dugout, and he waves at us with a smile. I return his wave and laugh when he stumbles over one of the bases. I glance at Rett, and she looks at me in a very knowing way.

I ignore it.

Eli is up to bat first. The first pitch is too high, but he hits the ball on the second one. It goes toward left field, and he makes it to first base. I watch as he lifts the bottom of his shirt up to wipe the sweat from his brow, catching a glimpse of the sprinkling of hair going down his stomach.

"Do they ever do shirts versus skins in this league?" Rett asks.

"Hmm?"

She laughs. "God, you are in denial. Do friends check out other *friends* the way you are blatantly checking him out right now?"

"I just happened to be looking that way." He bends down to tie his shoe, and his forearms flex with the motion. "And even if I was, there's nothing wrong with a friend appreciating another friend's aesthetic appeal," I say primly. "I appreciate your beauty all the time."

"Yeah, okay," she grumbles.

A few innings and ten mosquito bites later, the game ends and Eli's team wins when someone hits a home run. He's all smiles as we meet him at the bottom of the bleachers.

"Thanks for coming," he says, giving me a very sweaty side hug. He turns to Rett. "Good to see you again, Loretta."

"No hugs," she says, holding her hand up to stop him from hugging her, too.

"And here's Chris, our MVP for the night after that last play," he says, motioning for an attractive Black guy with wire-rimmed glasses to join us.

Chris jogs over, and I notice it's the guy who hit the home run at the end. He shakes our hands with a warm smile. "Nice to meet you all."

"Congrats on the win," I say.

He smiles shyly and reaches up to push his glasses up. "Eli is exaggerating. He had a pretty good run there in the fifth."

Rett leans over to whisper in my ear, "Are we going to have to talk about softball all night?"

I shush her with my eyes.

Eli bends down to zip up his backpack before putting it on. "I'm starving. You guys want to get something to eat?"

"Sure, we're down," I say. Rett and I didn't discuss getting dinner after this, so I hope she's good with me volunteering our acceptance.

Out of the corner of my eye, I see Third Base Woman approaching us. As she walks by, she shouts, "Hey Eli! This was fun!"

Eli turns to her and waves. "Maybe we'll be on the same team next time!"

"Hope so!" She shouts before getting into her car.

"Who was that?" Rett asks him, a sinister sweetness seeping into her question. I would normally discourage her intrusion, but I'm curious myself.

"Oh, that's Dani."

From our spot on the bleachers, I couldn't really see what she looked like. But up close, I'm seeing that she's maybe one of the most beautiful people I've ever seen. When Eli told me she was nice, I'm ashamed to admit I thought that was his way of saying he wasn't attracted to her. But if he invited her to play softball, they must have hit it off. Maybe he didn't want to rub it in after hearing how disappointing my date was.

I suddenly don't feel hungry at all.

Rett hums in a very disapproving tone, before locking arms with me. "Faye wants pizza."

I don't miss that her suggestion just so happens to be my ultimate comfort food. "I want pizza, or you want pizza?"

She grins. "Who doesn't want pizza?"

―――

WE DECIDE to go to the Italian restaurant in the strip mall next to the park. It smells like warm bread, and the air conditioning feels amazing after sitting outside in the sticky heat for the past few hours.

"Faye, what do you do for work?" Chris asks after we order a couple of pizzas. He's seated next to Eli, diagonally across from me.

"I'm an executive assistant at a software company. What about you?"

"I own a pet grooming business."

"Wow, that's impressive."

"Well, at the moment I'm a one-man show, so I don't know how impressive that is." He looks down and toys with the napkin-wrapped silverware. "Right now, I have a van I drive around to people's houses, but I just got a permanent space I'll be opening soon."

"So business must be good, then," I say.

Chris very humbly shrugs his shoulders and takes a drink of his water.

"I'm dog-sitting for my parents next week so maybe I'll call you up," Eli says.

"Sounds good. What kind of dog do they have?"

"Great Dane. She might be bigger than your van, though."

"I'm sure we could make something work. I went to a house last month and the lady had three Dobermans." He takes a sip of water. "I was so exhausted after that I don't think I moved for a week."

"I'm kind of jealous you have an active job like that," Eli says. "I hate sitting at a desk all day."

I snort. "As if you sit at your desk all day. You need to start wearing a sign at work that says, 'Don't talk to me unless you want to waste two hours.'"

Eli gives my foot a playful knock under the table. "Someone has to provide the office morale."

I make the mistake of looking over at Rett at this moment and she mutters the word, "Denial" under her breath.

Neither Eli nor Chris notice because they're now busy talking about how Chris once got an appointment to groom this guy's cat, and it went about as well as you'd expect. Chris found himself in urgent care requiring stitches because the cat had treated his torso like its very own scratching post.

"Well, if you ever want to help me out on weekends or anything, I could use it," Chris says to Eli. "Can't promise you won't also sustain any cat-related injuries."

"I might just take you up on that," Eli says. "You'll have to put an injury *claws* in my contract."

We all laugh at his stupid pun, even Rett giving a begrudging snort, and Eli beams at us in the way he always does when he's got all eyes on him. He loves being the one to make everyone laugh.

"I'll see what I can do," Chris says.

Chris seems like the kind of guy who probably gets along with everyone, easygoing in a way that makes you immediately at ease with him.

We continue eating and talking, and before we know it, it's almost ten o'clock. I can't stifle a yawn.

"I thought you were a night owl," Eli says, reminding me of our late-night phone conversations that have become something we regularly do now, almost every night. I hope we talk tonight because I kind of want to ask him about Dani.

"I may stay up late, but I have to do proper pre-sleep marination first. I'm usually queuing up a relaxing rug cleaning video right about now."

"Have you ever seen the yard mowing ones?" Chris asks me.

"Yes! I love those."

"They're just so satisfying," he says.

Rett leans back in her chair and crosses her arms. "This is why Faye has to do the fun list."

"What's the fun list?" Chris asks.

"It's nothing," I say, shooting daggers at Rett.

"It's not nothing," Eli says. "Which reminds me, what's next?"

I look around at them, vowing to kill Rett and Eli with slow and painful deaths and say, "Um, I think it's the small get together."

"I have an idea," Eli says. Hearing these words from Eli's mouth sends a spike of equal parts excitement and dread through me. "You should have a game night."

Rett looks skeptical. "A game night? Like Monopoly?"

Chris seems excited about this idea. "Game nights are the best. My friends and I used to have them all the time back in school."

"I guess I could do that? Would you guys come?"

"I'm in," Chris says. "Let me give you my number so you can give me the details."

He puts his number in my phone while I run through everything I need to do to prepare for this. It doesn't have to be a big thing, though. Just a few people over to my apartment. It will give me a good reason to do a good deep clean. Plus, Chris does seem really nice and maybe it'll be a good way to get to know him more.

Maybe it will end up being fun.

22

FAYE

GAME NIGHT IS GOING to be a disaster.

First, I am wearing the most uncomfortable jeans known to man. They are what I call "standing-up pants"— the second I sit down, it feels like my body is being cut in half. They do amazing things for my figure, but there's only so far I'm willing to go in the name of vanity.

Second, Chris has barely acknowledged my presence, too busy talking to only Dani. He's been slowly inching closer to her all night, but I can't really blame him for this. After talking to her when she arrived, I discovered that not only is she pretty, but she's smart and funny, too. I think I might even have a little crush on her.

Third, Cameron is on his way because I managed to accidentally invite him over when he texted me earlier today.

"This is going to be fun," Rett says, eating from a bag of chips while perched on a barstool in the kitchen overlooking the living room, like she's watching an episode of *The Bachelorette.*

I snatch the bag out of her hand. "These are for *all* of

my guests." I pour the chips into a large bowl I managed to fish out of the cabinet.

"By the way, where is bachelor number three?"

Oh yeah, and fourth, Eli isn't here yet. When he's around, I'm more at ease in situations like this. If he were here right now, I could look over at him, and he'd give me a look that says, *This isn't so bad. At least there's alcohol.*

"Guess he's running late." I check my phone for a text from him, but he hasn't texted me since last night asking if it was okay if Dani came. I was shocked when she showed up without him, assuming he meant he was bringing her as a date. "Come on, let's go join them so we're not being creeps in the kitchen."

"I told you, I'm not playing games."

"You don't have to play games. Just come sit over here." I give her a look that I hope communicates, *I need you.*

She hops off the stool and wipes chip crumbs off her palms on her pants. "Fine."

I only have a love seat to sit on, which Chris and Dani have already claimed, so I awkwardly take a seat on the floor, feeling like I have a paper towel tube wrapped around my waist.

Dani smiles at us after Rett and I join them. "What are we playing tonight?" she asks.

"Unfortunately, I don't have a lot of options." I gesture to the ancient Monopoly game I've had since I was a kid, and the Boggle that I'm pretty sure is missing a few pieces.

"You should have told me to bring something," Chris says, turning to Dani. "What's your favorite game?"

"Umm . . . don't really have one."

"I might have a deck of cards somewhere if we want to play a card game," I say.

"Let's play strip poker," Rett says suggestively.

Both Chris and Dani look nervous at this idea. "She's joking," I tell them.

Rett shrugs.

A quick knock at the door interrupts us, and Eli comes in with Cameron right behind him.

"Sorry I'm late," Eli says, looking apologetic.

"Same," Cameron says. "Band practice went late."

"You're just in time. We were just getting ready to play strip poker," Rett says.

"No, we weren't," I say, glaring at her. "Everyone, this is Cameron."

Cameron and Eli join us in the living room after depositing the beer they brought in the fridge.

Cameron takes a spot next to Rett. "Hi, I'm Cameron."

"I know," Rett says, deadpan.

"And your name is?"

"Rett."

"I like that name. Is it—"

Rett holds her hand up. "Yes, it's a nickname. No, I won't tell you what it's short for."

My eyes go straight to Eli, who is trying not to laugh.

We ultimately decide to play Monopoly in teams. Chris jumps at the chance to play with Dani. Cameron asks if Rett would like to be his partner. She looks over me, asking me if it's okay with her eyes. I shrug my permission, and she agrees to be his teammate as long as he's fine with making all the decisions.

Eli moves to sit next to me on the floor. "Looks like it's you and me. What piece should we choose?"

It's a little disappointing that Chris and Cameron didn't even glance in my direction when we were determining teams. Who the fuck did I wear these jeans for? "Hmm? Oh, I don't really care. You pick."

He picks up the top hat piece and mimics doffing the cap to me. "Ladies first."

I roll my eyes and try not to smile at his attempt to make me laugh. I wonder if I was a little too obvious about my disappointment. I roll the dice and try to put on a happy face.

We make it about forty-five minutes before everyone loses interest and starts talking amongst themselves. I get up to go to the kitchen to pretend I need another glass of wine, and motion for Eli to follow me.

"What's your take on this situation?" I gesture to the living room, where Cameron has cornered Rett and Chris has continued in what seems to be a relentless pursuit of Dani.

"Do you have any cookies?" He opens and closes a few cabinet doors, scavenging for sweets.

"Cookies are what you're worried about right now?"

"I just really could go for something sweet."

I give him a look that I hope conveys that sweet treats aren't my concern at the moment.

"I think we need to save Dani."

He ignores this this asks, "What about Rett?"

I hear Rett say to Cameron, "So do they do the lobotomies on the beach or . . ." and I know she's fine. She's completely in her element, fucking with him like that. "She can handle it."

"Looks like Dani can take care of herself." He points to where she's stood up from the couch, making her way over to us.

"I think I need to head out," she says. "Got a big day tomorrow."

I give her a hug. "It was nice meeting you. Thank you so much for coming."

Eli gives her a hug, too. "Want me to walk you out?"

"No, I'm good. Parked right out front."

I still can't figure out what's going on with Eli and Dani. I haven't had a chance to get any details from him. But they didn't arrive together, and now he's not even walking her to her car.

Chris looks around, like he's trying to decide who to talk to now. I guess this is my chance to go over and talk to him, but that prospect sounds exhausting at this point.

I catch Rett's eye, and she must see something on my face that makes her spring into action. She gets up and when Cameron moves to stand, she turns to him and says, "No, you stay." Cameron shrugs and takes Dani's spot on the couch next to Chris.

"Did you just command him to stay?" Eli asks, laughing.

She sighs. "Too bad he doesn't know the command for 'be quiet.' I can't listen to him talk for another two seconds." She jabs a thumb in my direction. "What's wrong with her?"

He looks down at me. "I think she's disappointed."

"I'm right here, you know."

"Well, the night isn't over yet," Rett says, giving me a very intense look that insinuates something I can't figure out. "I need to go, though. Eli, will you make sure she's okay?"

"I'm fine!" I just want to put on comfy clothes and wash my face.

On her way out, Rett gives Cameron a final command to leave, and Chris follows shortly after. I give them half-hearted goodbyes as the door shuts behind them.

Eli stays to help me clean up. We clean in silence for a few minutes before he asks, "Are you disappointed?"

"Kind of," I admit.

"Do you actually like either of them?"

Does that even matter at this point? I would have accepted just a whisper of validation for bringing out the vintage Levis out for this occasion.

"I *want* to like one of them."

"I don't think either of them is right for you."

"Why not?"

"Well Chris is a good guy, but he's too shy for you."

"You're the one who introduced me to him. You said he was nice. And then he just wanted to talk to Dani all night."

"He is nice, but I think you two are too alike. He was probably talking to Dani because she's more outgoing." He whistles to the tune of "Californication" while bringing the chip bowl in from the living room. "And Cameron is just full of himself."

"What's the deal with Dani? Why didn't you two come together?"

He scratches his beard. "We agreed to meet here, but I was running late, looking at an apartment." He picks up a couple of beer cans from the coffee table. "Also, Dani and I aren't . . . a thing."

"What do you mean?"

He tosses the cans into the recycling bin. "On our first date she told me she's already seeing someone. But she's cool and we get along as friends. I invited her tonight when you told me Cameron was coming, and I didn't want to be the odd man out." He doesn't sound disappointed, but there's some kind of underlying sadness in his tone.

I wash the chip bowl out in the sink. "I'm sorry things didn't work out with her. Romantically, I mean."

"Are you okay?" he asks, grabbing the dish towel and taking the bowl from me to dry it.

"Oh yeah. I guess I was kind of forcing it the whole

night." I laugh humorlessly. I am much more disappointed than I let on because there's no need to burden Eli with my insecurities right now. It sucks having the first two guys you pursue post-breakup end up not working out.

"For what it's worth, I think you can do better."

We finish cleaning up and he walks over to where the IKEA box is leaned against the wall. "Hey, you bought a dresser."

"Yeah, I've had it for a while. Just haven't felt like putting it together."

"You want some help?"

"You mean right now?"

"Sure, why not?" *Sure, why not?* His favorite question.

"No, you don't have to help with that."

Everything hits me all at once about tonight. The stupid fun list leading me to have the lamest "party" ever. My stupid uncomfortable pants. Rett not understanding that things like this aren't easy for me. And then there's Eli, always trying to help. "I can put it together myself."

"Why won't you let me help?"

"Because you've done too much. I can't pay you back."

"There's no payback required." He rubs his hands down his face. "It's not that complicated."

This is when I realize something. Eli is annoyed. He never makes snide comments like that. I hate to admit that I am almost excited by this side of him—he's usually so chill, it's almost inhuman. Maybe things not working out with Dani really is bothering him. Maybe he needs to do this so he can feel like something can come out of this night. Which is maybe what I need, too.

"If you insist." I grab a knife to open the box and hand it to him.

"It won't take us long," he says, running the knife

through the tape. "Do you have real tools, or will we have to use these things?" He holds up the plastic baggie full of screws and tools that come with the package.

"Do I look like I own real tools? Oh wait! I have a hammer!"

"Never mind, we can make this work." He pulls pieces out of the box and starts laying them out on the floor. He holds up the instruction booklet but doesn't even look at it before tossing it to the side.

"I'm going to change. Be right back."

I put on some bike shorts and my biggest, softest T-shirt, and I already feel ten times better. After taking my contacts out and washing my face, I feel like an entirely new woman. When I come back out, Eli is laying out the pieces on the floor. He glances up when I walk over, pausing to look at me for a second before sighing and continuing to spread out the pieces. He doesn't seem to be enjoying this at all.

"Are you sure you want to be doing this now? You seem . . . frustrated."

23

ELI

I AM FRUSTRATED, but probably not for the reason she thinks.

It's not because of things not working with Dani. Or because of anything Faye said. I'm frustrated at Cameron for being an idiot and at myself for introducing Faye to Chris, knowing that he would never make the first move with her. Since everyone left, Faye has tried to act like she's okay, but I can tell she's in her head about it. Even though she says it was fine and that she's not actually into them, I guarantee she's running through everything she said tonight, wondering what she could have done differently.

I'm frustrated at the battle I've had with myself for the last three hours because the handle I have on this crush is slipping by the minute. I guess I should be happy she changed, because those pants she had on tonight were designed in a lab to torture me.

But honestly, what she changed into doesn't help matters. Now, she's in her glasses and wearing these spandex shorts and huge T-shirt that just makes me want to curl up on the couch with her, instead of putting together this dresser.

Maybe if I talk to her about tonight, it'll help distract me from my own thoughts.

"Faye," I say.

"Yeah?" She's concentrating on screwing in a piece, and she's making this face that is so cute it's killing me.

"They're idiots."

"Yeah, I know," she says.

"I'd say you dodged a bullet with both of them. And look on the bright side, you've gotten a couple of dates out of the way. Gotta kiss some bad frogs or whatever the expression is."

She just hums in answer.

But I can't stop talking. "Can you imagine what either of them would be like in bed?"

She stops what she's doing but doesn't look at me. "Eli?"

"Hmm?"

"I don't really want to talk about their potential sexual prowess with you." She sits back and looks around. "Do you see another piece like this one?" She holds up what I think is the front of a drawer.

I sift through the other pieces. "No, don't see it."

She tosses the drawer piece aside. "If you want to continue this slow torture, go for it." She stands up and heads into the kitchen. "You still want cookies?"

I'm thrown by the change in subject. "Uh, yeah?"

"You like peanut butter cookies?"

"Uh, yeah?"

"Want to make cookies instead? Because if I have to play Tetris with this engineered wood for two more seconds, I'm going to explode."

I laugh and get up to join her in the kitchen. "Fine by me."

She takes out the peanut butter, eggs, and sugar and sets them on the counter.

"Is this all we need?" I ask.

"Yep, I used to make these all the time when I was little."

"Did you like to bake a lot?"

She takes out measuring cups. "Not really."

"Where did you grow up again?" I ask casually, subtly bringing up our old guessing game.

She gives me a sly smile. "Nuh-uh. Still not telling you."

"Why won't you tell me?"

She measures out the peanut butter and sugar into the bowl. "Now it's just fun to *not* tell you."

"You'll tell me someday."

She shakes her head as she slides the bowl down the counter to where I'm standing. "Can I tell you to crack two eggs in there, instead?"

"Yes, chef."

I add the eggs, and she hands me a spoon. "Just mix it all together until the dough forms," she says.

Her kitchen is so tiny that we keep brushing against each other with every move the other makes. She reaches across to take a dish towel from a hook next to the sink, grazing against my arm. I move behind her to throw away the eggshells, and we're pressed against each other momentarily. It's a dance we're doing, and it kind of reminds me of the swans circling each other at the pond.

She rolls the dough into little balls to place on the cookie sheet. "Do you think I'm mysterious?"

The question is so out of nowhere, I almost don't think I've heard her right. "What do you mean?"

"Rett says I'm bad at letting people know me. Just wondering if that's why—" She pauses and shrugs. "Maybe that's why Cameron and Chris weren't interested. Maybe I didn't try hard enough."

I was right—she has been overanalyzing the night. I take a bite of peanut butter to buy some time while I think of the best thing to say. Faye is an odd combination of open and closed. There's nothing intimidating about her, but you get the sense that she's never fully herself. She knows what to say to make you feel heard, but ask her anything personal, and she'll deftly steer the conversation back to you. "I'd say you're intriguing." I join her in shaping the cookies. "And I'd say Cameron and Chris are lazy."

"So, you don't think I'm hard to know?"

"I didn't say that." I playfully shove her with my hip. "You're worth trying to get to know, though."

She gives me a curious look before focusing on spooning more cookies onto the sheet. She places them in the oven while I set a timer on my phone. We take a seat on the stools she's placed by her kitchen counter—another tight space, where our knees bump against each other.

I decide to test something and don't move my knee away from hers to see what she does. She doesn't move hers away either, keeping it pressed against mine.

She folds a dish towel. Unfolds it. Folds it again. "I thought Andrew really knew me. But then when he asked me—" A few seconds tick away. But I don't say anything, even though I'm wondering what he asked her. Even though, I think I might know what he asked her. "He didn't know me at all."

She shakes her head as if to clear it out. "I'm sorry for even talking about this with you. He's a great person. You don't have to say anything."

"You can talk about anything with me."

"I know." She raises her eyes to fully look at me with a direct stare you rarely get from her. I don't want her to look away. I want to swim in those blue eyes forever.

I know.

Those two words make me feel . . . warm. More than a physical attraction kind of warm. Like, I want her to tell me everything, and maybe I could tell her everything, too.

She looks back down at her hands, still fiddling with the towel. "How are things going at work?"

"It's going okay. I'm still figuring things out."

"What were you doing before? In New York?"

"I was doing something similar, but it was a smaller company. More of a mom-and-pop kind of place that sold electrical parts."

The oven beeps, letting us know the cookies are done. Faye gets up to take them out and I watch the swish of her legs as she walks to the oven.

She places them on a plate to cool. "Do you like working in recruiting?"

"Does anyone like working in recruiting?"

She laughs. "I overheard Melissa talking about how you were fitting in well so far."

"That's good to know. My last job was . . . the opposite."

"What happened?" she asks, taking a cookie from the plate, and handing one to me.

"Well, I kind of got fired." It's not my favorite topic of conversation, but since we're talking about it, I might as well be honest. Not that I'm nervous to tell her, but it's embarrassing because I knew better.

"I'm so sorry. Companies pull that shit all the time."

"It wasn't layoffs or anything. It was something I did."

"You don't have to talk about it if you don't want to."

It was one of the worst days of my life. I've never felt the kind of shame I did that day. Turns out, companies do notice when you show up late to work almost every day but lie about it on your timecard. It was so stupid. I was so stupid.

It's not that I think Faye will judge me, and she obviously understands not wanting to talk about something difficult, but tonight just doesn't feel like the time to talk about my failures. "It's a long story, and I'm getting kind of tired."

"Yeah, same." She nods and fights a yawn.

I stand up. "Okay if I sleep on your couch for a bit? Don't want to drive yet."

"Of yeah, that's fine."

She goes into the bathroom, and I hear her brushing her teeth. She comes back out a few minutes later, tugging on the hem of her shirt as if she's nervous.

"Remember that night we talked on the phone about how sleeping alone sucks?"

I nod, unsure, but stupidly hopeful about where she's going with this. "Yeah, I do."

She swings her body around to gesture toward her bedroom. "You could sleep in here with me. If you wanted to."

My heart starts to pound. Sleep in the bed with her. Sleep in Faye's bed. In bed with Faye.

I need to calm down. She only wants someone next to her. It's not like she's champing at the bit to touch me like I am her. It's just sleeping. No big deal.

She must take my silence as need to explain herself. "It's just . . . we're friends, and—"

"I'll stay over." *I'll do anything you ask,* I think but don't say.

It's just sleeping.

I follow her into the bedroom.

———

"I FEEL PATHETIC," she speaks into the darkness.

"For asking me to stay with you?"

"I guess?" She plays with the edge of the sheet she's tucked under her arms. "You just get used to sleeping with another person next to you. I've gotten used being alone, for the most part. I don't mind my own company. Except at night, it's like—"

"Like you're literally the only person on the entire planet."

We're both lying on our backs facing the ceiling, but I feel her move so she's now on her side facing me. "Exactly," she sighs.

Why does she have to smell so good? Every time she moves, I get a whiff of her warm vanilla fruity-sweet scent. Does her skin taste as good as it smells?

"You're a good friend," she says.

I'm a terrible friend. To her. To Andrew. If either of them knew what I was thinking right now, I'd be sent into horny exile.

She closes her eyes, and I close mine. The air conditioner hums, but I'm hot with confusion and frustration. Her breathing has slowed, and I assume she's fallen asleep.

Until I hear her whisper, "Can I ask you for one more favor?"

I'm half terrified to hear what she could ask me right now. "Sure."

"Would you . . ." She covers her face with her hands.

The anticipation is fucking killing me. Does she want me to go to the couch? To get her another blanket? To leave her apartment and never see her again? I have never felt this antsy and nervous around a woman. My thoughts don't normally race like this because I don't give them time enough to.

"Do you want to cuddle?"

I release a breath that turns into a laugh. "I always want to cuddle," I joke, trying not to sound like I might spontaneously combust. If this is how I feel about cuddling her, imagine how it'd be to do other things?

Stop thinking about other things.

She rolls around so she's facing her window now and I rest my arm across her waist, careful not to grip her any tighter than she might want. "Is this okay?" I ask.

"Yes," she sighs, snuggling in close to me.

We both fall asleep almost immediately.

24

———

FAYE

EVERY AUGUST, our company has an employee appreciation party where they ply us with free food and alcohol, and we all get to pretend to have a good time.

It's always held in the largest conference room at the Marriott downtown, and I always spend the entire day dreading it. Andrew always came with me to these things because he's good at events like this, at making polite small talk with people. Tonight, I'm dragging Rett along with me for moral support.

As we make our way down the hallway, I already hear a cover band playing "Brown Eyed Girl." It's only a matter of time before Craig, our comptroller, takes hold of the mic for his rendition of "Bohemian Rhapsody."

"Is that a giant inflatable fish?" Rett asks as we approach the room's entrance.

"You mean Guppie? That's our company mascot."

She gives it a little poke with her index finger. "Weird."

"Come on, let's find the bar." I don't like to rely on drinking to make these events bearable, but a glass of wine certainly won't hurt.

Tonight, especially. I know Eli will be here, and we haven't talked much in the few days since game night. And when we did talk, it definitely wasn't about our little cuddling session.

On the way to the bar area, we run into Alexis and her husband, Brian. She's wearing a floor-length sequined gown and bright red lipstick. He's intently looking at his phone, seemingly oblivious to his surroundings.

I put on a bright smile. "Hi Alexis!" I turn to her husband and nod politely. "Nice to see you again, Brian."

He nods at me before looking back at his phone. Alexis smiles, huge and fake. "Faye! You look lovely this evening."

I smooth the front of my dress, the only semi-formal thing I own and the same one I wear every year. It's a simple black satin gown that wrinkles when I look at it wrong, but I still feel pretty in it and can't justify buying anything else.

"Thank you. Have you met my friend Rett?" I ask, knowing good and well they haven't. But that's just the kind of bullshit you ask at parties like this.

Alexis shakes her head. "I don't believe I have. Rett." She lets the name linger for a moment. "What an odd name."

Rett gives her the most fake saccharine smile I've ever seen. "I really love this self-care initiative Faye's told me about. It so rare these days to see a company prioritize making the office a more pleasurable environment."

I've got to get Rett away from my boss. Bringing her to an event, there's always a risk of some sort of debacle or unexpected event happening. She has a mesh sieve for a filter and gets off on antagonizing people, especially people like Alexis. She's fiercely loyal to her loved ones and it's nice to have her in your corner, but I need to make sure I leave this party with my job still intact.

Alexis lights up. "Yes! It is spectacular, isn't it? We really care about our employees, as you can see." She holds her arms up to gesture around her, fur stole slashing through the air as she polishes off her glass of champagne. "Maybe you should come work with us."

"Unfortunately, I already have my own terrible boss, so I'm not currently on the job market," Rett says with another grin.

I don't allow enough time for Alexis to get the gist of that comment before I guide Rett along to the bar. "We'll let you two get back to mingling," I say to Alexis.

"You've got to behave," I chastise Rett.

"Sorry, I just can't stand that woman. Do you think that's real fur?"

"It's faux mink. I ordered it for her last year when she was going through a vegan phase."

The bartender places a couple of napkins down in front of us. "What'll it be, ladies?"

"Riesling, please," I say. Wait, is that the one I like? "Sorry, actually make that a Chardonnay." I can never remember which one is dry and which is sweet.

"Sure thing, and for you?" he asks Rett.

"Cab Sav, please," she says.

I lean against the bar, already regretting my shoe choice, a pair of strappy black heels currently making permanent indentations in the sides of my feet. "We'll stay for an hour, tops, just so I can say I was here before we go."

"Fine by me. Hey look, Eli's over there."

She points toward the buffet line, and sure enough, Eli is loading up his plate with a pile of bacon-wrapped shrimp. He wears his simple black suit well, the bright white shirt sharp against the tanned skin of his neck.

He puts some fruit on his plate, and I watch as he tosses

a grape into his mouth. He licks the end of his thumb, and I feel . . . hot.

"When are you going to admit it?" Rett asks, handing me my glass of wine.

"Admit what?"

"That you want him," she croons.

I will admit that I wanted to look good tonight. That, as I curled my hair and put on my lipstick, I was thinking about him. That, while I was zipping up my dress, I thought about what he would think when he saw me in it.

I wanted to look good tonight *for him*.

She squints her eyes at me. "What happened after I left the other night? You're not telling me something."

I should have told her about what happened already, but part of me liked having this little secret rolling around in my head for a few days. "He hung out for a little. And then he stayed over."

She gasps and clutches my arm.

"And we—"

"Had sex?!"

"Shhh. No, we talked." I take a pause before mumbling, "There was also cuddling."

"What kind of cuddling?"

"What do you mean, what kind of cuddling?"

She gives me an exasperated look. "Arm over the waist, spooning you cuddling? Or your head over his heart cuddling?"

I watch Eli continue down the buffet line. He's already eaten half of what he'd put on his plate. "Arm over the waist cuddling."

"Caressing?"

I woke up and his face was buried in my hair, so close I could feel his beard stubble against the back of my neck. He was absently moving his thumb back and forth across my waist. I don't even think he realized he was doing it. "Some light caressing."

"And did you push your ass back against him?"

I give her a guilty look and hold up my thumb and index finger. "A little?"

She claps delightedly, and I can't help but laugh. "I'm calling it. You're going to fuck each other before the month is out."

"I don't know. It was nice, but I can't rebound with my ex's best friend."

"You keep saying that, but I don't think it's a big deal." She tilts her head and looks over to Eli again. He's now talking to Tina and gesturing about something so grandly that a grape rolls off his plate. "I like him, and he clearly likes you."

When Eli spots us, he walks over and he pulls me in for a hug, somehow managing to avoid spilling any more of his food. He always smells nice—like he's been out in the sun, with a hint of whatever simple bar soap and deodorant he wears that probably has a name like *Alpine Spring Morning* or *Rocky Beach Cliff*.

"Loretta, good to see you," he says to Rett. "Don't worry, I won't hug you."

"You save any shrimp for the rest of us?" she teases him.

Rett likes maybe three people in the entire world, so it means something for her to like Eli.

I take a sip of my wine and can't help but pull a face. Guess I was wrong about my wine of choice.

"Don't like your drink?" Eli asks.

"I always forget if I like Riesling or Chardonnay, and I chose the wrong one. It's fine, though."

"I'm going to get a drink," he says. "Do y'all want to sit together?"

"Yeah, we'll get some food and meet you at a table."

Rett and I load our plates and make our way to the seating area. The party is in full force now, getting more raucous by the minute. Last year, the party ended when our VP of Sales tried to do body shots with one of the hotel staff. Sadly, she's no longer with us.

She's not dead, she just got a job at Google.

We find Eli and when I sit down next to him, he slides a glass of wine over to me. "What is this?" I ask.

"Riesling."

"How did you know which one to get?" I didn't even mention I got Chardonnay before.

"Lucky guess," he says and takes a sip of his beer.

Rett practically obliterates my foot under the table. I yelp and give her a questioning look.

She nods to the glass of wine and takes a smug sip of her own.

"You excited for your interview?" Eli asks. He pushed my resume along and the team decided they'd like to interview me next week.

"I haven't had an interview in so long. I'm honestly terrified."

"We can do a practice interview beforehand if you want," he offers.

"That would be great," I say.

Rett gives my foot another stomp and I ignore her.

We finish our food, and I'm prepared to call it a night when Eli says, "Let's go check out the band."

"I think we're leaving soon," I say.

"I don't think so," he says matter of factly.

"Excuse me?"

"You can't leave already." He walks behind my chair and leans down by my ear, "That's not something Fun Faye would do."

I look up into his smirking face. "Fine, but I'm not dancing."

We get up and weave our way through the crowd. "Sure, whatever you say."

"I'm serious, Eli. You will not get me out on that dance floor."

The band area is packed, and I spot a few people from the marketing team belting "Don't Stop Believing." I need to get out of here.

Rett has her phone out with a look of concern on her face. "What's wrong?" I ask.

"I have five missed calls from my dad. Are you good for a minute? I should call him back."

"Of course. I hope everything is okay."

The song ends and the band begins to play "My Girl." Eli holds his hand out to me. "Alright Fun Faye, let's go."

Panic flares and I shake my head so hard my thoughts rattle. "No."

But Eli, being Eli, doesn't give up that easily. He smiles at me and I almost feel my defenses start to crumble. "Yes."

"I'll dance to the next one, I promise." A lie and he knows it.

"Two minutes. You'll dance with me for two minutes."

I quickly weigh my options. Either I wait for the next song, which could be something worse, or I suck it up through this one.

"One minute."

"Ninety seconds." He smiles and he's so handsome and it makes me want to say yes. It makes me want to do more than just dancing.

"Fine, but I'm setting a timer on my phone."

He beams in victory. "Deal."

"And, starting it now," I say, opening the app on my phone and starting the timer. He grabs my hand and pulls me over to the dance floor. I bring my other hand up to his shoulder to assume the classic slow dancing position. He guides us into a rocking motion.

"You look beautiful," he says by my ear, causing the little wisps of hair on my temple to tremble. We're about the same height when I'm wearing these heels.

"Thank you." I give his tie a playful tug. "You clean up nice, too. Kind of surprised you own this."

"Got it for my older brother's wedding a few years ago. Comes in handy for things like this."

"How many siblings do you have, again?"

"Two. Emmett is older, and Evie is younger."

"Do you get along with them?"

"We have the usual good-natured bickering, but I love them. The big reason I moved back was because I really missed my family."

"I'm sure they're happy you're back, too."

"What about your family? Are you close?"

"I'm close with my grandpa, but no siblings and I don't see my mom very often."

He nods and we sway for a few seconds. Maybe it's the song or that dancing with him makes me feel like sharing, but I find myself wanting to say more. It feels easy to talk to him in way that it never has with anyone else. I think of the conversation Rett and I had where she said I don't open up to people very easily, and I think about his comment the other night about how it's worth getting to know me. Maybe I should try to put in a little effort, too.

"It was her birthday yesterday. She just turned forty-three."

"She's pretty young. So, she had you . . ."

"When she was seventeen," I finish.

"Dang," he says.

I laugh. "Yeah."

"What about your dad?"

"It was kind of a one-time only thing with them, I think." We sway a little more and I catch myself momentarily laying my head against his shoulder. I straighten back up, remembering that I'm in a gray-carpeted hotel conference room surrounded by my coworkers, and not somewhere private. "I've never met him."

"I'm sorry."

"She had a hard time of it. I couldn't imagine having a kid that young."

"And did you have hard time of it?"

That is never a question I've had to answer, nor allowed myself to think about. I like to think I had a good time of it. I made good grades. I got a scholarship to go to NC State. I did all the right things. I guess it was hard sometimes, but it was just the reality of the situation.

The timer goes off, saving me from having to answer his question. I remove my right hand from his shoulder and unclasp my left hand from his.

"That was a fast ninety seconds," he says, slightly squeezing where his hand still rests on my hip. "Sure you didn't cheat?"

I agree, it went by really fast, but it's probably for the best. "How dare you accuse me of cheating?"

"I think I need another minute just to make sure," he teases.

"We had an agreement."

"What if I say please?" I have no doubt he's gotten away with so many things with that line and that face.

"There are plenty of others here who I'm sure would be glad to dance with you," I say. It's almost a challenge. *Are there others you want to be dancing with?*

"I don't want to dance with them."

I look away, feeling heat sweep up my chest. He's looking at me like he's the one challenging me now. *Are we thinking the same thing?*

"I should probably check on Rett," I say, breaking eye contact.

He nods. "I'll be in here if you need me."

I don't see her in the hallway or lobby. I try to call her but get no answer. She must have gone outside, so I send her a text before stopping by the bathroom on my way back into the party. There's a line so I pull up Instagram to idly scroll to pass the time. I swipe past a post that I almost don't register at first.

A photo of Andrew. It's a selfie of him and a woman.

"Faye, sweetie, the line has moved." I look over and Tina nods to the big gap I've left from not moving in line.

I need to be alone for a second, but there are people milling about everywhere. I spot the photo booth in the hallway that the company must have rented out, and it looks empty. I rush inside and close the curtain, taking a closer look at the photo he posted. It's the first photo he's shared in over a year. I think that's why I was so shocked to see anything from his account.

She's pretty, with strawberry-blonde hair and a bunch of freckles sprinkled across the bridge of her nose. He looks happy. I'm so ensnared with my stalking that I barely register the curtain opening and Eli peeking his head inside.

"Found a hiding spot I see," he smiles.

I hold my phone up to him. "Who is this?" I ask in what I hope is a very calm way. I feel anything other than calm. I feel . . . sick.

"That must be Emma," he says.

"Emma," I repeat. "Are they . . . together?"

"May I come in with you?"

I scoot over so he has room to sit down next to me.

"I don't really know much, just that he was going there to meet her."

I'm reeling at this information. This is not the Andrew I knew. He'd never do something like that. Maybe I didn't know him as well as I thought, either.

"I thought he—I thought—" I don't know what's causing me to have this reaction. I'm the one who ended things. I'm the one who didn't want to get married. It's my fault that Andrew went off to the Netherlands to meet a woman. Seeing him with someone has blindsided me in a way I didn't expect. "I didn't know," I say, suddenly having a hard time taking a full breath.

"Breathe." Eli places a hand on my back and moves it in a soothing motion. "You need to breathe."

"I'm sorry. I don't know what's wrong with me. Am I crying?" I reach up to touch my face and my hand comes away wet. "I never cry!"

"Maybe you need to cry," he says gently.

"I don't want to cry. I hate crying. My eyes get all swollen. Is this thing going to start taking our photo?"

"No, it's not on. It's okay. Come here." He pulls me into a hug, and I bury my face in his neck. This feels like when you're a little kid and you fall down and hurt yourself, but you don't really get upset until someone acknowledges that something is wrong. I'm full-on sobbing now, and it's embarrassing.

"I'm getting your shirt wet," is all I can think to say to him.

"I don't care."

The thing is, I don't think these tears are because Andrew is with someone new. I think it's more that the shock of seeing him with her has made me realize that I kept him from happiness for so long. He could have met someone else years ago. How much time did we waste together? How much time did I waste of his life, knowing I wasn't fully in it?

I also feel jealous that he found happiness so easily. And what a terrible thing to feel.

"I'm an awful person," I say.

He pulls me in tighter, and I adjust myself so that my legs are draped over his. "What are you talking about?" he asks.

I can't bring myself to voice my real thoughts. That I'm selfish. That in an attempt to be nothing like my mother, I became exactly like her. Because I knew Andrew was a good man, and I didn't want to be alone. "I just need a second."

We don't say anything for a few minutes, and with his continued soothing circles on my back, I feel myself beginning to calm down.

"You're a good hugger." This comes out muffled against the place where his shoulder meets his neck.

He chuckles. "Thank you."

"I'm sorry."

"You're understandably upset. It's tough seeing your ex with someone new."

"I just feel so terrible. I'm an idiot."

"You're not an idiot."

I pull away slightly, but keep my arms wrapped around

him. Eli is a good man, too. And it feels good being in his arms. It feels good being in his lap.

What the fuck? I am in Eli's lap.

"Why are you looking at me like that?" he asks.

"Like what?"

"Like you've just awoken from a coma and don't remember who I am."

I laugh. "I was just thinking I'm happy you're here. And also, that I'm sitting in your lap."

He smiles and says, "I'm happy you're sitting in my lap, too."

I snort, but it comes out as a sniffle. I lift my head up and we hold eye contact for a few seconds, smiling softly at each other. It feels like my heart is running a marathon in my chest. I was just crying in this man's arms over a failed relationship with another man. Another man who happens to be his best friend.

And then we stop smiling. "Are you okay?" he whispers.

I nod my head and lick my lips that suddenly feel very dry. The motion causes him to look at my mouth. Then he licks his lips, causing me to look at his mouth. I want so badly to kiss him, and I wonder if he wants to kiss me, too.

My phone buzzes. "Sorry, it's Rett." I answer, "Hey, are you okay?"

"I'll explain later, but it's my grandma. I'm heading back home tonight."

"I'm so sorry, is there anything I can do?"

"I don't think so. Are you able to get a ride? I hate that I abandoned you."

I meet Eli's eyes. "It's okay. Eli can take me home."

I'VE GOT to get it together.

Faye was just breaking down over another guy—one of my oldest friends—and here I am, unable to stop thinking about kissing her. The entire drive to her apartment has been silent, and for once in my life, I don't try to fill it with idle chatter.

It's simple. I will walk her to her door and go home. I will push all thoughts of kissing her out of my head. Before she got that call from Rett, the air inside that photobooth was charged with something that I don't think either of us have chosen to acknowledge yet.

What if we did acknowledge it, though? I felt closer to her tonight while we were dancing, not just physically, but it felt like she relaxed into me—letting me in for the first time.

I glance over at her and she's looking out the window. Some of her hair has fallen out of her bun, and it trails down the side of her neck. I want to reach over and brush it behind her shoulder or tuck it back into her hair. I want to take her hair down and run my fingers through it.

Upstairs.

Leave.

No kissing.

We arrive at her apartment building, and I find a parking spot out front. "I'll walk you up."

Her black dress shines in the moonlight, swirling around her curves, and I'm entranced. When we get to her door she asks, "Do you want to hang out for a little?"

I shouldn't, because my will power is hanging on by a thread, but nothing will ever give me the ability to say no to her. "Sure."

She unlocks the door, and we step into her entryway.

"I'm really sorry," I say.

She looks confused. "For what?"

"Tonight. I wish there was something I could do." It drives me crazy, knowing she's upset. Wanting to fix it, but not knowing how. Wanting to touch her, hold her, make her feel better.

Again, I wonder what she's thinking.

"I should apologize to you. I had a weird moment. It's just—" She leans against the back of her couch and starts to sniffle, like she's about to cry again. Her voice breaks as she shuffles around to sit on the couch. "It's—"

I rush over to sit next to her, completely at a loss for what to say. I place my hand against her back. "It's okay."

"It's these stupid shoes," she finally says and looks up at me, lip trembling. "My feet huuuuurt."

It's not funny, but I sort of laugh because it's so unexpected and cute. But I'm also relieved, because this is something I can help with, an action I can take to comfort her in some way. "Here." I tap my legs. "Put your feet up."

She smiles and swipes her hands across her cheeks. "I'm being dramatic. You don't have to take my shoes off for me."

"I want to," I say.

She turns and bunches her dress up so that her legs can swing up onto my lap. Seeing her dress pulled up, revealing a glimpse of her thighs is giving me ideas. More than just kissing ideas. I shift so that her feet aren't resting on what is becoming an obvious proof of where my thoughts are going.

I swallow hard and try to get my brain stem to instruct my fingers to unclasp the buckle on her shoes. They're black with tiny straps that crisscross all over her feet. She lays her head back and closes her eyes, letting out a sigh as I loosen them. They've left red marks all over her feet and I glide my hands over them, pressing my thumbs gently into the indentations. "No wonder you were hurting."

She sighs again and I swear it almost turns into a moan. "That feels . . . amazing."

I move my hands up to massage along her ankles and calves. Her skin is soft and smooth.

What if I just ask her? It never hurts to ask. "Can I ask you something?"

She turns her head toward me and opens her eyes. "Mm-hmm."

"Were we about to kiss earlier?"

Her eyes widen the tiniest bit, and I swear she glances at my mouth as she says, "I think so."

I continue running my hands over her arches, up her calves, and back down again. "Can I be honest about something?"

"Okay?" She huffs out a nervous laugh.

Fuck it. "I *really* want to kiss you."

Now it's out there—and either she wants to kiss me too, and I'll be sucked into the Faye vortex forever, or she'll reject the idea, and I can move on.

She sits up and scoots closer so that she's almost sitting

in my lap, almost the exact same way we were sitting in the photobooth. She rests her forehead against my shoulder and her voice is muffled against the fabric of my shirt. "I really want to kiss you, too."

Then she looks up at me, and her eyes seem to tell me that she's come to the same conclusion I have. We both want this, so what's the harm in seeing how it feels?

I place my hand on the side of her neck, with my thumb resting along her jaw. "Not a pretend kiss?" It's suddenly the most important thing in the world to me that this kiss be the most real thing I've ever experienced.

She grins and a wave of pink spreads up her neck into her face. She's so gorgeous, and I feel like I swallow my own heart waiting for her answer. "No pretending."

I press a soft kiss on the underside of her jaw where her flush always appears first. This spot has been taunting me all night, ever since our dance together. She places her arms around my neck, bringing us closer together. I kiss across her bare shoulder until I reach her neck. I take in her scent, the sweetness of her warm skin.

She leans her head to the side, giving me better access. I trail kisses up and along her cheek until I reach the corner of her lips. Then, I move to the other side and repeat this path, drawing out the anticipation, before finally bringing my mouth over hers.

It's tentative at first, like we're trying to figure out the rhythm of each other. We fall into pace easily, though, and I never want to stop doing this. It's been so long since I've made out with someone for the fun of it, just to explore.

Kissing Faye is really fucking fun.

I pull back for a beat to give us some air. I run my hands down her sides, and she's breathing so hard, I can feel her lungs expand beneath my palms. I'm breathing hard, too.

"Are we—" I don't even know what I was going to say, but I feel the need to check in. "Are you good?"

She smiles. "Yeah—I'm good. Are you good?"

I laugh. "I'm very good."

Then she gets a look on her face, like she wants to say something else, but is hesitant.

"What is it?"

"Can we . . . ?" She runs her hands along my shoulders. "Keep feeling good?"

I brush her hair behind her ear and nuzzle against her neck. "Tell me how to make you feel good."

She shivers. "Kiss me again."

I grab her by the waist and move her so that she's fully straddling me. She leans down and brings our mouths together.

Now our kisses become frantic, almost messy. We're not worried about keeping rhythm at all. It's less kissing, and more like consuming.

Her dress has ridden up further so that I can grab her thighs as she rocks her hips back and forth over me. I don't think I've ever been harder in my life, and the feeling is so amazing I'm worried I might come in my pants.

I don't even care if I do. I grip the sides of her hips and guide her to continue the motion. "Does that feel good?" I ask.

"Yes." She whimpers, and that sound alone almost sends me over the edge.

I kiss her neck and move the straps of her dress down to lightly bite and kiss her collarbone. I glide my hand over her ribs, wanting to touch higher, but seeking out her permission first. I think she knows what I'm getting at, because she places her hand over mine and guides it up over her breast.

She's not wearing a bra, and I can feel her nipples harden beneath my fingertips.

I pinch them through the silky fabric, and I watch her face to see if she likes it. "Do you like that?"

She tightens her grip on my shoulders and leans into my touch, so I take that as a yes. She continues grinding on my lap, and the only sounds that echo through her apartment are the rustles of our clothing and our heavy breathing.

"Eli, I think I might—" She quickens her rhythm and brings our mouths together. I bite and suck on her lower lip and she begins to tremble in my arms before she buries her face in my neck. "I'm so close," she moans into my shoulder.

I move my hands up to grip her ass while she rolls her hips over me. "That's it, Faye, you've got it," I coax.

"Oh God," she gasps as she comes, before relaxing against me.

I rub her back, allowing us both some time to catch our breath. That was the hottest thing I've ever done, and neither of us is even naked. I didn't even take my tie off.

Suddenly she stiffens and jumps off my lap.

"Oh my god, did I just—" she darts off toward the kitchen. "I am mortified right now."

"Faye, it's okay. It's more than okay, that was—"

"That was so embarrassing!" she interrupts and covers her face with her hands.

I take a couple of breaths and adjust myself as best I can before getting up from the couch and going over to her. "Don't be embarrassed." I reach up to pull her hands down away from her face.

"I can't believe I just did that with you, or more like *to* you. Did you . . ." she trails off and gestures to my crotch. "Never mind."

I fight the urge to laugh because she's worried about

whether I came or not. She escapes to the kitchen. I can't let her feel embarrassed about this, but I also don't want to make it completely obvious that I enjoyed that way too much, when she's clearly distressed.

"Wait, talk to me."

"I don't think I can form words right now. I mean I've never even—" She stops talking abruptly.

"Never even what?"

She hesitates, like she truly doesn't want to finish the sentence. After what feels like eternal silence, she says, "I've never had an orgasm with anyone else before." She grabs a glass from the cabinet and fills it with water. She faces away from me and chugs the entire glass. I think I hear her mutter, "Can't believe I just told him that."

I have no idea what to say. I'm doing the math in my head on how that could be possible. Did Andrew never . . .? Did no one before Andrew ever . . . ?

She continues, talking faster and with more words than I think I've ever heard her use at one time. "I mean, I've had orgasms before. Obviously. But, like, with myself. I've only ever been with Andrew and one other guy, and it just never happened with them. It's like a . . . mental block I've always had." She pauses and briefly looks me in the eye. "I don't even want to know what you're thinking right now. I'm sorry."

Sorry? For letting me take part in one of the most erotic experiences of my life?

"See? I've broken you," she says. "Normally you'd make a joke, or at the very least say *something* encouraging."

"I'm just processing," I say. "Do you want to talk more about it?"

I'm scrambling for what to say. Did I somehow cure this block she's had? Look, I'm not immune to the little ego boost that comes with making a woman come. But usually that ego boost is accompanied by a smiling, satisfied woman. Not one who looks like she's wants to run away.

And honestly, I didn't really do much tonight, other than talk her through it. Maybe that's what works for her. Maybe we can figure that out together.

She shakes her head vehemently. "Let's just forget this ever happened, okay?"

Like I could forget. I'll probably think about this for the rest of my life. I walk over to her. "If that's what you want."

"I think that's best, don't you? I don't want things to be weird between us now."

I run my hands down my face. "Things don't have to be weird. I want to do whatever makes you comfortable."

"Yes, let's just erase this night from our minds."

I feel a keen sense of disappointment. Now that I've dipped my toes in the water, I want to fully dive in. "Okay, yeah. Sure."

She nods her head like the matter is settled. "Thank you for being there tonight. Sorry for the whole emotional breakdown thing and then the . . . other stuff."

She heads over to her door, which I take as my cue to head out. Probably for the best, considering I need to get my head straight, too. But I can't leave knowing she feels that what just happened was a bad thing.

"For what it's worth, I'm proud of you," I say.

"Here comes the cheesy pep talk," she teases. "For what?"

"For not holding back." I lean down and place my mouth just by her ear. "And just for the record, you didn't hear me complaining, did you?"

26

FAYE

ELI IS MY FRIEND.

Eli is my friend.

Eli is my friend.

If I say it to myself enough times, I'm hoping I can eradicate the thought that keeps creeping like vines into my brain that Eli is my *very hot friend* who I made out with, and then dry humped to completion.

He didn't show up for our usual morning coffee, so I don't know if he's even at work today. I open Slack and check to see if his status has updated, but his name still has a gray circle next to it. I don't think he's missed a day of work since he started—I'm panicking, thinking it's because of me. I basically ran him out of my apartment, so maybe he's decided to leave the Southeastern United States again. But I felt so vulnerable in that moment, in a way that shocked me. I was overwhelmed, putting guards up just in case we'd done something we might regret.

For the record, you didn't hear me complaining, did you?

We've been flirtatiously circling each other for weeks now, but I didn't think anything like that would come of it.

Now, it's all I can think about. The way his hands moved over me, unhurried and certain. His mouth on my neck and his beard tickling my cheek. His strong thighs beneath me while I—yeah, not going there.

The delightful rush I felt when he praised me for not holding back.

And it's true. For the first time in a very long time, I let myself catch up to a feeling I've been chasing for a long time. But still, why couldn't I have sought out that feeling with someone besides my ex-boyfriend's best friend?

Since I'm not getting any work done, I decide to take an early lunch and try to call Rett again. I'd really like to get her perspective on the kiss.

I go outside and sit on one of the benches in the court-yard. A few other people are doing the same, taking their lunch breaks in front of the giant fountain. I take off my cardigan and call Rett.

She picks up this time. "Fifteen missed calls. Christ, is everything okay?"

I didn't realize I'd called that many times. "Sorry! How are things with your grandma? Is everything okay?"

"I'll tell you later. She's decided to be a little shit-stirrer, as always." I'm curious about what kind of drama Grandma Minnie has cooked up this time. "What's going on?"

"Something happened Friday night. With Eli."

"Okay, you should have called me thirty times. Tell me *everything*."

I tell her about seeing Andrew's Instagram post, crying in Eli's arms at the party, and then about the kissing, the dry hump session, and the orgasm confession. I catch my breath, not used to talking so much, or so fast.

"Hold on. He said, 'You didn't hear me complaining, did you?'"

"Yes."

"That's *so* hot."

"I know!" The woman on the bench across from me sends an annoyed glare my way. In a quieter voice I repeat, "I. Know."

"I knew you wanted him. I knew he wanted you." She cackles. "It's all coming together."

"I was hoping you would tell me it's a bad idea."

"Why? You clearly feel comfortable with him. He clearly wants to do stuff with you. I think you're on your way to checking off another item on your fun list."

I didn't even think about my list. Sex with Eli would mean more to me than just crossing off an item, and that's what's holding me back. But would I regret not exploring this thing between us? I do feel comfortable with him in way that allowed me to completely get out of my head—at least momentarily—and just enjoy myself.

"Maybe you're right."

"Don't overthink it, just go with your gut."

———

I FINISH MY BREAK, and as I exit the elevator by the door leading to the main stairwell, Eli steps out—like my thoughts have conjured him out of thin air.

"Hey," he says, grabbing my arm and pulling me into the stairwell.

"Were you just waiting in here for me to walk by?"

"No, but I'm glad I ran into you. I wanted to talk to you about Friday night."

It's stuffy in here and probably doesn't get a lot of air circulation. I fluff the skirt of my dress out to get some air flow around my legs. "We already talked about it. By deciding not to talk about it, remember?"

"I know we said that, but you and I both know I'm incapable of that." He paces back and forth, almost like he's agitated. "I can't stop thinking about it."

"Oh." I feel a little rush of excitement, knowing that he's been thinking about that night, too. "Where were you this morning?"

He stops pacing, pointing to his cheek, which I'm now noticing is a little swollen. "I was at the dentist with a fucking drill in my mouth, but I didn't even care because I couldn't think of anything but the vision of you grinding on top of me." He starts pacing again.

"I'm . . . sorry?"

"I don't want to pretend it didn't happen. In fact, I think it should happen again."

"I've been thinking about it, too," I admit.

His head snaps up and he looks at me. "You have?" There's a hopeful tilt in his voice.

"All morning," I confess. "I still feel a little mortified about it, but it was also . . . good." *Great job, Faye, really nailed it with that one.* I feel a nervous awareness of him. It's not a bad feeling, just the confirmation that he's no longer the Eli I've known, but something more complex.

"I want to help you with that too," he breathes out in a rush.

"Help with what?"

"The sex stuff."

"I don't know. . ." Why am in so much denial over this? Rett says to do it. Eli is making it clear as fucking day he wants to do it. But I can't seem to stop tossing up barriers. "We got carried away before, right? I don't know if it's a good idea for us to take it that far."

"I'm helping you with everything else on your list. I want to help you with that."

"Why?"

"Because we have fun together." He steps closer, and he doesn't touch me, but the way he's looking at me feels like he is. "Don't we?"

I try not to smile. And fail.

"Just imagine how much more fun we could have together."

Oh, I have imagined it. All night. All weekend. I'm imagining it right now. "Can I think about it?" As if I haven't done enough of that already.

"Of course," he says. "Are we still on for your practice interview tomorrow night?"

"Yeah, do you want to come over after work?"

"Sounds good." He holds the stairwell door open for me, and when I brush past him, he leans over. "See you then."

27

―――

FAYE

"THANKS FOR DOING this over the phone," Eli says. "I totally forgot I told my parents I would dog-sit for them this week while they're on their actual anniversary celebration trip."

Our practice interview is now a practice phone interview. I'm a little disappointed that we aren't meeting in person, but also glad we aren't in the same room right now. I'm half afraid of what I might do. And half afraid of what I won't.

"No worries. Where are they celebrating?"

"Spending the week in Hilton Head."

I decide to take a bath while talking to him, to hopefully loosen up and relax. "So, the anniversary party is not their real way of celebrating?" I take a fresh towel out of my bathroom closet and hang it on the hooks next to my shower.

"That's become more of an Evie project. She's going through a breakup, and planning a party is cathartic for her."

I understand, all too well, the post-breakup distraction phase. "That's tough. I hope she's okay."

I turn on the water and make sure the temperature is almost scalding before I get in.

"Are you washing the dishes?" he asks.

"No, I'm about to take a bath." I put my phone on speakerphone and set it down on the edge of the tub, ignoring what a bad idea that is. I don't have anywhere else to put it, though. I should buy one of those bath tray things.

"While you're on the phone with me?"

"Yes . . . ?"

He sighs dramatically. "I wish you had lied and said you were just washing the dishes."

"Why?"

"Because how am I supposed to be a good interviewer when my interviewee is naked in the tub?"

"Sorry, I didn't think about that. Very unprofessional of me." I find the fancy bottle of Anthropologie bubble bath Rett got me for Christmas and pour a couple of capfuls in. "Want me to put a swimsuit on?" It's fun to tease him, for once.

Another sigh on his end. "No." His voice sounds almost strained. "Do you use bubble bath?"

"Of course."

"What does it smell like?"

"Freshly baked cupcakes." I take my clothes off and slide into the water. I sigh at the warmth, already feeling more comfortable.

"You like smelling like baked goods."

"I guess I do." I take a sip of wine and hear the sound of him opening a beer bottle. "You know, you could take a bath," I say jokingly. I can't help but giggle at the thought of Eli's legs bent up above the water because he's too tall for the tub. "Then we can really take this professionalism to another level."

There's a long pause, and then I hear the unmistakable sound of water running.

"No way, you are not."

"It's only fair we both be naked for this." Now my head is filled with another image. Eli naked and wet, bringing the beer bottle up to his mouth and taking a long deep swallow.

"Is your hair up or down?" he asks. The splashing sounds continue as his tub fills with water.

"It's up. What does that have to do with anything?"

"Can you take it down? I like your hair down."

"You can't even see me."

"I have a good imagination. In fact, I have an idea," he says. I know this tone. He's feeling playful.

I take the clip out of my hair, and massage my scalp. "What's your idea?" I ask hesitantly.

"What if we used this as an opportunity for you to interview me, too?"

"And what exactly am I interviewing you for?"

"For sex."

I choke on the wine I was in the process of swallowing. "And how would that work?"

"Have you ever had phone sex before?"

"I mean, I've swapped sexy texts before, but not really."

"We could try it?"

"Are you serious right now?" I ask.

Do I want to do that with him? My body immediately responds with a resounding yes. I guess it doesn't hurt to see how it goes. If it's terrible, we'll know that we'd be totally awkward together sexually and we can laugh it off as this hilarious thing we tried.

But what if it's good?

When I don't say anything immediately, he says, "I can hear you thinking. Don't let it stress you out. We don't have to do anything." And I know he means it. He would never make me feel bad for not wanting to do this.

"Let's try it," I say before I can take it back. "If we start feeling weird, we'll stop."

"That sounds good." He clears his throat, and in a faux professional voice says, "So, Faye. Tell me about yourself."

Here goes nothing. I set my jam jar wine glass down on the edge of the tub and reach for my body wash. "For the last five years I have been working at Millionfish Enterprises, first as an intern, then as an executive assistant for the Vice President of Marketing." I see that my loofah is just out of reach.

"Why does it sound like you're drowning?"

"My loofah is hanging on the thingy I have on my shower head, and I'm trying to reach it without getting out of the water." It's impossible, but I refuse to stand up.

"Guess you'll just have to use your hands." The way he says this is so sultry, my toes curl in anticipation.

"Guess so. Anyway . . ." I squirt some body wash into my hand and start to wash my shoulders. "That was my first job out of college, so I'm excited to pursue other opportunities and grow my skill set."

"What are some tasks you've enjoyed in your current role?" I hear him get into the water, sighing before he asks, "And what part of your body are you washing right now?"

Oh my god, *it's starting*.

"Most of my tasks have been administrative, but I've found that I really enjoy reporting and putting presentations together." I take another sip of wine, careful not to let it slip out of my sudsy hands. "And I'm washing my shoulders and arms."

Was that how I was supposed to answer that? Shoulders and arms don't exactly exude sensuality. I have no idea how any of this is supposed to work, so I guess I'll just follow his lead.

"Can you tell me about a recent project you've worked on and then continue to walk me through the rest of the steps of your bath routine as well, please."

"Last week, I was able to pull our quarterly marketing metrics and represent them graphically using a software I hadn't used before. I really enjoy trying new things." I lather my hands up some more. "Next, I'm going to wash my neck and chest."

"I can tell you enjoy your work by the passionate way you speak about it."

He's giving me nothing, here. Maybe he's waiting for me to ramp things up?

"Absolutely. I find it extremely . . . stimulating?" I hold my breath, waiting for confirmation from him that I am doing this correctly, but again he gives me nothing. What is he waiting for? "Now, I'm running my soapy hands over my breasts, taking them down to my stomach . . ."

I think I hear a very low muttered "fuck" before he says, "What specifically are you looking for in a new role?"

"I'd like something more challenging, since I've felt a bit stagnant lately. I'd love to be in a position where I'm given expert *guidance* on how to best achieve my career goals." I hope that he takes the hint that I'd like him to tell me what to do next.

"I understand that. It's always great to feel that you're growing and expanding your skill set. Might I suggest lifting one leg and resting it on the side of the tub?"

"Okay . . ."

"Now, I'd like you to wash the calf of that lifted leg. Once you've done that, slowly massage the soap over your knee and thigh."

I do as he says. "My leg is getting cold. Can I put it back under?"

"Not yet. Do you have goosebumps?"

"Mm-hmm." Partially from being cold, and partially from the sound of his voice coming through my phone's speaker.

"Keep washing up to your inner thigh, but no higher. You can put that leg under after you answer another question."

"Okay, I'm washing my thigh now."

"Do you find that you usually take direction well?"

"Yes, I'm a very task-oriented person."

"That's good to know." I hear splashes on his end, and I wonder if he's washing himself now too. I am very turned on at the thought of him matching my movements.

"Put that leg under now and repeat on the other leg. Walk me through what you're doing. This is a good way for me to see if you can articulate your processes to others."

"First, I'm squirting more body wash into my hand and rubbing my hands together until they're slick and slippery. Next, I'm slowly rubbing the soap up my leg, really focusing on my thigh." The other night, that seemed to be a place he liked to touch, so I'm hoping he'll like that I'm mentioning it. "In circular motions, I'm running my hand up inside my inner thigh, higher and higher, and—"

"Stop. No higher."

"But that's normally the next part of my routine." I whine.

"You have to answer another question first." I can practically hear the smile in his voice. Oh, this is fun.

I sigh overdramatically. "Fine."

"After our kiss on the couch, did you think about it?"

I wasn't expecting this question, but I answer it without

thinking. "Yes, with some embellishments. Might have pulled out the massager a time or two."

He laughs and it echoes through the bathroom. It's the best sound in the world, starting with a low rumble I feel right down to the core of me, before it erupts into this spark of energy that's so *Eli*, it's the only way I know how to describe it.

"I like making you laugh," I say. "Because you're always the one making me laugh."

"Making you laugh is my favorite thing. What did you imagine, when you thought about it?"

"You touching me."

"Where do I touch you?"

"You pull the front of my dress down and palm my breasts in your hands."

"Do kiss them? Lick them?"

"Yes."

"While I'm doing that, do I pull the bottom of your dress up until I can touch between your legs?"

I lay my head back, finally rubbing my fingertips over my clit. "Yes."

"Can I slide a finger inside to feel how wet you are for me?"

"Please," I moan, pretending the middle finger I glide inside myself is his. "Are you touching yourself now?"

"Would you like me to?"

"Yes, I want us both to do it. Together."

"I'd like that, too. You can ask me questions now. Keep fingering yourself."

I take a ragged breath, trying to gain composure. "Right, so. Um, can you walk through what a 'day in the life' is like? Or, how a night would be . . . like . . . how things would continue tonight?" I can barely form a coherent thought, much less sentence, right now.

But he doesn't miss a beat. "Next, I'd insert another finger inside you and stroke myself with my other hand using the same rhythm."

The thought of that is almost enough to make me come. "That feels so good."

"Don't let yourself come yet. The interview isn't over."

"How long until the interview is over?"

He chuckles. "Until I say it is. Ask me another question. And quicken the motion of your hand."

"Why do you want to have sex with me?"

His answer is quick and without hesitation. "Because you're interesting and beautiful and funny. Because I want to know you like that. Because I want to make you come five million times."

I do a weird combination of a moan and a laugh. "Wow, that's a pretty lofty goal," I say.

"I think I could do it," he gloats.

I'm beginning to think so, myself. "That's all the questions I have for you."

"Thank you for your time today, Faye. You've been a great interview." He pauses, and I think he's starting to lose his composure now, too. "I think it would be very hard for me to find another candidate as talented as you."

"I wish I was with you. Touching you. Tasting you."

"Fuck, me too," he groans.

I let the sounds of our panting fill the silence. "Are you close?" I seriously don't think I can hold out any longer.

"Yes, let me hear you come for me first, then I will, too."

The sounds I am making and the sounds I hear from him are downright obscene, all wet splashes, gasps, and moaning. A few more pumps of my fingers and I come, exhaling his name in the process. It's not long before I hear him do the same.

Neither of us say anything, both trying to recover. After a few seconds he asks, "You alive over there?"

"Mm-hmm, think so."

"So did I get the job?" he asks with a chuckle.

I laugh. "When can you start?"

28

———

ELI

I'M WAITING in the stairwell for Faye.

It's the only place I could think of in the office where we can have some semblance of privacy, and neither of us have time to trek down to the duck pond. I didn't plan for the interview to take the direction it did, so I wanted to talk to her about last night.

She opens the door and steps inside—and it's hits me again, just how bad I have it for her. She's wearing a blue dress with buttons that run down the front, and all I can think about now is the fantasy we conjured up last night. I could slowly undo all those buttons. I could hold her up against the wall and kiss her and touch her in all the ways we fantasized.

"Hey," she says, shyly looking up at me through thick lashes.

I smile. "Hey."

"How are you?" she asks with a nervous laugh.

"I'm great. How are you?"

She crosses her arms. "I can't complain."

"Your hair is down," I say.

She reaches up and moves her hair to one side over her right shoulder, a slight grin on her face. Her eyes shine. "Yeah, I just felt like wearing it down today."

I love when she flirts with me. Those moments are few and far between, and I catch them like a greedy dragon to hoard in my lair forever. "You look pretty today."

She blushes and says, "Thank you."

"I just wanted to see you. Make sure we're good after last night. And to say that we can do a real practice interview sometime this week . . . without the other stuff."

She chews on her bottom lip. "Yeah, we're good. And that sounds good."

"Did you like what we did?" I have to know she liked it. I know I did, but I don't want her to be questioning anything. I hope she enjoyed it as much as I did.

She looks up at me and grins. "It was fun."

I wrap my arms around her waist, unable to keep from touching her. "I'd like to have more fun, if you're interested."

"I'm interested," she says.

"Come with me to my parents' anniversary party next weekend."

I meant to ask her to come over for dinner and swimming tomorrow night since I'm still dog-sitting, but this came out instead.

She furrows her brow. "Um, not exactly my idea of fun."

"Why not?" I move her hair so that her shoulder is exposed.

"Would I be, like, your date?"

I press my lips against her shoulder. "You'd be my *guest*."

She rolls her eyes. "Semantics."

"You'll like my family." And my family will like her. I'm starting to think I know why I've never brought anyone home to meet them.

It's because anyone else has never been Faye.

"I don't do well in those situations."

I caress the column of her neck, wanting to follow that pale blue vein snaking down under her jaw with my mouth. "Please?"

"You're not playing fair. I'd do almost anything you say right now if you keep doing that." She moves her head to the side, like she wants me to continue.

"So, you'll come with me then?"

Her eyes are almost shut, and her skin is hot beneath my fingertips. I need her so badly. "I didn't say that."

"Let's play a game. If I win, you come with me to the party."

"And if I win?"

I slide my fingers into her hair and massage the base of her scalp. "You won't win."

"What's the game?"

Great question. I hadn't thought that far ahead. "Can we kiss while I figure it out?"

She gives me playful shove and then rests her hands against my waist. "We can't kiss in here. What if someone sees us?"

She's right. Probably wouldn't be a good idea to get caught making out with a coworker on company time. "I just can't wait to kiss you again."

I feel her fingers hook inside the waistband of my pants. "Later," she says, with a new type of smile that I seem to have unlocked. A naughty smile. But why wait until later to be naughty?

"Here's the game. Go to the bathroom right now and

take your underwear off. Hide it somewhere in the office where only I would find it. If I find it, you're my date."

"You are bad! When did you become such a deviant?"

"You haven't said you won't do it," I challenge.

"You can't be serious about this. What if someone else in the office finds them?"

"Then it's their lucky day." We laugh together.

"We're at work. You work in HR for Christ's sake!"

"If you're too chicken, then forget it."

We stare at each other for a couple of seconds, and I think she might actually be considering this. "How much time will you have to find them?" she asks.

My pulse quickens. Is she really going to do it? "Let's say three hours?"

"Two," she says.

"Two and a half," I counter.

"Fine. Shake on it?" She holds her hand out.

"Kiss on it." I grab her hand and bring her wrist up to my mouth and kiss it the way I want to kiss all over her body. I watch her watch me. I kiss her palm, and then the tips of each finger. "Just let me know when you're done."

—————

IT WAS WAY TOO easy to find them. So easy, I wonder if she placed them where she did because she knew it would be a no-brainer for me.

"Good update, Katie. Sounds like you've got some good leads. Eli, how are things going? Eli?"

Melissa's question snaps me out of my daydream, and I force myself to be present for our weekly team meeting. We've been going around giving updates on current projects and I guess I missed that it's my turn.

"Sorry about that, didn't sleep well last night." *Because I was fantasizing about my best friend's ex-girlfriend masturbating in the bath, as one does. In fact, funny story. I have her underwear in my pocket right now.*

The first place I checked was behind the espresso machine, which was a stupid place to check because Faye would never put them in a high traffic area. Then I started thinking of places in the office where we'd interacted. The elevator? No. The stairwell? No.

Eventually, I went downstairs to the lobby and asked Tom if he had seen Faye down there at all since that morning. He said he saw her leave and head toward the back of the building a couple of hours ago, and that's when I knew.

The duck pond.

And there they were, taped beneath the picnic table, sealed up in a sandwich bag and wrapped in a paper towel with the words "Return to Sender" written on it. This detail, for some reason, majorly turned me on. Something about her taking the time to do that, knowing that I would unwrap them.

I resist the urge to touch them in my pocket. They're pale pink with little hearts on them, and it's like they're burning a hole through my pants, begging me to take them out. I can't stop thinking about her sitting at her desk in that blue dress with no underwear on. How nice it would be to kneel down and slide my hands up—

". . . heard there was an interview set this week with an internal candidate?"

"Uh, yeah, yes. Faye Wilson. She's worked here for several years, and the team is eager to speak with her."

"Excellent. Can't wait to hear more next week." She stands up, indicating that the meeting is over. "And hopefully you'll be able to get some sleep tonight."

I doubt it.

I haven't told Faye the game is over yet because I like the idea of her wondering what I'm doing. She's so shy in person about anything sexual, but after last night, I want so badly to draw out that part of her.

After the team meeting, I get back to my desk and send her a text.

Eli: Too easy.

Faye: You found them already??

Eli: I think you wanted me to find them.

Faye: I would rather die.

Eli: Don't be so dramatic.

Faye: Where are they now?

Eli: In my pocket.

Faye: Need them back now thanks.

Eli: Finders keepers.

Faye: You are a scoundrel.

Eli: A scoundrel? What is this the 1800s?

Faye: You're being one!

Eli: All joking aside, I would really love it you would come with me to the party.

This whole game was all in good fun, and if she really doesn't want to go, I'll be disappointed—but I'd understand. She doesn't like situations where she doesn't know what to expect, so I need to ease her mind.

Eli: Let me give you the details and if you decide you really don't want to go, you don't have to.

I text her all the details, from how many people will be there to what kind of food will be served. I send her a screenshot of the invitations Evie sent out.

Faye: Will Andrew be there?

I don't mention that Andrew was invited, but he won't be there since he's still gone on his trip.

Eli: No, it's just family and some close friends of my parents.

A few minutes pass and I wonder if she's going to reject me. My phone lights up.

Faye: Okay I'll go.

I'm smiling so hard it almost hurts.

Eli: Can't wait

Eli: I meant to ask you something else earlier. Want to actually take a summer Friday afternoon off and come swimming at my parents' pool tomorrow?

Faye: Should we do a scavenger hunt for your underwear to determine if I'll go?

Eli: Would totally do that but I'm not wearing any sadly.

Faye: Liar.

Eli: I'll make dinner too. I'm a great cook.

Faye: I'll have to be the judge of that.

Eli: So that's a yes, then?

29
___

FAYE

ELI'S PARENTS' house is in a beautiful historical neighborhood.

Every house looks at least a hundred years old, but they're all so charming. I imagine there's constant ambient noise of lawn mowers and children giggling on their bikes in the distance.

I pull up in front of the house, the cutest brick bungalow I've ever seen, and am greeted in the driveway by a little girl with a mass of dark curls in a hot pink swim dress. Standing next to her is a giant black Great Dane that reaches to the top of her head.

I get out of my car, wondering if I have the wrong address when she says, "You must be Faye." She adjusts the orange pool floaties on her arms and gestures for me to follow her. "Follow me, please."

She leads me past the front porch (complete with rocking chairs and giant potted ferns by the front door) to the side of the house, and down a flower-lined path into the backyard. When she opens the gate, the dog bounds in and runs up to where Eli is cleaning a small pool with a net. He turns at our approach, face lighting up. "I see you've met our concierge, Florence." He nods to the dog. "And her assistant, Pebbles."

Florence runs ahead of me, clearly eager to get the swimming started. Eli pulls me in for a hug and plants a kiss on the top of my head. "Sorry, I'm on last-minute babysitting duty this afternoon. Emmett is running late with a contractor at his house."

"That's okay." It's kind of nice to have a little buffer. Not that I haven't been thinking about being alone with him all day, but I feel a jittery anticipation about what might happen tonight. This will help take some pressure off.

Florence is already standing on the steps that lead into the water. "Come on in. The water's fine," she says with a twirl.

"Careful, Flo. Don't get in until I'm in there with you." She sticks her tongue out at him, and I laugh.

"You ready to swim?" he asks me.

"I love swimming." My grandpa had a membership to a neighborhood pool in our town. It was small, a little rundown, but it was basically my second home every summer.

He looks intrigued. "I didn't know that."

I'm already wearing my suit under my dress, so I take off my sundress and set it on one of the pool chairs. I grab my sunscreen from my bag and apply it everywhere I can reach while Eli finishes cleaning out the pool.

"Almost done, Flo," he tells her as he pretends to scoop her up with the net. "Just one last critter to fish out."

She shrieks. "I'm not a critter!"

She clearly loves him, and he clearly loves her. "I see you're the fun uncle," I say, walking over to the edge of the pool.

"Of course," he says, with a cocky grin on his face. "I'm her *favorite* uncle."

"I don't have another uncle," Florence says with a perplexed look on her face.

Eli and I share a smile at her confusion. He tosses a pair of purple goggles to her. "Can you stay on that top step until we get in?"

She nods excitedly and places the goggles on her head.

I hold up my sunscreen. "Do you mind getting my back?"

He squirts the sunscreen in his hand and rubs his palms together before massaging it onto my back and shoulders. "Need me to get your front, too?" he asks quietly by right ear. It's the same voice he used over the phone the other night.

"No, I think I've already handled that," I say.

"Suit yourself. Can I borrow this? Don't want to use up Flo's."

I hand him the bottle. "Sure."

I watch him rub the sunscreen on his chest and arms, the white streaks disappearing into his skin the way butter melts into a hot skillet. "Earth to Faye," he says.

"Hmm?"

He laughs. "I asked if you could get my back too."

"Oh, yeah, sure."

"Flo, I see you. Stay on that top step," he says to her. He turns his head toward me. "She's trying to be sneaky and see what she can get away with."

"Wonder who she gets that from?" I finish applying the sunscreen to his back. "Okay, all set."

He immediately dives into the deep end before the sunscreen even has time to set in. He pops his head back out of the water and slings his hair out of his face. "Want to practice swimming?" he asks Florence.

"If I can still wear my floaties," she says, with a little hop into the water.

I ease my way in and sit on the stairs, so I'm submerged from the waist down.

"Let's play a game," Eli says.

"Okay! What game?" Florence asks.

"It's called the telephone game," he says. "I'll stay down here and tell you something and then you have to swim to Faye and tell her what I said."

Florence's eyes light up as she turns to me. "Faye, do you want to play?"

"I would love to," I say.

I watch as Eli whispers something in Florence's ear. She paddles her way over to where I'm sitting and motions for me to lean down. She whispers, "Eli said that you're really pretty." I can't help the smile that blooms on my face.

I cup my hands around her ear and say, "Can you tell him that I think he's really pretty too?" She giggles and swims away. When I see her tell him, he makes eye contact with me and his smile is so big and beautiful that it makes my chest ache.

Oh, he's very pretty.

We play the telephone game a little longer, until Florence wears herself out. Eli wraps her in a towel and hauls her over his shoulder to carry her inside. She cackles all the way in. I dry off as best I can before wrapping my towel around me and following them inside.

Eli is standing with the freezer door open. "Alright, Flo. Here are dinner options. Chicken nuggets or . . ." He rummages around. "You good with chicken nuggets?"

She nods. "Is there enough for Faye?"

Eli looks over to me and grins. "Faye, would you like some chicken nuggets?"

"No thank you, I'm good."

"Faye and I are having grown up dinner later."

We sit around the kitchen island and not long after Florence finishes her nuggets, a man who looks like a more serious, but just as good-looking, version of Eli comes in through the side door.

"Emmett, this is Faye. Faye, this is my older brother, Emmett."

I go over and shake his hand. "Nice to meet you."

"You too. Sorry Flo crashed your date. I had to meet with a plumber."

"We had a good time," I say.

Florence bounds up to her dad and grabs his legs. "We played the telephone game!"

Eli takes a sip of his water. "Maybe we'll go without the floaties next time," he says with a wink.

Florence, suddenly shy, hides behind Emmett's legs. Obviously, she's not ready to go floatie-free.

"We'll head out so you two can enjoy your night. Let's go, Flo." He grabs her hand and gives me a wave. "Nice to meet you."

"Bye Faye!" Florence shouts as they leave.

After they leave, Eli saunters around the counter and loops his arms around my lower back. "Finally. I thought we'd never be alone." He snuggles into my neck. "Are you hungry?"

I turn my head and bring my mouth to his. It's a little awkwardly done, and he doesn't expect it. Very quickly, our mouths course-correct and we kiss each other with an impatient sweetness, like we've been waiting all afternoon for this.

"I guess that's a yes," he says smiling down at me.

"Actually, I am starving. For food," I clarify.

"I thought I'd make some chicken and veggies on the grill. Is that okay?"

"That sounds great."

We chat while he grills, and then we keep chatting more while we eat. He tells me about an apartment he looked at yesterday where the entrance had ten different locks to get inside. I tell him about a dream I had last night where I was trapped inside the conference room with Guppie, forced to complete a series of riddles to escape. I tell him the food is delicious. He tells me I look beautiful in the evening sun.

We finish up just as the sun is setting, hot and orange behind the tree branches.

"How do you feel about night swimming?" He leans back in his chair and places his arms up behind his head. This draws my attention to his tattooed biceps, to the sprinkling of hair that covers his chest and stomach.

I stand up and shed my towel. "It's a perfect night for it."

He watches me, and I don't feel self-conscious when he drinks me in. Because I see the same hunger in his eyes that I'm sure he just saw in mine.

This time, I dive in first. It's not my best dive, but I feel a little rush of adrenaline from it, anyway. I come back up to the surface and he's standing by the edge of the pool, looking down at me with an impressed grin.

Then he cannonballs in with a big splash. He doesn't come back up, though, and I look down to see his shadow beneath the water swimming around my legs. I know what he's doing, and I try to swim away before he can catch me.

I'm having an actual giggling fit as he chases me through

the water. I've felt this giddy energy bubbling beneath the surface all afternoon, and it's finally coming out.

When he catches me, he pulls me toward him and I wrap my legs around him as I loop my hands behind his neck. His skin is still slippery from the sunscreen he put on earlier.

I'm still laughing when he kisses me. He pulls away and both of us are a little out of breath. "Shit, I'm out of shape," he says.

"Same, my lungs are on fire."

He holds onto me and spins us around slowly. "Thank you for having dinner with me," he says.

"Thank you for making me dinner."

I feel a drop of water slide down into my cleavage and I feel his eyes follow it. "I like hanging out with you," he says. "I like kissing you."

He kisses me again, and somehow I feel light but grounded, too. Like I fit here, with him, and this pool is a magical place where outside worries don't exist.

"All day at work I thought about this," he murmurs against my cheek. "Your wet skin under my hands. Grabbing your hips and kissing your neck."

Even while kissing, the man can't stop talking. I huff out a laugh, and he stops the trail of kisses he was running across my collarbone. "What?"

"Nothing," I say innocently.

He hefts me up and tightens his grip on my thighs. "Tell me."

"I love how much you talk. Like you have to say what you're thinking, or you'll die."

He smiles and it's almost sheepish. "I don't even know what I'm saying half the time."

"I bet you got in trouble a lot for talking in class."

"Yeah, but I always got to sit next to the girls like you." He kisses my shoulder. "The 'pleasures to have in class.'"

I laugh because it's true and we just look at each other, smiling and swaying in the water. I reach up to brush his hair back. "What's next?"

"What do you mean?"

"I mean . . ." I don't know how to ask this, but I really think we should talk about things before taking this any further. We're entering dangerous territory, despite all the warning signs, such as, maybe you shouldn't fuck the person who is quickly becoming your best friend—who is also your ex's best friend. "We should probably talk about this first."

"I agree." He hasn't stopped kissing anywhere his mouth can reach.

"Are you even listening?"

"Mm-hmm," he says, face buried in between my boobs. "Definitely listening."

I lift his face up to look at me. "I need to know something." He moves so that he's at eye level with me. "You helping me with the sex stuff . . . it isn't like a pity thing, is it?" I don't think I could stand to know he's only interested in that just because he feels sorry for me after failing twice to find someone to sleep with.

"Pity?" He shakes his head as if he can't comprehend the question. "If anything, you'd be taking pity on *me* for all the things I've wanted to do with you."

Oh. "What kinds of things?" I ask. I'm greedy now and I want to hear him say it.

He licks his lips. "The first day I saw you again in the elevator, I thought *damn, how is she more gorgeous than I remembered?* Then, I thought about that fucking vibrator and if you used it that entire weekend." He runs his hands along my waist, sliding his fingertips under the band of my bathing suit top. "Then, I thought about you coming in my lap so many times, it's a wonder I've been able to function at all." He grinds against me, and I can feel his hardness so close to where I want him to be. "I want this with you, not because of your list, but because I—because you're all I think about."

I lift my hips to meet his and move that we're pressed together as close as we can possibly be. "Want to know a secret?"

He uses his fingertip to follow a drop of water down my chest, tracing a circle over my heart. "I want to know all your secrets."

And I'm starting to want to tell him every single one.

"I may or may not have accidentally fantasized about you the first time I used that vibrator."

"Accidentally?"

"Yeah, I sort of just let my mind wander. You were some type of ranch-hand and we were having a rendezvous in the barn."

He bursts out laughing at this. "Farm fantasy? I'm banking that one for later."

"So you don't want this to be a one-time thing?"

"I have a feeling one time won't be enough for me. What about you?"

I swallow down a lump that forms in my throat, not knowing what to say. My thoughts want to spiral, thinking of all the reasons we shouldn't make this a one-time thing, much less a many-times thing. I'm scared to express these thoughts out loud, like it'll burst the bubble we're in right now. Instead, I kiss him, hoping that's answer enough.

He pulls back. "I'm starting to get a little pruny. You want to see upstairs?"

"You're not showing me the basement? I wanted to meet your roomie, Santa."

Another sheepish smile. "Since my parents are gone, I get to sleep in the office that's also a guest room." He pulls me closer and his deep voice rumbles in my ear. "Santa doesn't need to see what we're about to do."

An expectant shiver runs through me. "In that case, I'd love to see upstairs."

30

FAYE

WE STOP to dry off before going inside, so we don't track water through the house. It's a quiet walk up the stairs, anticipation buzzing in the air along with the steady blast of the air conditioning. Goosebumps break out over my skin from the sudden chill.

He leads me into a gorgeous room that looks so cozy, it could be the set of a Nancy Meyers movie. A walnut desk covered in stacks of books and papers sits on one side of the room, and an antique bed with blue floral bedding is on the other.

"This is lovely," I say.

He clicks the door shut behind him and he leans back against it. "My mom loves interior design."

I tighten the towel wrapped around my chest. "Is that what she does for a living?"

He shakes his head. "No, she was a teacher, but now she works part-time at a bookstore downtown."

I walk over to the desk and idly flip through one of the books on the top of a stack, *Field Guide to the Birds of North America.* "And what does your dad do?" I'm stalling, unsure of what to do, where to stand, how to act.

I feel him step up behind me. "Accountant." He slides his arms around my waist, reaching through my arms to remove the book from my hand and place it back on the desk. "And amateur bird-watcher."

"Do you ever go bird-watching with him?"

He puts his mouth against the nape of my neck and speaks against my skin. "Sometimes." He moves his hands down my hips to graze the bottom edge of the towel, skimming his fingertips over the tops of my thighs.

"That sounds . . . nice."

He glides his hands up, bunching the towel so he can run his palms over the inside of my thighs. "You're nice," he says, moving his caresses over my legs. "You're so soft."

I roll my neck to the side, relaxing into his touch. "You said that to me in my fantasy."

"Oh yeah?" He runs his mouth over the top of my shoulder. "What else did I say?"

"You asked if you could touch me."

"Can I?" He moves his right hand further over, almost between my thighs. "Touch you?"

"Please," I sigh.

I spread my legs a little to give him easier access and he slides a hand into my bottoms, running his fingers over me. I place my hand over his to guide his motion.

I feel his breath against the side of my neck. "Yes, show me what to do. Show me what you like."

A whimper builds in the back of my throat as I guide him to put his middle finger inside me. God, how is this so good? He adds another finger, and I melt back against him.

"I want to kiss you while I do this," he says.

I turn around so that I'm facing him and our mouths

come together as he backs me against the desk, fingers moving in and out inside me. I wrap my arms around his shoulders, holding myself up. I rock shamelessly against his hand and suck his tongue into my mouth.

"Fuck, Faye," he groans. "Can I go down on you?"

"Yes," I sigh. "But I should shower first."

"Why?"

"Because we've been outside swimming and sweating all afternoon in ninety-degree heat."

"But I bet you taste like summertime." He drops to his knees and looks up at me with a playful grin. "Like sunscreen and pool chemicals and freshly cut grass."

I snort. "Don't make me laugh."

"Why not?"

"Because it's not sexy," I say in a mock-sultry voice.

"Really? Because I've never been so hard in my entire life." He palms himself over his shorts and I feel his breath against the front of my swimsuit bottoms. "May I?"

"Yes, you may."

He kisses my lower stomach first, then lower and lower until he's practically making out with me through my suit, still touching himself while he does it. It's such a hot visual, I don't think I'll ever have trouble coming up with a fantasy ever again. It's right here in front of me.

He pulls my bottoms down and traces a finger over my hip bone where my tattoo is. "I wondered where this was." He leans down and runs his tongue over it while sliding his hand over me. I'm so wet, there's barely any friction.

I can feel his eyes on my face as he slowly massages my clit. And then his mouth is on me, and I buck my hips forward, grabbing his head as he licks.

He pauses. "Yeah, definitely a hint of chlorine."

"Stop. Talking," I say, playfully pulling his hair.

"I thought you liked when I ran my mouth."

"I'd like you to run your mouth somewhere else," I say, nudging my hips forward.

He laughs. "So needy. You want me to run my mouth here?" He licks me slowly. "Or here?" Then he moves the tip of his tongue right where I want him, and I grab his head to hold him there.

"You're so annoying," I moan.

"You like me," he says, sliding a finger inside me. "You like this."

He licks me again and my legs are trembling, I'm so close. I school my breathing, telling myself it's okay if I can't come from this. It still feels amazing.

I focus on the sensation of his mouth on me until finally the release crashes over me and I'm coming, coming, coming, so hard.

He stands up and crushes his mouth to mine, turning us so that he can lead me to the bed. He guides me down and kisses his way down my neck and chest. I lift myself up so I can reach to untie my top. I'm fully naked now, and his hands are on me immediately, everywhere.

"I've wanted to do this since that day we went shopping. I wanted you to wear that dress *for me*."

So, he was jealous I bought that dress for someone else. Why is that so hot?

"Roll over," he says.

I roll onto my stomach, and he trails a fingertip from my lower back up to the nape of my neck. His hands feel rough on the soft skin of my shoulder blades, and I relax into the bed as his massages my back. His hands move lower, and he brings them down to my ass. "And those pants you had on at your game night. I was trying so hard not to just look at you all night."

I see what he's doing now, walking me through how much he's wanted me as he touches every inch of me. When he brings up these moments, I think of the times I wanted him, too.

Then his hand is between my legs again and I arch my back as he inserts a finger inside of me and I rock back into it.

"I hope you see it now," he says, his voice thick as he drives his finger inside me again and again.

I don't do anything but whimper in response as I continue riding his hand.

He brings his mouth down by ear. "How much I want you."

"I want you too," I say as I come again, swift and fleeting this time, and almost over before it begins. I bury my face into the bedding. He's still touching me, running his hands over my back like now that's got the chance, he doesn't want to break contact.

When I gain my bearings again, I sit up and guide him to lay back on the bed. "My turn," I say.

He props himself up on the pillows. "Your wish is my command."

I run my fingertips over his face and along his jawline in a delicate touch over his beard that makes him shiver. "When I first saw you again, I remember noticing this. I thought *wow, he's a man now.*"

He chuckles as I scatter kisses along his neck over to his ear. "I was so aware of you in this new way." I nip at his earlobe. He moans and I file that away as something he likes.

I need him to know how much I've been wanting him, too.

I move my mouth down his body, following the trail of

hair from his chest to his lower stomach. "At your softball game I watched your hands as you bent down to tie your shoes." I sit up and grin down at him, lifting his right hand up so that I can kiss the index finger where his silver ring rests. "And I wondered what they would feel like touching me." I let go of his hand and he glides his thumb over my nipple before grazing his knuckles down my stomach.

I slide my hand into his trunks and run it up and down along his length. He groans and lays his head back against the headboard. I clench my thighs together. "I can't wait to feel you inside me."

He springs up, clearly just as eager for that, and he reaches into his pocket to pull out a condom.

"Have you had a condom in your swimming trunks all day?"

"Always prepared," he grins.

I slide his trunks down his legs and he puts the condom on. I straddle him and place him at my entrance, lowering myself onto him slowly, until he's fully inside me.

"Oh, Faye," he says. "You feel so good."

I rock my hips back and forth and it feels amazing, how deep he is. "I love how you say my name."

He holds onto my hips as I increase my pace, watching his face now. He doesn't close his eyes or shy away from me looking at him. He does the opposite, holding my gaze as if there is nothing he'd rather be seeing. I roll my hips more slowly now, and he clenches his eyes shut before suddenly turning us over.

I wrap my legs around him as he drives back into me.

He stops moving for a moment. "Sorry, you on top like that . . . I wasn't going to last much longer," he says with mild chagrin. It's charming to see that expression on his face because it doesn't happen very often.

He begins moving in and out of me again, deep and slow. Bringing his mouth down to mine, he repeats my name—barely a whisper against my lips—with each thrust.

The headboard bangs against the wall in pace with our panting, until he moans into my mouth as he comes.

We stay locked together for a few moments, breathing hard, cuddling and touching. Reluctant to separate from each other.

He gives me a long, deep kiss before getting up to throw the condom away. The sheets are sweaty, but I pull them over me. I press my hands against my hot cheeks, feeling flushed and overwhelmed. That was . . . something I can't even form a thought around yet. Everything about it felt so instinctual, so right.

I didn't know it could be like that.

When he comes back into the room, he sprawls out next to me, but on top of the covers. Then he seems to think of something and turns his head to look at me. "Did you come just now?"

"No . . ." I trail off, toying with the sheet. "But that's okay."

He moves the sheet aside so he can run his hand across my stomach. "I want you to come one more time."

"Oh my god, Eli, it's fine." I pat his head affectionately. "You did good."

He dives under the sheet and moves down so that his head is back between my legs, forming a tent. "I *need* you to come one more time," he says, muffled against my lower stomach.

I giggle at how silly it is to be talking to a sheet-covered head and pull up the top of it so I can see him. "Now who's the needy one?"

He runs his hand over me. "*You* are, based on how wet

you still are." He pulls the sheet back over his head. "And I'm not done exploring."

I lay my head back against the pillow. "Alright, carry on then. Let me know if you need a headlamp. Or some trail mix."

He gives my hip bone a playful bite before continuing his expedition. It's not long before he has me coming again sooner than I thought possible. He pokes his head out from beneath the sheet and says, "Only . . . four-point-nine-million to go?"

I laugh bursts out of me, and he captures it from my mouth with his.

31

FAYE

THE SOUND of paper rustling wakes me up.

I peek my eyes open, and the room is bright, with light streaming in through the window next to the bed. I hear a low, muttered, "Damn it" and roll over to see Eli sitting at the desk. The back of his hair is sleep-mussed and sticking up every which way. It's so endearingly boyish.

"What are you doing?"

He turns at the sound of my voice and holds up a notepad. "Shoot, sorry if I woke you up. I was writing you a note."

"What does it say?"

He sits on the edge of the bed and holds the paper up so I can see it.

"*Have breakfast with me?*" is written next to a rudimentary sketch of a plate of waffles. He drew a heart at the bottom with his name below it.

"I messed up the drawing," he says, leaning down to kiss me on the forehead. "I think my waffles want to be pancakes."

"I like them. Can I still have it?"

He hands it to me and I bring it up to my face to hide my smile. It's so incredibly cute, I feel like a giddy thirteen-year-old.

He looks at me, expectantly. "Well?"

"I'd love to have breakfast with you," I say.

We get dressed and decide that he'll drive us to breakfast and then back here so I can get my car.

———

THE FURTHER WE get away from his parents' house, the more nervous I begin to feel. That giddiness I felt after reading his note is becoming blacked out by an impending sense of uncertainty.

It feels like I'm leaving a fantasy world.

"Where are we going, anyway?" I ask him.

"It's a surprise."

"You know I hate surprises."

"You'll like it, I promise."

I glance over at him and he's happily tapping his thumbs against the steering wheel in tune to the music. Not a care in the world.

Meanwhile, I am freaking out over last night. Over the past twenty-four hours, really. I knew that my list had nothing to do with why we wanted to have sex with each other, but I didn't think it would be this . . . transformational for me.

I feel vulnerable, like he's seen a part of me I can't take back. Not that I want to take last night back, but there's this longing now for something that I can't have. I try to silence the voice in my head that says, *You don't even know what you want. You're going to hurt him, too.*

I look out the window and watch the scenery pass us by.

It's still early but already hot, and the asphalt shimmers on the highway as we drive.

"Do you want me to ask what's wrong, or would you like to stew a little longer?"

"Nothing is wrong. I'm just tired." It's true. We didn't exactly get much sleep last night.

He leaves it alone at that. And then he pulls into a parking lot, and I see where he's taking me.

My spirits lift a little when I see the familiar yellow sign. I smile over at him. "I *love* Waffle House."

"I know you do." He opens his car door. "Come on, cranky, there's nothing a little sausage grease won't solve."

It's not busy at all, and we take a booth by the window. I stare down at the laminated menu and the words and images run together into a mass of imaginary text that promises, "*Waffles first, worries later.*"

It's hard to be in a weird mood when you're seated beneath big, globed lights with a plate of syrup-drenched waffles in front of you.

The waiter comes by to take our order, filling our mugs up to the brim with coffee.

Eli immediately takes a sip, slurping loudly to avoid burning his mouth. "Ah, I love diner coffee."

"You like all coffee." I smile at him, hoping to dispel the tension I created because I can't just exist and enjoy a moment. I have to chew on it like a piece of gum that went stale hours ago.

He leans back in the booth. "So . . . let's have at it."

"Have at what?"

"Our first argument. I feel like it's about to happen." He rubs his hands together like he's excited at the prospect.

"What are you talking about?"

"You spent the whole drive here looking out the

window like I was driving you to the gallows. Something is bothering you." He tilts his head. "Or annoying you."

"I'm not annoyed." I take a gulp of coffee, and it burns the roof of my mouth. "Ouch. I'm . . . confused."

"Okay," he says patiently. "What are you confused about?"

"Us!" That comes out way louder than I mean it to. A bit softer, I add, "How are we supposed to be around each other now?" We were supposed to talk all this through before having sex, but clearly we got derailed.

"Look, I'm just gonna say it. The sex we had last night was the best I've ever had."

I fidget at this, feeling heat rise up my neck to my face. His hair is still wet from showering—a shower we took together—and I'm only human. I know how that stubble along his jaw feels against the inside of my thighs now. I know what it feels like to curl up in the security of his arms. "It was amazing," I say, unable to keep the tiniest hint of despair from my voice.

"Why do you say that in such a sad way?"

"Sorry, I don't mean to sound sad. I just don't want us to regret anything." There's also the Andrew-sized elephant in the booth with us that we haven't talked about. "And I don't want to hurt anyone."

He looks at me sincerely, and I know he understands. "We won't hurt him."

I swallow, not ready to give up the fight. This need to convince myself and him that we can't do this is overwhelming. *Get out while you still can*, or whatever.

"There's something else, isn't there?" he asks.

What about feelings? I want to ask him, but we haven't even begun to broach the subject of something more than sex between us. After last night, I'm scared to acknowledge this other thing floating out there that I think he feels too, but I'm not completely sure. "I don't know if I can do a casual thing with you. You're used to that, but I'm not."

There's a brief flash of annoyance on his face before the waiter arrives with our food. Is he annoyed that I'm over-thinking this?

"Do you want a relationship with—" he pauses and clears his throat. "Are you looking for a relationship?"

I hesitate because *of course* he asks up front like that, and it makes me squirm. I don't know what I want, and that's the fucking problem.

"What are you looking for right now?" I move my hand back and forth between us to imply that I'm asking what he's looking for with us. I also recall how he wanted to start trying to find someone, after realizing he's never been in love before. Are we going down that road, or am I going to keep him from finding that with someone else if we continue whatever *this* is.

He takes a bite of his hash browns and doesn't answer for a few seconds. "I think we owe it to ourselves to keep exploring this."

"What happens when we get tired of each other?" I ask. I fold my straw wrapper into an accordion to give myself something to do with my hands.

"That's not going to happen."

I pick up my fork and set it back down. "But it might. I think we just say the casual sex thing has been checked off the list and go back to being friends."

It's a pathetic defense and I know he sees how weak it is. He sighs and taps his fingers on the table. "Faye, you and I know we're never going to be just friends. We passed that point after I gave you instructions on how to get yourself off in the tub."

"You're just bringing that up to get me flustered."

"You're very cute when you're flustered. You get this red splotch right under your right ear. I want to kiss it."

Damn him for countering my pathetic defense with his charming one. "My splotch is not cute. And you can't kiss me in a Waffle House." I toss the straw wrapper at him.

He holds the menu up, hiding our faces, and leans over to kiss me on the cheek.

"Hey," he says to get my attention. "I understand how you're feeling, and I don't want to do anything that would cause anyone harm. But I want to keep spending time with you."

I want that, too. So much. But I'm scared. "Promise me one thing."

"Anything."

"Promise me if you meet someone you want to pursue, that you'll do it, and not feel bad for me."

"Faye . . ."

"Promise," I insist. This somehow gives me comfort—he'll have the freedom to leave our arrangement whenever he wants.

"Believe me, when I decide to pursue someone, you'll be the first to know."

32

FAYE

"I CAN'T DO THIS."

"Yes, you can."

I'm in my kitchen, FaceTiming Eli while I fix my coffee before heading to the office.

"I'm going to forget everything I've ever accomplished. They're going to be mean to me."

I slept maybe three hours last night and my eyelids feel like sandpaper. I didn't want to wake him up early to bother him with my mini meltdown about my interview this morning, but Rett is still back home, and I didn't want her to feel obligated to help me when she has so much going on right now. I talked to her briefly on the phone last night to check in to make sure she was okay, and to tell her that she was right about Eli and I having sex before the month was out. Her response was to scream, "Yes!" over and over for thirty seconds straight.

"Once you're there, you'll feel better," he says. "And why would they be mean to you?"

"Because it's going to be obvious that I've never done anything even remotely close to this job and they're going to be annoyed I've wasted their time." I set my phone down so that he's now facing my water-stained ceiling. "I'm sorry I called and woke you up. I don't even think I can be perceived right now. I'll call you later."

"Can you pick up the phone and look at me? I need to tell you a story."

I pick it up and there is his lovely, sleepy, handsome face. He's laying in bed, and it hurts how much I want to be there with him, forgetting about the list, the job, everything. "You can't distract me."

"It's a story about you. Do you remember the first time we met?"

"The football game, junior year?" I remember going to the tailgate with Andrew, our first outing together as a couple, and meeting Eli and some other friends.

"No. Well, I guess that was the first time we officially met, but we actually spoke to each other briefly before that."

"We did?"

"At freshman orientation. You were in my group."

I don't recall meeting him there. All I remember is being led around campus on a hot July day in North Carolina, and having to make huge decisions about my future as a seventeen-year-old. "Are you sure?" I ask.

"We were doing this icebreaker activity where they passed a roll of toilet paper around and asked each of us to take some, but they didn't tell us why."

I groan. "This I remember."

"I was sitting next to you, and you took *so much* toilet paper."

"Why are you making me relive this?" Why don't I remember Eli being there?

"Then, when they said we had to tell a fun fact about

ourselves for each section of toilet paper we'd grabbed, I'll never forget the look on your face."

I remember looking down at how much toilet paper I had in my hands and thinking, *this is it, I'm going to have to switch schools*. By fact number ten, I was making everything up. "Needless to say, I do not know how to play the clarinet." I am laughing now, because I can finally see the humor in it.

"I remember thinking you were so cute."

"Why are you even bringing that day up?"

"Because it helps you remember that even if you majorly fuck this interview up, it's not the end of the world. Just another random blip in your life that no one will remember."

"Clearly you remember it, though."

"I only remember that because it's you."

I don't know what to say to that because what I really want to ask, *Why didn't you talk to me then? Why didn't I know you before everything else?*

"But I really don't want to fuck this up."

"What's the worst thing that could happen?"

"I'll answer a question so badly they'll think I'm the dumbest person they've ever met, and tell me to get out because they can't even conceive of giving me this job."

"Okay, let's say that happens. Then what?"

"Well, I wouldn't get the job."

"And then what?"

"I'd have to keep working a job that is sucking the life force out of me."

"You wouldn't have to do that. You could look for another job. You could work for another company. You could do anything you want."

When he says it, I believe it. That I could decide to do

something and do it. I don't tell him the true worry that's been in the back of mind. That I don't actually want this job at all. That I'm pretending to want it, because it feels like I should. I made my list on a whim and I'm suddenly feeling very silly about it. "Yeah, I guess you're right."

"I know it's not easy, but I know you'll do great." He gets out of bed and walks me along with him to his kitchen. "Want to meet up for dinner tonight?"

"Maybe. Can I text you later?" I'm worried the interview will put me in a weird mood and I'll just want to be alone without bogging him down with another "fix Faye" moment. He would understand.

He looks like he's going to say something else, but all he says is, "Sounds good. Good luck."

MY INTERVIEW IS at ten o'clock, so the moment the clock strikes 9:45, I set my status to busy and head down to the fourth floor. Eli told me to ask for Anna, the operations assistant. She started working here not long after me, so it will be reassuring to see a familiar face to calm my nerves.

I smile at her in greeting. "Hi Anna, how are you?"

"Hi Faye." She reaches out to shake my hand. "Come on back. I hope it's okay that a couple of other people will be joining us."

"Of course," I say, even though my heart rate skyrockets. We walk into the conference room and apparently a couple of people means *five* other people. I wonder if Eli knew this interview would be with multiple people.

She gestures for me to take a seat at the head of the table.

Ryan, the person who would be my manager, is directly

to my left. Every time I've ever seen him, mostly during company meetings when he provides operations updates, he's smacking his gum. Today is no different. He smiles and pops a stick of Extra into his mouth before kicking things off. "Why don't we start with a little bit about you, Faye."

I give the spiel I've practiced with Eli countless times. At this point, I'm so separated from the words it's like I'm talking about someone else.

When I finish, he looks down at my resume as if seeing it for the first time. "I had no idea you'd been here so long." He frowns down at the paper. "And in the same role?"

I'm taken aback, because Eli told me that the fact that I've been at the company so long was a huge factor in me being good candidate. We didn't prepare for the scenario in which that wouldn't be a good thing. I nod and smile stiffly. "Yep!"

"She's always been Alexis's right hand." This is from Mary, another assistant on the team. She parks next to me most days. Always crooked. "I think I saw you at the party. You were dancing with Eli."

"Oh, yeah." I shift uncomfortably in my seat, confused by the comment. "We were."

She leans forward, excited. "Are you two dating?"

My face heats. I don't like the direction the conversation is taking, especially on a job interview. I fumble for the words. "No, we're . . . friends."

She looks around at the others and laughs gregariously. "I thought you two were an item."

"Nope, we're not."

Do they think that Eli and I are dating, and that's why he put me up for this job? I uncross my legs and cross them again. My thighs are stuck together with sweat. This interview is not going well, and I don't think I'm the only one who thinks that, based on the throat clearing Ryan does to get us back on track.

The group then asks me some of the other questions that I had prepared to hear. And maybe it's just me being overly sensitive to the fact that maybe these people think I've been fucking my way to the top, but no one seems engaged. I mean, everyone knows interviews suck for all involved. Nobody wants to spend their time interviewing someone. Maybe that's it, and they just want to move on with their days.

They all kind of look like someone is holding them hostage in this room with me.

After each person has had a chance to ask me a question, Anna turns to me. "Do you have any questions for us?"

I feel a bit of pressure lift at this point, because this means I get to assume some semblance of control over the conversation now. I take a sip of the water that someone had set out for me before I arrived. "What do you all like best about your roles here?" I'm hoping this question might bring a little animation into them.

Anna is the first to answer by saying, "Oh, the company culture for sure." I wait for her to elaborate on that, but she ends her sentence there, looking expectantly at the others in the room. I don't mention that I am already well versed in the "culture" here, if that's what you want to call it.

Callie, the director of operations, answers next. "The work is very rewarding." Again, no elaboration. Am I supposed to ask them to elaborate? Eli and I didn't talk about what I should do if the people interviewing me didn't want to answer any of my questions.

The rest of the group answers with similarly vague responses. At this point, I just want to be out of this room. "I think that's all I have for you," I say. And then it's like a weight has been lifted from the room and they all heave a collective sigh of relief.

We stand, and Anna says she will escort me out to the elevator. "It was nice speaking with you all. Thank you so much for the opportunity," I say in the most polite voice I can muster.

"We will be in touch," Anna says, pressing the *Up* button for me.

And that is that. I head back to my desk, and I sit there for a few moments before waking my computer up, dumbfounded at how odd that was. No one was mean to me like I was worried about, but instead this feels somehow worse. I didn't expect an interrogation about Eli, followed by polite neutrality. I really didn't expect to feel even more invisible at this company than I already do. Maybe they saw me and immediately knew I wasn't a fit, so they just went through the motions.

Either way, I'm relieved it's over.

Maybe Alexis isn't so bad. At least she doesn't act like a robot.

33

ELI

AFTER PICKING up takeout from Faye's favorite Indian restaurant, I head over to her place. Based on the brief text exchange we had earlier to decide on dinner plans, I couldn't tell if the interview went well or not. But as soon as I give her a hug when I arrive, I notice something's off. She radiates tension and refuses to look at me.

By the time we finish eating, I can't stand it any longer, and decide to try to press her for details about the interview.

"How did it go today?" I ask.

She sniffs. "It was fine, I think."

"So, you're feeling good about it?"

"I'm not sure," she says, busying herself with placing the lid on the rice we didn't eat.

I don't push anymore, because clearly, she doesn't want to talk about it. I tell her about my day instead, hoping to ease some of her tension by letting her know about a call I had with a candidate that involved him forgetting to put the phone on mute while he peed during the call. This would usually get at least a chuckle out of her. But she just smiles in a distracted way.

"Want me to stay over tonight?" I ask.

"No, that's okay. I'm not really in the mood."

"I meant just to stay with you. It seems like something is on your mind. Are you sure everything is okay?"

"I think I'm just going to shower and go to bed, so I won't be good company."

As if that matters to me. I would stay with her if she's breathing fire down my throat or not talking to me at all. I know something is bothering her and I hate that she doesn't feel like she can tell me.

"You know it's not a burden for me to stay with you," I say.

And that was the worst thing I could have said.

"I don't think I'm a burden," she says shortly, grabbing the takeout containers and taking them into the kitchen. I can practically see the wall she's put up. A wall I don't mind scaling, if it means I can help her.

"That came out wrong. I just mean I don't care if you're good company. I don't care if we sit in silence or watch a movie. I don't care if you sleep in your bed and I sleep on this couch. If you need someone, I'm here. That's all I'm saying."

She doesn't say anything, and I watch her wipe down the kitchen counters that aren't even dirty. She's scrubbing them as if it's her personal responsibility to rid them of decades of invisible grime.

"I could maybe go for a movie," she says, so quiet I'm not sure I even heard her at all.

"What's your comfort movie?"

She folds up the kitchen towel and hangs it over the edge of the sink. "Probably *Rosemary's Baby*."

"*Rosemary's Baby* is your comfort movie?"

She smiles the tiniest bit. "I know it's fucked up, but yes. I used to watch it a lot when I was younger."

"Isn't that the one where she's pregnant with Satan's baby? You watched that as a kid?"

She shrugs. "I know, but I used to skip the really scary parts because I mostly just loved her outfits."

"*Rosemary's Baby*, it is."

We decide to watch the movie in bed on her laptop. Or I guess I should say, Faye watches the movie, and I watch Faye watch the movie. She doesn't even know she does it, but she mouths the words to basically the entire thing.

When it gets to the part where Rosemary returns from the hair salon with a new pixie cut, I watch Faye mouth along with her, "*It's Vidal Sassoon.*"

"He's such a dick," I say.

"Hmm?"

"Her husband. Saying that about her haircut."

"Oh yeah, he's the worst. Just wait. You have no idea."

We watch for a few minutes longer and I can see where Faye's fashion influence comes from. I can easily imagine her, as a kid, watching this and admiring the dresses.

"What would you say?" she asks. "If your wife came in with a new haircut you didn't like?"

"I'd say, 'You look cute, let's make out.'"

She rolls her eyes in the way I now know means she's trying to resist my charms. All I ever want to do is make her roll her eyes at me. "You're so unserious."

"I'm dead serious. I'd go down and kiss Vidal Sassoon right on the mouth for making my wife feel so beautiful."

"Okay, okay," she says, playfully brushing me off. "I get it."

She moves so that her head is resting against my shoulder. "One time my mom came home with bleached blonde hair, and the guy she was married to at the time made her get in the car so he could drive her back to the salon and demand a refund."

"That's awful."

"Mark. He was terrible. He used to bring me those red cinnamon candies. Who eats those?" She chews on her thumbnail. "He was some kind of manager at the local bank. I think he ended up going to prison for embezzlement."

I'm curious about Faye's upbringing but never know a good way to ask without making her feel pressured to talk about it. "How old were you when that happened?"

"Probably fourteen or fifteen."

"Did your mom change her hair back?"

She snorts. "No, but that also coincided with her hat phase, which I'm now realizing isn't a coincidence. She's getting married again next month."

"Really?"

"Husband number five. Marsha loves being a bride."

"Are you going to the wedding?"

"No, she doesn't really need me there."

She doesn't sound sad when she says this, but she sighs right after, like she's resigned to it. Her mom may not need her there, but what does Faye need?

We finish the movie and lay in silence together. She rubs a circle on my chest with her index finger and I run my hands through her hair. My fingers snag a little on the waves.

"I'm sorry," she says.

"For what?"

"For the way I acted earlier when you asked me if I was okay."

"You don't have to apologize."

"Still, I was being pouty," she says, making a figure eight pattern across my chest with her fingertip.

I give her a little squeeze. "It's okay."

She moves her head to look up at me. "You seem tired, too. Everything okay with you?"

I didn't think it was obvious, but I am exhausted. I've been staying late almost every day this week to get on top of my workload. It feels like no matter what I do, I can't seem to get on track. The system we use for managing tasks is almost painful to use—there is so much information to input when we have a call with someone.

"Just some work stuff I'm dealing with. Trying to get into the swing of things."

"Is there anything I can do to help?"

"No, I just struggle with it sometimes. It can be hard for me to focus."

"Is that what happened with your last job? The same trouble?"

"In a way, I guess. I have a hard time staying motivated. You know when you *know* you need to do something, but it just feels impossible for no good reason? That's how that job was."

"What do you mean, for no good reason?"

"I just dreaded going in to work. Like, more than usual. And then I started showing up later and later, and they were so old school, we had manual timecards." I sigh, but the flood gates have opened, and I want—need—to get this out. "I lied on my timecard about when I was coming and going. They found out and fired me immediately. It was so embarrassing. I felt awful."

I wait for her to gasp or express some kind of shock that

I did this. Instead, she just holds onto me tighter and says, "I'm so sorry that happened."

And I think that's all I needed to hear. When I told my parents, they asked me what I was thinking, doing something like that. I told Andrew and he said nothing, but shook his head as if wondering how I could have fucked up that bad. I *knew* I fucked up and when I kept hearing it from everyone else, it made it that much worse.

"Why did you dread going in so much?"

I twirl a strand of her hair around my index finger before letting it unravel. "There's a lot I like about what I do. That I *should* like about it. I do like talking to people about the kind of jobs they're looking for and making those connections. But the whole office environment is something I have a hard time with." I playfully give her a little shake and kiss the top of her head. "I think I like this job because I can see you every day as a distraction."

She lifts herself up onto her elbow and looks at me with apprehension. "I don't want to be a distraction."

I wrap my arms around her and pull her back down. "Sorry, it's not you that's a distraction. It's my own brain. I'll figure it out."

"Based on what I know of Melissa, she'd probably want to know if you're struggling with something. Maybe you can talk to her about it."

That's not a bad idea. "I have a one-on-one meeting with her later this week so maybe I'll bring it up. She's kind of scary, though."

She wraps an arm around me again, locking back into place. "You can win her over, I'm sure."

We enjoy the silence for a bit, and I must doze off for a second because I'm startled awake by her saying, "The interview was kind of weird."

So it was the interview, then. "Weird how?"

"Everyone was nice, but no one seemed engaged."

That seems odd, because I got the impression they were looking forward to talking with her. "I wouldn't read into that."

"Yeah, I'm probably overanalyzing. They also got super sidetracked, wanting to talk about you."

"About me? Why?"

"Mary, who really shouldn't focus on anyone but herself and her shitty parking job, kept pressing me about details about us."

"What details?"

"Like, if we were together. Because she saw us dancing at the party."

"What did you say?" Faye and I haven't really talked more about what exactly we're doing here, with each other. Not that I think she'd be totally honest about our relationship, or friendship, with a coworker. Still, I find myself holding my breath for her answer.

"That we were friends."

"Maybe she was just trying to make the interview feel more casual."

She shrugs. "Maybe. Did you know I would be interviewing with a bunch of people at once?"

"Didn't I tell you that?"

She shakes her head.

"Fuck, I'm sorry. I really thought I mentioned it." How could I forget to tell her that? She was already nervous about the interview and then I added that surprise into the mix. It feels like my heart rises into my throat.

I really need to be better.

"It's okay. It's over now. I won't ask about other candidates because I'd rather not know, but do you know when they're making a decision?"

"You're the best candidate for it, easily. I think we're meeting on Friday since they're eager to get the role filled."

"If I don't get it—"

I stop her before she can continue. "You're going to get it."

34

———

ELI

"FAYE ISN'T GETTING THE JOB?"

Melissa takes off her glasses and sets them on her desk. "We're going with another candidate someone on the team brought in. They said Faye seemed like a great person but is not qualified for this role."

This is bad. I made Faye think she was a shoo-in for this job. How am I going to tell her this when I brushed aside her worries about the interview?

"I don't think Faye should have even been put up for this role."

"I disagree." This comes out more combative than I meant. I ease my tone and ask, "Why do you say that?"

"I know you two are friends, or maybe more than that based on some of the notes from Mary, but we can't be offering positions just because we're friends. This is a business, and I'd like to make sure we're crossing t's and dotting i's. Not wasting anyone's time."

So not only am I about to disappoint Faye, but now my manager thinks I'm bad at my job for trying to offer favors to my friends. Or worse, that because I made Faye dance with me at the company party, everyone thinks she's sleeping with me to get a job? It's so stupid and I feel heat rise up the back of my neck. I don't mention that ninety percent of people get their jobs through connections.

I think I might key Mary's car.

"I'm sorry if they feel that I wasted their time. And I assure you, I think Faye would be great in that role."

"Well, decision's been made already."

"Who is the person they're offering it to?" This is the first I'm even hearing of an outside candidate. Wouldn't this be information I should be made aware of?

"Someone that Anna went to school with. They used to work together at another company, and I like the initiative she showed to bring her in."

I want to scream. I want to snap her glasses in half. The same thing I'm being reprimanded for is the same reason she's praising someone else. I feel like I'm going insane.

"Can I tell Faye?" The least that I can do is have this news come from me, since this is all my fault.

"Sure, that's fine. Now, let's discuss your next assignments. I think it might be best if you and I work on them together. I may have let the baby chick out of the nest too fast."

Great, now I'll have a babysitter.

When I get back to my desk, I see that I have a missed call and voicemail from Andrew. He's probably confirming I can pick him up from the airport next week, but I'll have to listen to it later. It's bad, but part of me isn't ready to face the fact that he's coming back, and Faye and I will no longer be able to avoid discussing our friendship that has evolved into much more than that.

Right now, I need to think about when and how to tell

Faye that she didn't get the job. I also have a ton of emails to sift through. It's going to be a long day.

I get a text from her a few minutes later.

Faye: How did your meeting with Melissa go? I hope she was able to offer some help.

Shit, I completely forgot that I wanted to talk to Melissa about how things are going at work, but I got so distracted by the conversation about Faye. I can't talk to her about this over a text, though. I'm also not sure I can talk to her about this today at all. I'm feeling overwhelmed with everything and need to get my thoughts in order.

Eli: I actually didn't get a chance to talk to her about my issues. We had some other things to discuss.

I could tell her now and just rip the band aid off. But I can't bring myself to do it. This fucking sucks.

Faye: I'm sorry. Maybe you can find another time.

Faye: No pressure, but would you want to come with me to my grandpa's tonight? I don't know if I'll want to go on Sunday if we get back late Saturday night.

I sit up in my chair. Faye's grandpa is this sort of enigma to me. She's told me bits and pieces about him, and she's mentioned she visits him each Sunday, so he's clearly an important person to her. Asking me to go with her feels like a huge step.

Eli: I would love to.

Eli: Are you going to blindfold me so I can't see the name of the town you grew up in?

Faye: That's a great idea.

If I tell her today, would she change her mind about coming to the party with me?

It's a weight on my shoulders and I'd be selfish to keep this from her all weekend, but I really want us to have fun tomorrow. And I really want to meet her grandpa. I don't want to ruin our weekend with bad news.

35

———

ELI

WE PULL up to a small brick house with a Ford pickup truck in the driveway that I'd love to take a closer look at. It's tan with white stripes down the side, and I'd guess it's probably an '85 or '86. I snap a picture of it to send to Emmett since he drives one very similar.

"I see the driveway still isn't fixed yet," Faye says as she's unable to avoid hitting a big hole where the gravel needs to be filled in. She sighs. "I called someone last week about it."

I grab the grocery bags from the trunk before we walk inside, screen door squeaking closed behind us to announce our arrival.

"That you, Bambi?" her grandpa yells from inside the house.

"It's me!" Faye shouts. "You can put those bags on the counter," she says to me.

We walk into a kitchen that reminds me so much of my grandma's—the same stale coffee smell with a hint of cigarette smoke. I set the grocery bags down next to a pile of mail. "Bambi?" I ask Faye.

275

"He calls me that," she says with zero enthusiasm.

"That's adorable. Can I call you that too?"

She shakes her head. "Hell no."

We walk further into the house into a living room that looks like it hasn't changed in decades. The only modern-looking item in the room is a sixty-inch television in the corner. Her grandpa is sitting in a recliner positioned right in front of it.

"I brought a friend," she says, giving her grandpa a hug.

"A friend? Didn't know you had one of those."

"Funny," Faye says, gesturing to me. "This is Eli."

"Nice to meet you, sir," I say, going over with my hand extended.

He gives my hand a firm shake. "You like movies, Eli?"

I join Faye on the love seat. "Sure, I love movies."

"This is one of my favorites," he points at the screen. I see Cillian Murphy walking through deserted London streets in a pair of teal scrubs.

"Is this *28 Days Later*?"

He seems impressed that I know it. "I like to nap to it."

This man naps to zombie apocalypse movies? That explains Faye's comfort movie of choice. I turn to her and lean in so that only she can hear me. "So much about you makes sense to me now."

She tries not to smile. "All those empty streets? Nice and quiet."

"I was admiring your truck when we pulled in. My brother has one just like it."

"Oh yeah?" He perks up. "Had it forever. Still runs pretty good."

"Yeah, Emmett fixed his up a few years ago. I'd love to find one to do the same." I've always wanted a project like that—something I can fix with my own two hands.

"I'll keep an eye out. There's always somebody selling one around here. One of my buddies I see at Roy's fixes up trucks and resells 'em."

"I thought you were scaling back on Roy's," Faye says.

"It's my watering hole, girl. I can't just stop going."

"What is Roy's?" I ask.

"It's a restaurant, if you want to call it that," Faye says.

I think I understand the dynamic she has with her grandpa. She tries to take care of him, and he stubbornly refuses.

I look around the living room and there are a few photos on the wall. I see a school picture of a girl that has to be Faye, smiling a big, gap-toothed grin in a neon green shirt.

There's another photo of what looks like a much younger version of her grandpa with a pretty brunette woman. I wonder if that's Faye's mom.

Faye must catch me looking. "That photo is so embarrassing. I had grape jelly all down the front of my shirt."

"That just makes it more genuine. You were a kid who ate a PB and J that day. I love that."

"That's my grandpa and my mom in that other picture. Before grandpa lost all his hair," she says a little louder in his direction.

"You look like her."

She nods and hums in agreement as she stands up. "Hey Gramps, why don't we show Eli your garden," Faye suggests, smoothly steering our conversation in another direction.

We head outside to the backyard, where a small garden sits along the chain-link fence that marks edge of the property. It's overgrown, so I'm guessing it doesn't get a ton of upkeep.

Her grandpa walks over to one of the plants. I can't tell

whether it's a vegetable or a weed. "It's gotten a little leggy with all this rain we've had."

"What do you have in here?" I ask him.

"Tomatoes when the bugs don't get 'em, cucumbers, carrots, some potatoes."

"Nothing like a fresh tomato from the garden," I say, and I hear Faye snicker.

"Bambi hates the garden," her grandpa says, brushing her off.

"I don't hate it." Faye bends down to pluck a tomato from the vine. "It's just a little much for you to take care of."

"Nah, it's fine," her grandpa says.

Faye just looks at me and shakes her head in a way that signals her surrender to her grandpa's stubbornness. I get the sense this is an argument they've had plenty of times before, and Faye has lost it each time. It's becoming clear where Faye gets her reluctance to accept help from.

"You want to take some of this with you, Eli?" he asks me.

I look at him and then I look at Faye, silently asking her permission. She smiles. "You don't have to."

"No, I'd love to."

He goes inside and brings out a grocery bag. "Here you go, have at it."

About twenty minutes later, my plastic bag is full of tomatoes and cucumbers, and I get into Faye's car for the drive back.

"I think he liked me."

I expect her to playfully disagree or say something vague in response, but she says, "Yeah, I think he did. No small feat. As you can tell, he's a little prickly."

That makes me feel like I've won the fucking lottery.

"I don't mind prickly. I'm glad I got to meet him." As we

pull out of the driveway I notice the hole again. "Want me to help fill that some time? I can borrow a shovel from my brother if your grandpa doesn't have one."

"Sure, that would be a huge help."

This also makes me feel like I've accomplished a great feat. Faye is accepting my help without asking what she can do for me in return.

Now's my chance to bring up the job. But we just had a great afternoon together and I don't want to ruin the mood. Maybe I can find a chance to mention it before the party tomorrow.

36

FAYE

"I NEED to tell you something before we go in."

Eli's been nervously fidgeting the entire drive from my apartment to the party. I thought maybe it had to do with him being worried about his speech. I offered to help him with it earlier this week, but he said he would "let the inspiration come to him when he's up there."

Now I feel uneasy, like something else is wrong. If he's showing this much discomfort about it, I'm scared it's something to do with the party itself. "Okay . . ."

We pull into the driveway of his parents' house, and I notice there are cars everywhere, lined up and down the entire street.

A woman darts out of the house and runs down the front path. "That would be Evie," Eli says. He seems tired, too. He's got bags under his eyes like he hasn't slept well.

My stomach churns. "What do you need to tell me?"

He scratches at his chin—he has a light five o'clock shadow from shaving last night—and turns toward me. "I should have told you sooner, but—"

He's interrupted by persistent tapping on the driver's

side window. Evie motions for Eli to open the door. "Why haven't you been answering your phone? We have an ice emergency."

He gives me an apologetic look. "It's not life or death. I'll tell you after."

That doesn't help matters for me, but I can't help but go with it. We get out of the car and Eli introduces me to Evie.

She has a bubbly way about her that I like immediately, and I'm beginning to think Eli's entire family is attractive. Her light brown hair is perfectly curled, and she's wearing a simple black tank top tucked into a pair of high-waisted white shorts that highlight her curvy figure.

"I *love* your dress," she says. I'm wearing a vintage baby-blue shift dress that Rett and I found while thrifting one Sunday afternoon. It was one of those magical moments where the perfect clothing item was hanging from an end cap, like it was waiting there for me. "Anyone ever tell you that you look like Liv Tyler?"

I glance at Eli. "I've heard that a time or two."

"Eli, why didn't you tell me you were dating Liv Tyler?"

He winks at me. "Because I'm not dating Liv Tyler."

Eli starts to walk up the driveway, but I pull him back before we go further. "Are you sure everything is okay?"

"I'm sure. I'm sorry to make you worry, but it's nothing that should get in the way of tonight."

"Okay," I say, reaching up to straighten his collar. He's wearing the shirt he bought when we went shopping. He seems a little more relaxed now that we're here, except he's got the shirt buttoned all the way up.

"Hang on." I undo the top button of the shirt and my knuckles graze against his neck.

"Don't unbutton too much. This is a classy affair,

remember? Can't be showing too much skin." He grabs my hand. "Come on, this will be fun. I promise."

———

SO MANY PEOPLE are packed into the backyard that I can't even see where the yard begins and ends.

"Who are all these people?" I ask.

"I think Evie invited every acquaintance my parents have."

That's an understatement. No wonder the street was so packed.

Eli spots his parents, and we walk over to them. I met them years ago when Eli and Andrew were moving into the apartment they shared our senior year. I remember his mom being stylish and friendly, and his dad being a bit of a strong, silent type. I'm not sure if they even remember me.

Patti pulls Eli in for a hug and then does the same for me. "Good to see you again Faye, I hope you like hugs," she says.

I smile at her and it's easy to see where Eli gets his charm from. "I'm not opposed to them."

Eli's dad holds his hand out and I return his very solid shake. "Good to see you, Faye."

"Eli, introduce Faye to everyone," his mom says.

"Everyone, this is my friend Faye," he shouts out to everybody in the vicinity. It was so loud I think I've now been introduced to the entire neighborhood. They all shout their *hellos* and *nice to meet yous.*

I wave awkwardly. "Hi, nice to meet you all."

"I'm so happy you could come." She turns to give Eli a side squeeze. "Eli was so excited when he told me you were coming with him."

I wipe my palms on my dress, nervous at the attention. "Thank you so much. Is there anything I can help with?" I ask.

"Let's go see if the kids need help with the shrimp. We're doing a big seafood boil, and could probably use all the hands we can get."

We go inside and Eli immediately grabs an apron with a cat on it that says, *Hiss at the Cook*. Emmett is already preparing the shrimp, and Eli doesn't hesitate to start helping. "Faye, you remember my brother, Emmett," he says, gesturing to his left and almost slinging shrimp guts all over the place.

"Hey, watch those hands," Emmett says as he turns to me. "Good to see you, again."

"You, too."

"Wait, you've already met her?" Evie asks, somewhere between a yell and a shriek.

"Yeah, the other night," Emmett says.

"Not fair. I wanted to meet her first."

"It's not a competition," Eli says with a laugh.

I don't know if I'm flattered or even more nervous now that everyone in his family seems so eager to meet me. Clearly this night is important to Eli and I'm curious about what has Eli told them about me. About us.

Florence comes rushing into the kitchen, her poofy green dress twirling around her.

"Flo, no running in the house," Emmett chides.

"Sorry," she says. "I'm playing hide and seek with Pebbles."

"Pebbles is surprisingly good at hide and seek," Eli says.

"She'd probably like to stay hidden to keep you from trying to ride her like a horse," Emmett says. "You have to stop doing that."

She jerks a thumb at Eli. "Eli said she's my trusty steed!"

Everyone looks at Eli for an explanation as to why he'd allow a child to ride a dog like a horse, but he just shrugs and steals a carrot from the veggie tray. "Sue me for enriching the kid's imagination."

Florence pulls at my hand. "Faye, will you help me find her?"

I squat down so that I'm at eye level with her. "Where was the last place you saw her?"

Eli removes his apron and tosses it over a bar stool. "I'll help too."

Florence leads us outside to the front porch. "There. By that chair." She points to one of the white rocking chairs.

Eli slowly marches around the chair and mimics the action of bringing a magnifying glass up to his eye.

Florence giggles. "What are you doing?"

"Looking for clues. Aha!" He points to the corner of the porch. "Paw prints."

Florence gasps and rushes over to take a look. "Those aren't paw prints. That's just dirt."

Eli smiles over at me. "Guess I need to get my eyes checked." He looks around some more, continuing the pretend detective game. "Hey, Flo. Maybe she went into the backyard. Go find your grandpa and we'll meet you there."

"Good idea!" She jogs around the side of the house, leaving Eli and I on the porch.

He comes up behind me and wraps his arms around my waist. "How are you doing so far?"

I turn my head slightly, feeling the scratch of his stubble against my face. "Surprisingly good."

He nuzzles my neck. "Surprisingly?"

I shake my head but can't keep from smiling and leaning

into him for a split second before extricating myself. I turn to face him. "I'm a little nervous, but loosening up. How are you?"

He seems confused that I'd ask. "Me? I'm great."

"Food's almost ready!" Evie shouts from the side of the house.

"I like this dress, too," he says, running his hands over my sides before squeezing my waist. "It's the same color as your eyes."

I give him a quick kiss. "We should head back."

Eli places a hand at my back and guides me down the path to the backyard. I feel him messing with the line of bows that run down the back of my dress. "Don't mess with the bows!"

"I like them. This is like a present I can unwrap later."

"I'm serious!" I swat his hands away, unable to stop giggling at his playfulness. We're still laughing together as we round the corner and step through the gate into the backyard.

And the first person I see is Andrew, standing there watching us.

37

FAYE

ELI MUST NOT SEE him yet, because he doesn't seem to notice that I've stopped and that I'm not taking the hand he's reached out for me to grab. He looks down at me, confused.

"You said he wasn't going to be here," I say.

Is this what Eli was trying to tell me when we pulled up? The thing that he thought wouldn't have any effect on us having fun at this party?

"Who?"

Andrew starts to make his way over to us and I watch the shock register on Eli's face when he finally sees who I'm talking about.

"Oh, fuck." He turns, grabbing my shoulders. "Faye, I swear I didn't know."

I shrug him off, not wanting Andrew to see any more of our blatant display of affection.

I breathe deeply, preparing myself for whatever awkwardness is about to come. Maybe Andrew didn't see Eli playing with the back of my dress. Maybe all he saw was us coming through the gate, laughing, because friends laugh together, right?

Maybe I should leave.

Eli smiles at Andrew's approach, but I see the tightness in it. "Who invited this guy?" he jokes, pulling him into a hug. "Are these for me?" he asks, gesturing to the bouquet of flowers in Andrew's hand.

"Tried to call you yesterday to tell you I was coming." He holds the flowers up. "These are a gift for your mom."

There are a few seconds of awkward silence that feel like six years, before Andrew turns with a simple but surprised nod in my direction. "Faye, it's good to see you."

Was Eli ignoring Andrew's phone calls? I need to talk to him privately so we can discuss how to play this, but there's no time. Since we're about to start eating, it would be too obvious for Eli and I to suddenly disappear. That would make Andrew even more suspicious.

"Hi," I say, forcing a smile. "Good to see you, too."

"*Surprised* to see you here."

"Faye came with me for moral support," Eli explains in a rush. "She's been helping with my speech."

Andrew nods, but I know as clear as the sky is blue, that his brain is working out why the fuck I'm here right now and that it probably isn't for moral support. Also, Eli is completely lying to him. I have no idea what he's going to say in his speech.

"You two match," he says, and it might as well be an accusation.

Eli and I both look down at our outfits. I didn't even realize it until now, but the blue stripes in his shirt are almost the exact shade of my dress. Eli and I glance at each other quickly, both awkwardly smiling. Every cell in my body riots against what's happening right now.

"Andrew!" Patti rushes over to greet him with a hug and I've never been so happy to see a person. I expect to see his usual tense reaction to being hugged by someone, but he seems to welcome the embrace. "These are for you, Mrs. Miller." He hands her the flowers.

"Oh, they are gorgeous. Thank you, sweetie. Everyone come sit down, we've got place cards for everybody."

Red-and-white gingham tablecloths cover a line of tables set up in the backyard. There's heaping piles of food on the tables, and it smells amazing. Each seat has its own place setting, complete with name cards. Seeing my name next to Eli's makes me want to smile, but I feel like I'm not allowed to.

We take our seats, and Eli leans over and says, "Looks like I've got the best seat in the house."

I know he's trying to put me at ease, but I don't want him to flirt with me right now. But I also want him to never stop flirting with me, ever.

I point to the melted butter sitting right in front him. "Because you're next to the butter?"

His face gets serious. "Can we talk?"

I shake my head and can't help but feel a bit exasperated. This should not be happening. I should not be here. "We can't talk now, and you know it."

I gesture to where Andrew has made a stop to see Eli's dad. "I didn't forget you, Mr. Miller," he says, placing a small box down on the table.

"Puro Vintage cigars? Where the hell did you get these?"

He smiles, polite as always. "I have my ways."

I brace myself for Andrew to notice that while he's seated on one side of Eli, I am on the other. He says hello to a few people on his way over and he pauses momentarily before taking his seat.

Eli nudges my knee with his under the table, a nonverbal assurance that he's there and that we'll get through this evening. I give my head a slight shake that I hope he sees as my nonverbal signal that if we're going to get through this evening, he needs to stop trying to touch me.

"Everybody dig in," Eli's dad says. It's a welcome distraction when everyone begins to fill their plates. Some of my anxiety subsides, lost in the chattering of guests.

I've always wanted to experience a family gathering like this, everyone laughing and talking over each other. After watching the way Andrew interacts with Eli's family, I can see that's he's probably drawn to the camaraderie as well.

He found a family with Eli.

I glance out of the corner of my eye and watch Eli and Andrew for a few seconds. I try to keep myself from doing it, but with the two of them in front of me like this, it's difficult not to compare them. Andrew is high strung and excitable, while Eli is relaxed and spontaneous. Andrew's dark eyes are kind yet discerning. Eli's eyes are warm, a little mischievous. Maybe what makes them so different is also what makes them such good friends.

Does that make me the interloper?

I shuffle my food around on my plate and wonder what I'm doing here. And what Eli and I are doing? My grandpa liked him. I like his family. I don't know what to do with that.

Evie moves to stand at the front of the table. "And now, with a few words to celebrate our favorite couple . . . my second favorite brother."

Eli gets up from his seat and walks over to her. "Thank you, dear sister."

"Does someone have music ready for when he goes over his allotted time?" Emmett asks.

Eli grins. "They've made it thirty years, so what's five extra minutes?" Then, he takes a swig of his drink, and I see a hint of nerves in his demeanor. I may be grappling with the discomfort of this situation, but so is he. He meets my eyes, and I give him a small smile of encouragement.

But he doesn't break eye contact with me like he should. Why is he staring so intently at me like that? I give my head a confused shake, not wanting to draw attention.

He finally looks away. "I had a speech planned where I was going to tell a story about the time when I was about sixteen, I caught Mom and Dad smoking weed right over there." He points to the edge of the yard between the garage and the neighbor's fence. "Don't worry, Mom, I'm not actually going to tell that story. And don't worry, Dad, I'm not going to tell Mom that you gave me the roach from the joint later that night."

Everyone laughs and turns to look at his parents. Patti gives Steve a mock-chastising look.

Eli continues, "Burnt the shit out of my fingers trying to smoke that thing." He shuffles back and forth. "I like that story, though, because the only reason I discovered you were over there was because you were giggling so loud. And I think on some level, I must have subconsciously thought, *That's what I want someday*. To be with someone I can laugh and have fun with like that."

He clears his throat. "Then I was going to say something like, 'Here's to many more years of laughter together' or something corny like that. But lately I've been thinking..."

"Shocker," Evie buts in and everyone chuckles.

"I've been thinking it's more than laughter that gets you through thirty years with someone. There are tears and hard times in there, too. I've watched my parents have fun with each other, but there's more to it than that."

He looks at me, his honey-brown eyes so earnest I can't move or breathe. "They know each other in a way that no one else ever will. They tell each other everything. They support each other. They get on each other's fucking nerves sometimes."

"Language, honey," his mom says, blotting her tears away with her napkin.

Everyone laughs, but I don't. Because I'm starting to sense something. That, while technically he's giving this speech to his parents, what he's really doing is telling something else.

What he's really doing is telling me.

"They love each other," he says raising his beer bottle, not once taking his eyes off me.

But I must be imagining things. Eli doesn't *love* me. He *can't* love me. I've always had a runaway train for an imagination, and surely that's all this is. I'm so lost in my thoughts I barely register that Eli has finished his speech and we're all raising our drinks.

He turns to his parents. "Love you both. Now is when I'll say cheers to many more, et cetera, et cetera . . ."

He drains the rest of his beer as all the blood drains from my face.

I glance briefly at Andrew and he's not even looking up at Eli, but right at me. He's one of the most intelligent people I've ever met, able to find patterns that most people would never see. He's compiling everything he's seen tonight into a Faye and Eli folder in his brain, coming to the same conclusion that I have.

What Eli and I share is beyond friendship now.

When Eli takes his seat again, I'm unable to make eye

contact with him, feeling the sting of impending tears behind my eyes.

"I'll be right back," I say. "Need to use the restroom."

A look of concern passes over his face before he smiles softly and says, "Okay."

"That was lovely," I say, barely above a whisper before I weave through the guests and make my way inside the house. I'm relieved when I find the half bath next to the living room unoccupied. I shut the door and look at myself in the mirror. I almost laugh, even though nothing about this is funny. I'm pretty sure when someone gives a heart-warming speech, that is also a not-so-thinly-veiled confession of feelings, you're not supposed to look as terrified as I do now.

I take a few seconds to re-do my bun and gets my thoughts in order.

This is the moment I think I'm supposed to decide what to do. I'm supposed to look myself in the eye and tell myself to buck up and tell him how I feel, too.

And there it is. *What do I feel?*

I feel scared, sure, but that's too easy. What's hard is admitting that everything he said in his speech is the very thing I've always wanted, too. Fun, friendship, safety, and love. And those are all things I can't keep denying that I feel for him.

But if there's anything I've learned in life, it's that just because you want something doesn't mean you'll get it.

I touch up my lipstick and give myself a big, fake smile.

38

———

ELI

IT'S TAKING everything in me not to follow Faye into the house.

I didn't mean for my speech to the take the direction it did. I had planned to tell the funny pot story about my parents, give the toast, and that's it. But then I looked out at my family and friends, sharing this moment of celebration together and Faye shifted so clearly into my focus.

The sun was setting behind everyone and there she was, cast in its golden glow. She was smiling softly the way she does when she's not thinking about how others are seeing her, like she does when she's watching a movie she loves or is showing me something funny Rett sent her. Like she does when it's just us two, sharing each other's company.

She was all I could see. And I felt it.

I'm falling in love with her.

The moment just felt so right to tell her, like if I didn't take the opportunity to say something I'd lose my nerve. I didn't even think past that, I just started talking and then I couldn't stop.

Fuck.

I discovered my mistake when I got back to my seat and Faye looked pale, her soft smile wiped away to reveal a tense set to her jaw. She looked like she was going to pass out or puke.

I watch her stop to allow Florence and Pebbles to zoom across her path. She gives Flo a sweet smile and wave and I feel my heart break a little.

This party is not going the way I thought it would. I imagined introducing Faye to everyone and . . . I don't know, showing her how well she'd fit here. With me.

I look over at Andrew and he's watching her, too.

"Is she okay?" he asks, as we get up from the table.

Everyone disperses to refill their drinks or stand around talking. I notice Emmett standing by himself away from everyone, pretending to be interested in the hedge growing along the back fence. I wonder how he's doing tonight. If he's missing Mara and wondering, like me, if he's made too many mistakes he'll never be able to fix.

"Yeah, uh, she said she needed to go to the restroom."

He nods, taking a sip of his drink.

I don't know what to say to him. I want to apologize, but where do I start? With the dead plant? With missing his calls?

With falling in love with his ex-girlfriend?

My mom and dad make a beeline for me before I get a chance to say anything to him.

Mom has tears in her eyes, and she gives me a tight hug. "Honey, that was beautiful." She pats my cheek. "We are so lucky to have you—our sweet, funny boy."

Dad claps me on the back and says, "Great speech, son."

I've never felt this confusing muddle of emotions before. Where I clearly did something so right, based on how my parents and everyone else reacted. But also, something so wrong. I feel selfish for basking in the pride of my parents' praise while the woman I care about is currently feeling upset over what I said.

My parents are pulled into another conversation, leaving Andrew and I standing alone. I look over to check to see if Faye has come back outside, and see that Evie is standing with her, arms flailing animatedly in conversation. Faye is smiling politely, listening to whatever my sister is rambling about.

"I'm sorry I missed your calls yesterday. Busy day with work."

"It's okay. I was going to see if you could still pick me up from the airport, but I got an Uber."

"Is everything okay? What happened with the trip?"

He shrugs. "Long story. How did things go with the plants?"

Maybe I'm paranoid, but I sort of think he's asking to trap me in a lie. The lie being that I replaced the pothos plant that I think I killed in the hopes that he wouldn't notice. Surely, he hasn't had time to comb through his entire collection yet and confirm everything is as he expected.

Right?

Fuck, this is such a stupid thing to lie about.

"I killed the pothos," I admit. "It had two brown leaves and everything I googled wasn't helping and then I freaked out thinking you'd freak out and then I went to the store and bought one."

"Okay . . ."

"I'm sorry."

"Is that all?"

"What do you mean?" My God, he knows everything doesn't he? I'm not a Catholic, but I feel like I'm in confession. I *want* to tell him everything. I *need* to tell him everything.

"Hey Andy," Evie says, seemingly appearing out of thin air next to Andrew with an impeccably timed interruption. "Did you see our new pool? I was thinking about night swimming later."

"Don't have my trunks with me, unfortunately."

"Who said you need those?"

Andrew just shakes his head and drinks his beer, wisely choosing not to engage with my sister. Evie loves to embarrass him, and I'd think her crush on him was kind of cute if I didn't feel so uncomfortable right now.

Out of my periphery, I see Faye walk up to us. A bit of color has come back to her face, and I hope she's okay.

I need to talk to her, alone. But I don't know how.

"I've been trying to convince Dad to put in a hot tub next," Evie says.

"Hot tubs can be tough to maintain. They can carry disease if they're not kept up properly," Andrew says, distracted.

Evie looks at him like he just said he doesn't like chocolate cake. "Have you ever had a good time in your life?"

"Sorry if getting Legionnaires' disease isn't my idea of a good time."

"Of course, you know the actual name of the disease," she says, rolling her eyes. Then she turns to Faye. "Faye, you'll back me up. Don't you think we need a hot tub, even though they are apparently riddled with bacteria?"

Faye cautiously looks at me, and then Andrew, before shrugging casually. "That's what antibiotics are for, right?"

"Exactly!"

Faye glances in my direction, but immediately reverts her attention to the beer bottle in her hand.

"Do you need another drink? We can go grab one." I hope she takes the hint that I want to go somewhere to talk.

She brushes me off. "No, I'm good."

She's avoiding talking to me, then. I should expect that, because what exactly do I want to say to her right now?

Sorry I just confessed to maybe being in love with you in a speech in front of my entire family. Can we go have that "define the relationship" conversation that we've been too scared to have?

Florence dashes over carrying sparklers in her hands. "Time for sparklers," she says, handing them out to us. "Dad says we can spell words out with them. I'm going to spell my name."

Faye takes a sparkler from Flo's hand. "Well, you have a beautiful name, so I can't wait to see it," Faye says to her.

Florence beams up at her as if she just told her she hung the moon.

We congregate together in the yard by the pool and our fearless leader, Evie, makes her way to the front of the crowd. "Everyone line up in two lines to create a path for Mom and Dad to walk through," she says, shuffling us around and into position.

"Evie-bear, we don't need to do this," Mom says.

"Yes, you do! It's what you *do*, Mom. You and Dad walk through while all of us hold up our sparklers. I'll take a photo of you two smiling. It will be gorgeous. It will be happy. It will be *perfect*."

Mom exchanges a worried look with Dad before they both shrug and move to stand at the edge of the path we've created for them.

Since everyone is distracted by the sparklers, I take my chance to get closer to Faye. I lean down so only she can hear me. "You okay?" The question feels completely empty at this point, but I don't know what else to say.

She nods but doesn't smile at all. Not even a fake one. "Yep, I'm good."

"You going to spell out your name?" I ask. I don't like when people are mad at me, or I can't get them to give me some kind of reaction. No reaction from her feels like I'm losing at a game I forgot I was playing. I think I'd almost prefer if she was behaving like Andrew is right now.

By which I mean, I watched him disappear into the house when everyone was lining up and haven't seen him since.

"That might be too advanced for me. Maybe I'll do a heart." She pauses and shakes her head. "Or a star."

She and I have come to a fork in the road, and we have to decide what path to take. I want to follow the one that might have some difficult spots, but it leads to the cliff we can look out at the world from. She's still standing at the trailhead, unwilling to share the journey with me.

"Count of three!" Evie shouts.

I light my sparkler first and turn to light Faye's with mine. How long can I wait for her to decide I'm worth the risk? How do I prove to her that I *am* worth it? That's she's worth it.

On the third count, I spell out her name in huge swooping letters.

———

MOST OF THE guests leave in a flurry of hugs and goodbyes until it's just Faye, Evie, and I left standing in the yard. We walk together toward the house and sit down in the pool chairs.

Emmett comes out of the house with a sleeping Flo tossed over his shoulder. "We're heading out. This one crashed shortly after Aunt Linda's famous chocolate cake." He gives my shoulder a squeeze as they walk past us. "Good speech."

I swallow a lump in my throat. "Thanks, man. Drive safe."

We sit quietly, all of us seemingly lost in our own thoughts.

Evie breaks the silence. "What's wrong with him?" she asks, gesturing to the kitchen window where we can see Andrew moving around the kitchen.

"He's stress cleaning," Faye and I say at the same time.

I look at Faye. She looks anywhere but at me.

Evie looks at Andrew for a few more seconds, calculating. "I think a night swim is in order."

"I don't know, Eves," I say. I'm exhausted myself. "Maybe another time."

"Yeah, I'm kind of tired too," Faye says. She gives Evie an apologetic smile. "Sorry."

Evie releases a sigh before hopping up from her chair. "Well, I'm going to put my suit on because the summer is almost over and I'm getting another swim in." She walks inside and pauses to say something to Andrew, probably asking if he wants to swim with her. He shakes his head and watches her bound up the stairs.

It's true, the summer is almost over. It always seems to end both too soon, and not soon enough.

I look over at Faye and her eyes are closed. I reach over and graze the back of my index finger against her arm and keep my voice low and soft. "Faye, baby, you ready to go?"

She peeks her eyes open and for a moment we just look at each other. We're finally alone and I can't read her at all.

Not sure if she just heard that "baby" endearment slip out. I'm doing that a lot tonight, saying things to her I've been wanting to say for a while, but managing to choose the worst time to do it. She sits up and nods. "Let me go use the restroom and grab my purse."

We head inside and Andrew looks up at our entrance.

"Sadly, looks like the party is over," I say. I feel myself trying to be casual and it sounds so stupid to my own ears. Like the three of us aren't all very aware that this party is beyond over.

Faye smiles carefully at Andrew. "It was good to see you," she says.

He smiles carefully back at her. I want to scream this is so awkward. "Good to see you, too."

"I'll be right back," she says before heading down the hallway.

"I drove us here," I explain. "I'll just run her home and come back." I grab a glass from the cabinet. I feel like my fight or flight has been engaged, I'm so nervous. This is my best friend, and I'm terrified to be in the same room with him. "You want some water?"

"Sure."

I take another glass down and fill them both up, biding my time before I take a seat on a stool across from him.

He takes a sip of his water. "So, what's up with you and Faye?"

I pause, glass halfway up to my mouth. "What do you mean?"

"You guys are different around each other. More familiar. It's almost like you're . . . together or something." He shakes his head as if it's so hard to believe, it can't possibly be true.

This need to tell him the truth is going to claw its way

out of me. I'm scrambling, thinking of the best way to broach this subject, knowing Faye will hate me if I tell him about us. Knowing that I can't keep this a secret from my best friend anymore. "We're not . . . together exactly."

"What do you mean by *exactly*?"

"It's . . . I don't know"

"Are you sleeping with her?"

I don't say anything which I guess is answer enough for him.

He bounds off his seat and the stool screeches across the floor. "What the fuck?"

"It's not what you think," I say.

"I think you're sleeping with my ex-girlfriend behind my back."

"I'm not just sleeping with her. I . . . care about her." I stand up, pacing now. "It's complicated."

"Yeah, I guess it is. What are you thinking? What is *she* thinking? How long has this been going on?"

"I feel awful keeping it from you and I'm sorry." I take a steadying breath. "I'm sorry it's hurting you to hear about it, but I'm not sorry it happened."

"Was that your plan all along? You fucked up so bad in New York you decided to come home and take my life? Live in my apartment—check. Date my girlfriend—check."

That hits me right in the chest, because what he's saying isn't exactly *not* true. "Come on, you know that's not what I did."

He slides his glass around on the countertop. Back and forth, back and forth. "I knew you always wanted her. I could see it back in school, the way you talked to her and looked at her."

I had a crush on her, sure, but at the time it felt more like curiosity. I wondered about her like you do when someone is interesting in a way you can't put your finger on. Maybe he saw my own feelings before I did, but that doesn't mean I was waiting in the wings to swoop in and steal her while he was away.

"Andrew, please." This is going so off the rails, I don't know what to say to make him understand. "It wasn't something I planned."

"Are you in love with her?" he asks incredulously.

I don't answer immediately, knowing how crazy it probably appears to him.

"Oh my god," he says. "You are."

"I didn't mean to be." I try to gather my thoughts. "It started with me helping her with some things. Job stuff, around her apartment . . . and it just became more."

"I can't believe this." He laughs, but not a funny way. He laughs in way that is almost terrifying, like when someone reaches a breaking point and they are on the verge of full hysteria. "You can't be with her," he says, and now it sounds like he's almost sorry for me, which makes me feel even worse. "She's going to find out you're not serious about her and then she'll be alone again. She won't have you. She won't have me."

And then I feel another emotion wash over me so quickly, I feel like I've been doused with hot water. I'm suddenly angry, too, at the unfairness of our situation. He and Faye are not together anymore. Faye and I can be together if we all just work through this. I need us to work through this.

"And were you serious about her?" I ask.

He's taken aback by my question. "I asked her to marry me. Of course I was serious about her."

My stomach drops. So, he did finally ask her to marry him, then. "Why did you wait so fucking long to ask her?

You bought that ring before graduation." I remember him showing it to me and asking me what I thought about it. I didn't know much about rings, but I knew that they seemed happy together. It was the moment I came to the realization that I needed to leave, and start my own life.

He looks at me, bewildered, and sits back down on his stool. "I don't know . . . I wanted to be sure."

"Sure about what?"

"About her. You know how she is."

"I know she's amazing and it didn't take me six years to figure that out. It took me six seconds. I'm glad I wasn't here to watch you drag your feet with her."

I regret the words as soon as they're out of my mouth when he crumples over and buries his head in his hands. "I wasn't dragging my feet. I wanted to—I was trying to be who she wanted. I *loved* her. I don't want to see her get hurt." His voice breaks a little, and I feel like a monster. "I don't want to see *you* get hurt."

I'm tired—so tired. I deflate onto a stool. "I won't hurt her. I am serious about her."

"And how does she feel about you?"

I can't answer his question. Because that's the same question I've been asking myself, too.

He looks at me for a few seconds before shaking his head. "I hope she'll let you love her." He gets up and places his empty glass in the sink.

When he leaves, he doesn't storm out in an angry rush, but walks stoically over to the door, closing it with a soft click behind him.

39

———

FAYE

I DIDN'T MEAN to eavesdrop.

When I came out of the bathroom and got closer to the kitchen, I could tell that Eli and Andrew's conversation was heated. I've never heard either of them speak to each other that way. I've never heard either of them speak to *anyone* that way.

Eavesdropping on a conversation where you're the main issue of discussion is not something I ever wanted to experience again. It makes me feel like I'm six years old, hearing my mom and grandpa talking about me. My mom had met someone and wanted to move to another state to be with him.

"What about Faye?" my grandpa had asked. They were sitting at his dining room table, and I had been outside playing with my new jump rope. They didn't hear me come in the door.

She tapped her cigarette against the side of the amber glass ashtray. "Can't she just stay with you?"

He looked at her in his exasperated, yet stern kind of way. "She needs her mother, Marsha."

"She doesn't need me when she has you." She reached over and placed a hand on his forearm. "I had you, and everything was fine."

My grandpa just shook his head and sighed with the deep kind of fatigue that he always seemed to have. "If that's what you want," he said, defeated.

Overhearing loved ones discussing your future is hard when you're a kid. It's even harder when you're an adult and they're hashing out all the ways you've managed to fail them.

I could see it back in school, the way you talked to her and looked at her.

You bought that ring before graduation.

. . . it didn't take me six years to figure that out. It took me six seconds.

Worst case scenario? I'd say we're there. All my fears about what would happen if Eli and I got involved are coming true. I'm sick with guilt.

Eli doesn't know I'm standing there, but I watch him for a few seconds before I make my presence known. He puts his palms on top of the kitchen counter and hangs his head down. I want so badly to comfort him and tell him everything will be okay.

I mentally count to three before I step into the kitchen. I try to make my voice neutral, as if I didn't just hear him and my ex-boyfriend talking about how difficult I am to love. "Hey."

He pops his head up, almost like he forgot I was in the house. He straightens up and takes an empty glass over to the sink. "You ready to go?"

———

WE DRIVE IN SILENCE, which is fine by me.

My mind is a hamster wheel, spinning round and round with questions and memories. How do we move forward from this? How do we make everything feel normal again?

I look over at Eli's side profile. His face is serious and his hands are tight on the wheel. He looks as tired as I feel, and as sad. I want to place a comforting hand on his thigh, and I want him to place his hand over mine and give it a reassuring squeeze.

He turns and catches me looking at him.

"Sorry," I say, embarrassed about being caught staring.

"I like when you look at me." Gone is the playful glimmer I'm used to seeing in his eyes. It's been replaced by a solemn survey of my face that seems to ask, *But do you see me too?*

I believed him when he said that he's serious about me, even if Andrew didn't, and I don't know what I should do with that declaration.

I turn away to look out the window and watch the streetlights pass. "Did you know you called me 'baby' back there?"

I don't know why this is what I choose to bring up right now, but it's where my exhausted brain decides to go.

He heaves a sigh. "It slipped out."

"I liked it," I admit, taking my hair down and leaning back against the headrest. Might as well make this worse. Might as well pick the scab, right?

"You did?" He sounds almost hopeful.

"But I don't think you should call me that."

"Why not?"

"Because I can't be your baby."

"Why not?" he repeats.

And how does she feel about you?

He deserves someone who can be with him fully. To stand out in the light with him, experiencing nothing but the joy of getting to be with him. Someone who doesn't hesitate to tell him how she feels.

"Because you're like this fun, frolicking dolphin, bouncing on the waves."

He sniffs. "A dolphin, huh? And what does that make you?"

"A moody old eel, living deep in an ocean trench."

He hums. "Maybe I can evolve and become one of those fish with the weird light things hanging over their heads. Then, I can come see you."

"You're ridiculous."

"You're the one who said I was a dolphin."

We're quiet again and I hear the distant rumbling of thunder, a summer storm getting ready to blow through. I keep waiting for him to tell me what he's thinking. I keep waiting to have the courage to tell him anything myself. But I know I won't.

This drive has felt like a slow, silent goodbye.

Eli pulls in front of my apartment building. He doesn't move to open his door and instead turns toward me. "Okay if I just drop you off?"

"Yeah, that's okay."

I get out and we don't say goodbye to each other. He stays parked on the street until he sees me make it to my door.

40

FAYE

I GET the email at eight o'clock on Monday morning.

We appreciate your interest . . . Have decided to go in another direction . . . Wish you luck . . .

I didn't get the job.

I sit with this news for a second, and honestly, after how that interview went, despite Eli's certainty that I would get it, I'm not surprised. It doesn't make the disappointment any easier, though. I wonder if this was the news Eli was hesitant to tell me. That would make sense. That would also make things much easier—if me not getting the job was our biggest hurdle to overcome.

I'm half tempted to conjure up a fake sickness just to avoid the weekly Monday morning meeting. It wouldn't even really be that fake, that's how terrible I feel. I didn't sleep at all last night, tossing and turning, wondering if Eli was okay. We haven't talked or texted since Saturday night.

He's become the bright spot I looked forward to on my Monday mornings, and I dread going into this meeting with the weight of the weekend on my shoulders.

I'm tempted to head for the elevator and go straight

home to bed, but I find my feet following the familiar geometric-patterned carpet into the large conference room. For the first time in five years, I'm one of the last people to arrive. I take a seat in the back corner.

My eyes are immediately drawn to Eli, the back of his head visible over the others. He's sitting toward the front, and I watch him quietly say something to the person sitting next to him, giving me a view of the side of his face. He's smiling and looking like his usual carefree self. Is this just a façade he's wearing today? Is he hurting as much as I'm hurting? A sick part of me hopes so, because when I look at him, all I feel is hunger—deep, like I haven't eaten all day and my stomach is eating itself.

The meeting starts with its usual mundanity, updates from sales, updates from product, but I don't even listen. All I can do is watch Eli, searching for any signs that he's not okay. I analyze every minuscule movement he makes. He scratches his chin. He sits up in his seat. He laughs at a dumb joke the CFO makes because he can't stand for anyone to feel uncomfortable. I think what I'm actually doing is collecting these images so I can file them away as something I can pull out on a rainy day, like an old photo album.

Don't forget him. Don't forget how great he is.

As soon as the meeting ends, I head straight for the exit, needing to be alone. I get back to the illusion of privacy within my cubicle and my phone lights up with a text.

Eli: **Can we talk?**

———

THE DUCK POND IS EERILY quiet today.

The sun's tucked itself in behind the clouds, casting the

whole scene in a gray haze. I'm standing just behind a clump of tall grass that grows along the water's edge. It's itchy against my ankles and feet, but I don't move.

I hear Eli coming down the path, grass whispering against his legs. His footsteps stop just before reaching me.

I turn around. "Hi."

He puts his hands in his pockets. "Hi."

As he continues walking toward me, I feel an ache start to bloom in my chest. The conversation we're about to have is not going to be fun at all.

"I got an email about the job this morning."

His eyes go wide before he looks down at his feet, shaking his head. "Shit, I asked them to let me tell you. Every time I tried to bring it up, I just—I'm so sorry."

I turn back to look out over the water. "Was it because I didn't send them a thank you email?" I joke, and it's hollow.

He moves to stand next to me, and he doesn't reach for my hand, but I can feel the phantom press of his palm against mine. "We'll find you something else. Something better."

Still, he wants to help me. Still, he's so sure that something better could exist.

I watch his eyes scan the pond. "I was hoping our swans would be here," he says.

The way he says "our swans" brings to mind the other things that we've shared, too. Our laughter. Our kisses. Our hearts.

Our mistakes.

"I heard you and Andrew fighting," I confess.

In my periphery, I see him jerk his head in my direction. "I wouldn't say we were fighting . . ."

I press my sandals down on the grass, smashing the

blades out as flat as I can. "I think we should cool things off."

He turns so he's facing me. "Don't do this," he says, a pleading desperation in his voice.

I can't look at him. I'm a fucking coward and I can't look at him. "Do what?"

"Run away from me."

"I'm not running away," I lie. "This was always going to end at some point, right?"

"It doesn't have to. What are you afraid of?"

I'm afraid of letting myself admit that I might be falling in love with him. Or worse, that I'll accept his love the way I accepted Andrew's, and I'll end up using it as a safety net so I don't have to face my own insecurities. I'm afraid of being like my mom.

Mostly, I'm afraid of losing him.

"Are you still in love with Andrew?"

Is that what he thinks? That I've been buying time with him while I wait to get Andrew back?

"No. I . . ." I trail off, unsure of how to even finish the sentence.

"You what?" He sounds exasperated. "Please tell me what's going on in your head."

So many years spent keeping my own feelings so close to my chest, it's not easy for me to express them. But I feel his frustration and I understand it. I'm frustrated, too, with myself.

"Sorry we can't all wear our emotions like a giant marquee across our face. No wonder Andrew found out."

"I'm sorry that I don't want to put caution tape around my feelings for you anymore."

"I need to get back to my desk," I say, turning to walk away.

He steps forward to block my path. "Are you worried Andrew will hate you if we're together?"

"No."

"Then what is it?"

"I'm worried he'll hate *you*. He's like a brother to you, Eli. And hearing the way you were talking to each other. I felt sick about it."

"I can work this out with Andrew. And Andrew cares about you. He wants you to be happy." He places his hand over his heart, tapping it against his chest. "Tell me *I* don't make you happy."

"What if I can't make you happy? Because I can't be what *you* want, Eli. I think you have this fantasy in your head that we'll be like your parents. Your friendship means so much to me. It can't be more. I can't do more than that."

"I don't believe you."

He doesn't believe me, or he *can't* believe me?

"Where do you see yourself in the future? Are you married with kids? Do you take your dog for walks around the cute neighborhood you live in?" I take a shaky breath. "Do you have the love that your parents have that you talked about in your speech?"

He doesn't say anything, just looks off into the distance.

"Because I don't see that in my future. Your speech was so lovely. *You* are so lovely." My voice breaks. "And you deserve someone who can appreciate you without any reservations."

"We can't control the future, Faye." He takes my forearms in is hands. "I'm just asking you to try. With me. I don't want anything more than I want you."

That feels like a kick to the stomach. "You say that now, but you'll meet someone else who wants those things. I can't keep you from finding that. So, we have to go back to what we were before. Friends." The sting of tears is like daggers behind my eyes, but I don't let myself cry yet. "I don't want to hurt you."

He looks at me, pleading now. "Being just friends with you would hurt me. I'm falling in lo—"

"Please don't," I interrupt him. If I hear him say those words I will break. "Please."

"But I am. I can't help it." He steps forward, until he's so close me that I have to lift my chin to look at him. "I'm falling in love with you, Faye. Please let me."

"I can't." A tear escapes in a slow procession down my cheek. He wipes it away with his thumb.

"Can I tell you why?"

Why does he have to be so wonderful? Why do I have to be so broken?

"Every day I wake up and I can't wait to see you. To hear about your day and tell you about mine. Make you laugh. Talk about nothing. Talk about everything. I thought I was just curious about you, and I'd satisfy the curiosity and move on. But that curiosity will never go away, because it shouldn't. I want to spend every second I have figuring you out because I love being able to know you. You may not be easy to know, Faye, but you're easy to love.

"I'll spend the rest of my life convincing you to be with me. And if you won't have me, then I'll spend the rest of my life missing you." His voice trembles, like he's holding back tears, too. "Because I'd rather miss you forever than pretend I'm just your friend."

I wrap my arms around his waist and bury my face in his chest. This debilitating fear has turned me into the worst version of myself. Because it'd be so simple to just tell him the truth.

That I'm falling in love with him, too.

But telling him would only make things harder, and I don't trust myself to love him the way he really needs. It's easier in the end to let him go now, so he can move on. He doesn't need me the way the thinks he does.

He kisses the top of my head, holding his lips there, gaining strength and giving me comfort.

I hope she'll let you love her.

He lifts his head and removes my arms from his waist. "I hope someday you'll let me," he says before walking back up the path.

41

——

ELI

I FEEL stripped down to my bones.

Walking back to the office, I'm like a zombie, running on nothing but pure instinct to follow the same paths and hallways that have become familiar to me.

But everything is wrong. I no longer see possibility in this place. I see it for what it really is to me now. A place I fell in love. A place I felt like a failure. A place I can't make myself work or think the way I'm supposed to.

So where does that leave me?

I didn't look back as I walked up the path, but I wanted to. Half hoping Faye would come sprinting through the grass to make her very own confession, that she's in love with me, too.

But who would do that after being backed into a corner the way I just did to her?

I keep my focus on making my feet move, one step at a time, and head straight for Melissa's office. While I'm baring it all, I might as well continue this honesty kick. Let's keep this party going. What do I have to lose at this point?

I peek my head in and tap lightly on her door. "Knock, knock."

She looks up but doesn't stop typing as she says, "Eli. What can I do for you?"

I stall for a second to decide how to approach this conversation. "How do you do that? Keep typing while talking?"

She shrugs. "Lots of practice, I guess."

"Impressive." I step further into her office. "Do you have a minute?"

She rolls her chair around to face me and gestures to the chairs in front of her desk. "Sure, have a seat."

I sit down. "I just talked to Faye." My voice cracks on her name, and I clear my throat. "I didn't know an email was going to her this morning, and I didn't have a chance to speak with her before it went out."

"Sorry about that, there must have been a miscommunication there."

I fidget in my seat, steeling myself for what I want to say.

"Is there something else?" she asks impatiently.

"Yes, sorry. I've just been thinking. It's just . . . well . . . I hate this job."

Not exactly the most elegant way of putting it, but my chest unclenches a little after saying it, so I'm taking that tiny bit of relief while I can get it.

Her brow furrows. "You . . . hate it?"

"I really hate it."

"I'm sorry to hear that. What's going on?"

"I just don't think this is the company for me. Or the role for me, honestly."

"I wish you had come to me sooner. Is there anything I can do to help? We really can't afford to lose anyone right now."

It's not lost on me that she says "anyone" and not "we can't afford to lose *you* right now."

I stand up. "Can you give me just a second?"

She's so clearly bewildered by this conversation and my behavior, and I can't blame her. But I need to check one thing before I do what I'm pretty sure I'm about to do.

"Okay . . ."

I step into the hallway outside of her office and walk over to the wall of windows that overlooks the courtyard. I dial Chris' number.

"Hey Eli, what's up?"

I hear dogs barking in the background. "Hey, sorry to call you while you're working, but I had a question."

"No worries, I've gotten pretty good at pretending I have an extra limb or two."

"I'm sort of hoping I could help with that. Any chance you're hiring?"

He lets out a surprised laugh. "Actually, yeah, I could use some help."

"Any chance you want to hire me?"

"Yeah, let's talk details at our game tomorrow."

"Sounds good. See you then."

I hang up and go back into Melissa's office. "I think I'd like to quit." I wait to feel regret after saying those words. But I feel relieved.

"Let's not jump to quitting just yet. What about some additional training? Or a mentorship?"

"I'm sorry, I just don't think I can make it work here."

She heaves a sigh. "That's unfortunate, Eli. I was really looking forward to seeing how you'd grow in the company."

The corporate bullshit never ends. They don't care at all. She didn't once ask what's made me so eager to quit, she's so focused on how this affects her. I don't fully put the blame on her. She's another cog in the wheel, too. But I'm tired of feeling like I'm struggling up a never-ending hill.

Also, pretty sure my job is going to be taken over by some AI bot named Janet soon enough, anyway.

I nod. "Thank you, but I think I'd like to find another path."

———

AFTER DROPPING my work badge off with Tom, I drive around aimlessly until I find myself parked in front of the very old house Emmett just bought.

I think it's Victorian—white, with frilly trim around the porch. It looks a little haunted, honestly.

His truck is in the driveway, so I know he's inside. When I get out of my truck, I hear a saw running. I open the front door with an ominous creak and step inside. This is the first time I've seen the house, and I thought everyone was joking when they said he'd purchased what amounted to a pile of moldy planks.

But I know Emmett, and he can see the potential in it. That's all that matters.

I move toward the sound of the table saw and find him in the kitchen. Or, what I think used to be a kitchen. I don't want to startle him while he's using dangerous equipment, so I wait until he stops to yell his name.

He jerks up. "Christ, Eli. What the fuck?"

"Sorry," I grimace.

He looks confused to see me. "What are you doing here?"

I sigh. "I don't know."

"Bad day?"

I nod. "Bad day."

He walks over to the side of the room and reaches down for a sledgehammer. He passes it, along with a pair of safety goggles, to me and nods at the kitchen cabinets. "Have at it."

I love my big brother. No questions asked, he just hands me this giant tool, basically saying, *Try working out your feelings on some old cabinets.* I spend about thirty blissful minutes destroying things before I tire out.

I grab a bottle of water from his cooler and sit down on top of it.

He picks up the sledgehammer and knocks a shelf down. "Do you want to talk about it?" he asks.

"For once in my life, I don't know what to say. Other than I'm officially a fuck up."

He chuckles and gestures around him. "Look who you're talking to. I bought this trash heap to try to prove something."

"To prove what?"

"We all make mistakes." He breaks down the last piece of wood that seemed to be hanging on for dear life. "Doesn't mean you are one."

"Fuck, man. Are *you* okay?"

"I will be. And you will be, too." He places a two-by-four onto the table saw. He hasn't stopped working once since I got here. "Everything can be fixed."

Is he telling himself that, or me? "It just feels impossible. Like, every time I try to do something right, it doesn't go the way it should. I try to be good at my job. I try to be a good friend. A good son. A good brother. A good person."

"What makes you think you aren't those things? You help all of us out so much. Especially with all the shit going on with me right now, and you stepping in to help watch Flo sometimes. She adores you."

I shrug. I've never thought about any of those things as having any meaning, other than I love my family and friends, and would do anything for them.

"You just need to find what works for you. There's nothing wrong with you. We all have to find ways to navigate life's bullshit." He takes off his safety glasses and massages the bridge of his nose. "Sometimes things have to break so you can build them back up again."

I go over and give him a hug. We both linger in it longer than we ever have, like we both needed one.

"You got anything else that needs breaking?"

42

———

ELI

IT TAKES me two weeks of mild to moderate pestering, but I finally convince Andrew to meet up to talk.

Just like the first night I met him, we're standing at the bottom of the ladder that leads to the roof of the elementary school.

"It seemed taller before, didn't it?" he asks.

"Yeah, it did." I place a foot on the first rung of the ladder, which has gotten much rustier than before, too. "Come on, let's see if anything else has changed."

"What if they have cameras now? If I get arrested because of you, that'll be the final nail in the coffin, just so you know."

"We won't get arrested." I don't think we will, anyway. It's a Sunday night at nine in the evening, and I don't know what I was thinking come up here. It just seemed like a cool, full-circle thing. "We'll just be quiet."

We climb to the top and I shine the flashlight of my phone over the area. I see a pile of candy and Doritos wrappers. Guess we aren't the only ones who hang out on roofs.

I look around a little more, not because I'm super interested in what I might see up here, but because I suddenly don't know what to say. He's waiting for me, I'm sure. I know I need to fix this rift between us somehow. How do I apologize for the thing that I could really use his advice on right now?

I know I was sleeping with your ex and I'm super sorry about not telling you, but also can you help me figure out what to do?

"Everything sucks and I fucked up," I finally get up the nerve to say.

"You're going to have to be more specific." He kicks around an empty Mountain Dew can. "You mean the whole losing your job thing, or sneaking around with my ex-girl-friend thing?"

I knew he wouldn't make it easy. Not that I deserve for it to be easy. "Both. But I didn't really lose my job. Techni-cally, I quit."

"So, what are you going to do?"

I take it he's talking about the job, which is the least contentious thing to talk about first. "You're looking at the newest employee of Clean Fur Smell."

"Do I even want to know?"

"I'm in the dog grooming business now."

He almost huffs out a laugh. "Is this a permanent career change?"

At my softball game the other night, I talked more to Chris about how I lost my job. *Lost* is such a funny way to describe becoming unemployed. Like, you just misplaced it somewhere and need to retrace your steps in order to find it again.

We decided I'd start working next week. I figured, if he needs the help, why not spend time bathing puppies while I figure out my next move.

"No, just for the time being while I decide what I want to do with my life." Because I will figure out something that works for me.

He takes a seat on the building's ledge. "That's good."

It's go time, Eli. Let's really make this apology count.

I look down and kick my feet around. "I'm sorry," I say. It's simple, but it's the truth. He'd appreciate some brute honesty from me. "I really didn't mean for anything to shake out the way it did."

He crosses his arms. "I overreacted the other night."

"No, you didn't. You had a very normal reaction." Maybe an overreaction for the way he usually tempers his emotions, but he responded exactly the way I would expect someone in his shoes would have.

"It's just hard." He sighs and it's weighted. "When things don't go the way you think they'll go."

I sit down next to him. "Yeah, that's for sure."

"Are you two . . . together now?"

"That's another part of my fuck up."

"How so?"

"We don't have to talk about that. If it's weird."

"It's absolutely weird, but I've been thinking about it, and I could see how you two would be good together."

I feel a shred of hope, like this is his way of saying he would be okay with Faye and I being together. It's a hope I'm terrified to have, because having his blessing means nothing if Faye herself doesn't want to be with me.

"Too bad I scared her away."

"What do you mean?"

"She overheard you and I talking about her after the party."

Andrew grimaces. "Oh no."

"And then I told her I was falling in love with her."

"That was quite the speech you gave, looking deep into her eyes the whole time." He scratches the back of his neck. "Let me guess. That didn't go over well?"

"I basically called her a liar and told her that I couldn't be her friend anymore." I can't stand even thinking of that day and how shattered her face looked when I said this to her. "I think I just got scared of losing her and overcompensated by just . . . telling her every feeling I have."

"Faye likes time to process. Hope might not be lost yet. She looks at you—" he picks at his cuticles. "In a way she never looked at me."

My chest tightens. If he saw this too, that means I wasn't imagining it, the softening of her gaze when she looks at me.

"I really am sorry."

"I know. And by the looks of you right now, I think you've suffered enough as punishment."

I look down at myself, at the ketchup-stained shirt I haven't changed in days. I need to shave. I haven't had a good night's sleep in weeks. "I look like shit, huh?"

"Take a shower. Eat a good meal. Go for a run. It'll be okay."

I chuckle at his pragmatic approach to solving heartbreak. Looking up at the clear night sky, I feel emotional, and grateful for the people in my life. "Hey, I never got a chance to ask, why did you come back early?"

"Let's just say Amsterdam wasn't for me."

"You mean the city or the girl?"

"Both, I guess."

I think about the selfie Faye showed me, of Andrew and Emma smiling at the camera. "You seemed to be having fun. What went wrong?"

He doesn't answer right away, and I give him time.

"Can I tell you something and you swear to God you won't laugh?"

"Um . . . sure?"

He exhales heavily. "I think I'm bad at sex."

I can't help it, but I do bark out a laugh because it's such an unexpected thing for him to say.

He gives me a look like, *You said you wouldn't laugh.*

I try to ignore the specter of Faye in the corner of this conversation, considering what she told me about her lack of—

Yeah, not going to go there. "Why do you think that?"

"Because Emma told me."

"Wow."

He lays his head back. "Yeah."

"What did she say exactly? Maybe this is just some kind of misunderstanding."

"We had just . . . you know . . ."

"Had sex?"

"Yeah. And before I even had a chance to put my boxers back on, she's telling me that we got that out of our systems, and she doesn't think we're compatible."

"Okay, but not compatible doesn't mean you're bad at sex."

He shakes his head. "There's more. I asked her what she meant by that since we have so much in common. And she said, 'Andrew, you fuck me like you're rushing through your to-do list.'"

"Oh no, you're kidding."

"I wish I was."

"That's brutal, but don't read too much into it. And hey, some people might be into that. A man who knows how to get things done with efficiency."

He snorts. "It's hard not to read into it, though." That

would be a blow to the best of us, but someone like Andrew who hates being bad at something was probably on the way back from the Netherlands, reading *She Comes First* on the plane.

"Look on the bright side. You won't have to have a long-distance relationship."

He scoffs. "I think I might put a pause on any kind of relationship for a bit." He stands up and brushes off the back of his pants and ending the conversation. "I really do hope things work out with you and Faye."

43

FAYE

I NEED to get out of this apartment.

I've holed myself up inside, using up two weeks of my well-earned PTO hours. Instead of the usual comfort I feel at being in the safety of my own space, I feel like I need to claw my way out of my enclosure.

I'm aimlessly scrolling on my phone and see a post from a local movie theater that they're showing a screening of *Death Becomes Her* for a Meryl Streep Appreciation Week.

Before I can talk myself out of it, I splash some cold water on my face and slide on my scuffed-up pair of Birkenstocks. I don't bother changing out of my sweatpants and baggy T-shirt, because there's no way I'll get out of this apartment if I have to wear real pants.

As I drive to the theater, I have a torturous, but hopeful thought. Maybe tonight the fates will intervene with my current heartbreak problem. If Eli and I are meant to be together then he'll be at this movie tonight, too. He'll be walking down the street and stop at the theater to see the movie's name written on the marquee, and he'll think, *Faye probably likes this movie. I should go see it.* Then, I'll walk up the sidewalk and see him standing there, waiting in line to buy his ticket. Like the final scene of a film, he'll turn and see me coming and we'll both break out into a run as we sprint to meet each other.

But life isn't a movie and when I arrive at the theater, there are a few people standing outside, but none of them are Eli.

I buy my ticket, a large Diet Coke, and a pack of Skittles before heading inside to find a seat. It's more crowded than I anticipated, but I'm able to grab a spot in the back row. The movie starts, and I welcome the couple of hours of distraction it provides. I should look on the bright side— maybe I ruined the one chance I'd ever have to be happy with someone, but at least I didn't drink an elixir that promises eternal youth, only to find that it will eventually make my body melt away like a wax figure in the noonday sun.

The movie ends and I fall in line with the crowd as we head out.

"Everyone gets what they deserve in the end, huh?" It's the woman standing behind me and as I turn around, I'm shocked at who it is.

"Alexis?"

I barely recognize her in the dark theater, but she looks like she's been through it. Smudged mascara, hair that hasn't been brushed in a few days, and an unmistakable bad aura surrounding her. She's probably thinking the same thing about me right now.

She gestures for me to keep walking because I had stopped in the middle of the aisle. "Do you want to get a beer?" she asks.

"Um, sure?"

We walk to a bar next door, and it's swarming with

college students since it's a Thursday night. There is a group of girls in front of us getting their IDs checked by the bouncer. They're bouncy and giggly, excited for what the night might bring.

We get to the front and I start to dig in my purse for my ID.

"Don't worry about it," the bouncer says. "You ladies go ahead in."

Alexis looks at me and shrugs before stepping inside.

"Should we go somewhere else?" I yell over the sound of cheers for the girl currently flopping around like a ragdoll on the mechanical bull in the back corner.

"Nah, come on."

We take a couple of seats at the bar, and she orders us the Thirsty Thursday special, a shot of fireball and a lukewarm Coors Light.

"You look as bad as I feel," she says.

I throw the shot back. "I was thinking the same thing about you." I never speak to her with this level of candor, but how else should you talk to the boss you're about to get drunk with?

"What's this mystery illness that's been keeping you out of work for the last two weeks?" She doesn't ask this in her usual cool tone, but I almost detect a hint of worry in her question.

"Oh, the worst kind," I say, tapping my palm against my heart. "I think I'm lovesick."

"Yeah, me too," she says, clinking her beer can against mine.

"I think I might be unable to accept love."

She nods. "I think I might be getting a divorce."

"Alexis, I'm so sorry."

She brushes that off and shakes her head. "I'll be fine. I'm just really going to miss him."

"You don't think you and Brian could work it out?"

"Brian? No, I'm going to miss Conrad."

She's lost me on this one, and I think I've misheard her over the screaming girls. "Conrad? The massage guy?"

"I'm leaving Brian." She sighs wistfully. "But Conrad doesn't believe in monogamy. Which is sad, because the man had a way with his hands."

I look down into my can of beer. "Yeah, he seemed . . . talented."

She cackles and I jump in my seat. "Will you be back to work on Monday?"

I wasn't expecting that change of subject, but welcome it wholeheartedly over any more talk of her failed marriage or Conrad's magical hands. "Sorry, have things been chaotic without me? I'll be sure to catch up on everythin—"

She stops me with a hand over my forearm. "I'm going to let you in on a little secret."

I don't know if I can take any more of this woman's secrets. I take a sip of my drink.

"It's all fake, you know," she says.

"What is?"

She sits up and fixes her hair, bringing the Alexis I know back into focus. It's almost eerie how quickly she can go from the woman I've been talking to tonight to the woman I've been borderline fearful of for the last five years.

"So why do you do it?" I ask.

"Because I thought I had to. But none of it matters. They're all a bunch of fucking leeches."

I don't disagree. "Is your advice that I need to fake it, too?"

"Hell no. I'm telling you to get out while you still can."

I laugh. "I applied to another job in the company," I confess.

"I know you did. And I'm sorry they didn't offer it to you."

"You are? Why?"

"Because I've been selfishly hoping that you'd never stop working for me. Which is exactly why you should stop working for me."

"That job wasn't right for me, anyway. I knew it but had a hard time admitting it."

She stands up. "How about this? On Monday, we'll talk. About career stuff." She sways and grabs the back of her stool to balance. "I'm calling an Uber." She slaps a hundred dollar bill on the bar, and with a wave she's gone before I even register that our conversation ended.

I sit at the bar for a few minutes, reeling over tonight's events and revelations. Turns out Alexis is a real person who makes mistakes, too. She's still kind of aloof and odd, but she seems eager to help me, in her own way.

Maybe the fates intervened tonight after all.

44

FAYE

THE NEXT MORNING, I'm up bright and early, painting my living room.

I decided on a sage-green color. Or at least it looked sage green in the store. I run the roller over the wall and it's coming across a little more . . . neon than I wanted.

Too late to turn back now.

This is my latest attempt at busying myself so I don't have to think about anything else, only home projects. If I come up with enough tasks to complete, I won't have to face any of my problems. Very healthy.

A knock at the door interrupts me. I look through the peephole and rip the door open so fast I almost remove the years of paint that have been painted over the hinges.

Rett is here, and I know things will be okay.

Her eyes land on the scene behind me. Sheets and blankets acting as drop cloths tossed over everything. The chair I've been using as a ladder, laying sideways on the ground. Takeout containers littering the floor.

Then she looks at me, and her eyes go wide at the sight

of what might be the world's worst case of breakup bangs to ever be seen.

"Oh no," she says, pulling me into the second hug she's ever given me. The first was right after I gave the engagement ring back to Andrew. Two Rett hugs in a single year. I must really look awful.

"Are they that bad?" I ask, reaching up to press them down on my forehead.

The concern on her face turns to determination as she guides me toward the bathroom. "Come on."

I sit on top of the toilet while she attempts to fix the mess I've made of my hair. I'm so grateful for Rett in this moment—for her steadfast friendship and unwavering support. I feel tears start to well up in my eyes, thinking of what it's going to take to fix the mess I've made of my whole life.

"Don't cry. They're really not that bad." She steps back to view her progress. "You have the perfect facial structure to pull off a short bang."

I sniffle. "I just don't know what I would do without you."

She starts snipping again. "Good thing you won't ever have to find that out. Now, what do you think?" She places her arms on my shoulders and leads me to stand in front of the mirror. They're a little short for my liking, but they definitely look better. Plus, it's just hair. It will grow. "Thank you so much," I say, tears starting up again.

"Have you talked to Eli?" she asks our reflections.

Just hearing his name hurts, like shards of glass piercing through all of my vital organs. I've picked up my phone to call him every single night since the party, but haven't been able to follow through. Something else has been nagging me too, as I've replayed that fight I overheard between Eli and Andrew.

I wasn't dragging my feet...

I was trying to be who she wanted ... I loved her.

"I think I need to talk to Andrew first." If I had resolved things with Andrew and really told him all my fears and feelings, so much of this would have never happened. Talking to him feels like the first step in getting the closure we never had. Then, I can move forward with making things right with Eli.

She looks at me, green eyes approving. "I think you're right."

"Although, who knows if he'd want to see me. You should have seen his face that night. He was ... distraught."

"I think you should try."

I take a deep breath as I pull up our text thread. The last time we texted was about the suitcase. That feels like ages ago—so much has transpired since then.

I type out the text before I have time to second guess or overanalyze it.

Faye: Would you like to go for a walk with me?

We used to go on walks together all the time, at local trails or parks. Plus, if we're outside and moving, maybe it'll give our conversation some room to breathe. "There," I say, putting my phone in my back pocket.

He texts back almost immediately, though.

Andrew: I would like that.

Some of the tightness in my chest loosens. We decide to meet later this afternoon at Dix Park. "He said he'll meet me."

"I'm sure he wants to talk to you, too." Rett steers me out of the bathroom. "Now that your bangs aren't looking like Weird Barbie anymore, let's finish painting your key lime pie living room."

———

"I'M KIND OF surprised you agreed to see me."

My voice cracks on the last few words, and I really don't want to cry in front of him right now. He shouldn't have to be the one to comfort me. I thought I was done crying but seeing him has brought on the waterworks again.

"I'm glad you texted me," he says, silently passing me a tissue without drawing attention to it. He has bad allergies and never goes without a pocket full of Kleenex this time of year. "I wanted to talk to you, too."

"I'm so sorry. For everything," I say.

He puts his hands in his pockets and pays close attention to our steps as we walk. "I'm sorry for anything you might have heard the other night. I was having a rough day."

"Please, you don't have to apologize to me for that. I didn't mean for anything to happen how it did."

He half smiles. "That's almost exactly what Eli said to me."

"So, you've talked to him?"

"Yeah, we're okay now."

"You and Eli are . . . good?"

"Yes," he confirms before concern creases his brow. "Are you . . . good?"

The tears start rolling again before I can stop them. "I hurt him. I didn't want to hurt him."

He places a hand lightly on my back. "Faye, it's okay."

"I ruin everything. I messed up. He was so—" I stop, realizing how inappropriate this is, even in my current emotional state. "I kept you from being happy. I'm keeping myself from being happy."

We stop at bench, and he gestures for me to have a seat. "What do you mean you kept me from being happy?"

"Well, we were together for so long and so wrong for each other."

He looks down the path, gathering his thoughts before he responds. "The reasons we didn't work out aren't your fault. It wasn't anyone's fault."

"But I'm losing everyone now. I'm losing him. I lost you."

"You haven't lost me." He holds his arms out to the side. "I'm right here, aren't I?"

"He told me he loved me." I take a shuddering breath. "He told me he loved me and all I said back was 'I can't.'"

"Do you love him?"

A fresh batch of sobs bubble to the surface. "Yes, I think I do."

"You need to talk to him and tell him how you feel."

"I'm scared."

"This is your chance at happiness. Take it. You deserve to be loved. Don't let fear keep you from experiencing that." I can't help the laugh that comes out after he says this. He shrugs and looks down bashfully. "Or something. Fuck if I know."

"That was very poignant. Have you been reading self-help books?"

He smiles wryly. "Something like that."

"You deserve that, too, you know."

He nods. "Yeah, I know."

We sit in companionable silence for a few minutes, just enjoying the sounds of birds and crickets. It's good just to sit here with him, together, but lost in our own thoughts.

"What if he says he doesn't want me anymore?"

"Trust me, that isn't the case."

"How do you know?"

"I happen to know where he is right now if you want to find that out for sure."

I hug him, and his arms tighten around me, telling me that things may be different now, but we still have each other.

45

ELI

"CHARITY . . . IS THAT A FAMILY NAME?"

The beagle looks up at me with droopy, sad eyes that seem to communicate that she didn't choose her name, she didn't choose to be here, and it'd be great if we could cut the chitchat and get this bath over with.

I slide the brush over her fur. "A dog of few words. I could learn a thing or two from you."

She slumps down with a little grunt.

"I hear you got into a bit of a mess involving a scheming squirrel. That's rough."

Another glare.

Making sure the water is lukewarm, I run the nozzle over her fur. "Keeping an air of mystery. I like it."

I squirt some shampoo into my hands and run it over her fur. "Squirrels can be annoying, huh? They seem to be one of the more conniving creatures of the animal kingdom."

Chris swings open the door that leads to the lobby area, just as I'm lathering up the shampoo. "Who are you talking to?"

"Charity, of course. I like to make small talk with them." Charity looks over at Chris as I give her ears a good massage. "See? She likes it."

Chris just shakes his head. "Someone here to see you," he says, holding open the door.

I peek out to see Faye standing there. I think I'm imagining her, until she gives me an awkward wave. "Hi," she says, stepping inside the room.

"I'll be out here if you need me." He winks at me as the door closes behind him—a subtle nod to the confession that he and Dani made after one of our softball games that everyone at game night, except Cameron, was in cahoots to get Faye and I together.

We just stand there, staring at each other, neither of us saying anything. I drink in the sight of her. Her hair is tousled up on top of her head, and she's wearing a tank top with a pair of old overalls on top of it. Her bangs are messy, like she's gotten them sweaty and brushed them away from her face.

Wait, she has bangs. "I love your hair."

She reaches up, like she forgot they were there. "Thanks. I think I got a little scissor happy," she says.

I notice she has paint splattered on her clothing and in her hair. "Have you been painting again?" I ask.

She looks down at herself. "Oh, yeah. My living room." Charity gets restless and makes a low groan, probably wondering why I stopped scratching her ears. "You're busy. I'm so sorry. I should've called or texted."

"What color?" I ask. *Don't leave.*

"Hmm?"

"What color did you paint it?" *I miss you.*

"Oh." She frowns. "Green."

"Green's a pretty color." *Why are you here?*

She shakes her head. "Rett says it looks like I live inside of a key lime pie now."

"How are you?" *Do you miss me, too?*

She adjusts her ponytail. "I'm good. Are you liking the new job?"

"I am. It's temporary while I find something that fits what I'm looking for, but I can't complain about getting to hang out with dogs all day."

She smiles and walks over to give Charity a head rub. "Good for you. I'm glad you're doing what's best for you."

"How are things at good ol' Millionfish?"

"I've actually been on vacation for the last couple of weeks. I also had a very interesting run-in with Alexis. We're going to talk on Monday about what's best for me, career-wise."

"That's great. I'm glad you took some time off."

She shuffles on her feet.

"I found a place to live," I tell her, hoping that if I keep talking it'll encourage her to say what she came here to say. "It's a little apartment I'm renting above someone's garage, but it's nice for now."

"That's awesome. You seem to be doing well?" she says, her voice straining a little.

I'm taking steps to make my life better in many ways, but none of that matters if Faye isn't in it. Why is she here? I feel hopeful, but I'm scared to hope for anything.

She straightens her shoulders like she's gearing up for what she wants to say next. "The reason I came here is because I'd like to ask you something."

My heart speeds up. "Okay . . ."

"Would you like to go on a date? With me?"

She's so awkward. She's so cute. She's so perfect. "I would love to."

"Friday night?"

I nod. "That works."

She nods. "Okay. Cool. I'll text you later with details."

"Sounds great."

She turns and leaves, the door swinging shut behind her. I stand there baffled for a few seconds before I can register what just happened. Then, I'm so full of excitement, I resist the urge to pick Charity up and swing her around with glee.

46

FAYE

IT'S a perfect evening for a date.

The weather is finally cooling off and the fresh change in season has given the city a burst of energy.

I pull up in front of Eli's apartment and wipe my palms on my dress. I'm nervous, but excited too. In all the times we've hung out together, we've never actually gone on a real date. It's nice to be nervous for a date that you're actually looking forward to.

I go up the stairs and give his door a soft knock. It opens almost immediately, and my heart firmly lodges itself in my throat when I see him standing there.

He's styled his hair in a different way, his usual waves pushed back from his face. His facial hair is trimmed, and he looks so good I swoon a little. Our eyes stay fixed on each other as he steps back to hold his arm out for me to come in.

"Hi," I say, breathless. I don't think I've taken a single breath since he opened the door.

He leans down to hug me, wrapping his arms around my lower back. "You look beautiful," he says into my hair.

His hug makes my nerves completely subside, and I'm left feeling the familiar warmth I always do with him.

"Thank you." I wore the dress I bought that day we went shopping. I also exfoliated my body within an inch of its life and based on how he's looking at me right now, I'm glad I did. "You look very handsome."

He looks down at his outfit and smirks. "Hope you don't mind the Hanes white tee."

"I don't mind it at all." He looks like Eli. Relaxed, comforting, playful Eli. "Sorry I'm a little early."

"That's okay. I've been ready for two hours," he admits. "I was a little eager."

I smile up at him. "I was too." I look around his place. It's s single room, with a small kitchenette in the back. It's small, but tidy. "I like your place."

"Yeah, it's been good to have my own little spot. You want to sit down?" He gestures to the couch.

I take a seat, and then it's quiet. We both look around, as if thinking of something to say. Then we make eye contact and both start laughing.

"Can I get you something to drink?"

"Water would be good," I say.

He grabs a couple of glasses from a shelf and fills them at the sink.

"Did you have to work today?" I ask.

He hands my glass to me. "My dad brought Pebbles by for a spa day."

This makes me giggle, imagining the giant dog sitting there with cucumber slices over her eyes. "Good for Pebbles."

He turns toward me, inching a little closer. "Did you have any pets growing up?"

I look down at my glass. "There was a stray cat that

used to come around sometimes, and I would always leave food out for her. I named her Possum." I laugh at the memory. "I would sit by the screen door of my grandpa's kitchen and watch for her to come up. But every time I opened the door, she'd run off." I haven't thought about that cat in years.

"I'm sure Possum appreciated you leaving food out for her even though she was scared of you."

"Yeah, it was always disappointing, though. I wanted so badly to pick her up and cuddle her." I feel embarrassed about that for some reason.

His gaze wanders over my face. "You should get a cat."

I laugh. "Maybe I should. I'm surprised you don't have a dog. You seem like the type that would have a golden retriever or a chocolate lab that you bring around to breweries."

His eyes sparkle with good natured mischief. "Why do I feel like you're making fun of me?"

"I'm not making fun," I take a sip of my drink to hide my smile. "Just making an observation."

He checks the time on his phone. "It's 6:30. Should we head out?"

I fiddle with the edge of my dress, suddenly hesitant to leave. We have a seven o'clock reservation at a restaurant downtown, where I was planning to give my whole spiel. But that feels wrong. It doesn't feel like us.

This, us sitting together on the couch talking, feels like us.

"Actually, can I . . . can I tell you something first?"

He leans forward, looking at me in his intense, but gentle way. "Of course."

The butterflies in my stomach are back and they have teeth that tear at my stomach lining. It's silly, but I feel like

I'm about to hand him my heart. He already has it anyway, but it's like I'm fully acknowledging it now.

"I want to tell you more . . . about me." I laugh. "I know that sounds ridiculous, considering how long we've known each other. But I know that I'm not exactly an open book."

He nods his head, encouraging me to go on. "Okay."

I clear my throat. "Two truths and a lie."

He smiles and it's so sweet I want to eat it.

"When I was six, my mom left me to live with my grandpa for about five or six years. One night, I overheard her telling my grandpa she was leaving, but I thought she meant she'd be gone for like a week or something. I don't know, I was little. I even felt kind of excited because my grandpa let me watch all the *SpongeBob* I wanted."

He reaches over and gives my hand a squeeze.

I turn my hand so that my palm lies in his. "But then weeks passed, and she didn't come home. Then I started freaking out, thinking she was dead or kidnapped or whatever my little kid imagination conjured up. Finally, I asked my grandpa where she was." I take a sip of my drink. "Long story short, I didn't see her again until I was thirteen, shortly before I started high school."

"That must have been hard," he says, brow furrowing with concern.

"I felt like I didn't even know her, like she was some stranger who showed up one day, expecting everything to be fine."

"I'm so sorry that happened to you."

"I had my grandpa, at least. Not many people can say they had someone there for them."

"Still, you were just a kid. You should have been worried about math tests and field trips."

"I had this fear, I don't know, that I would become her.

Because when Andrew and I broke up, I felt so guilty. I didn't want to be alone, but I didn't want to stay with him, knowing that I wasn't ever going to marry him."

His thumb runs back and forth over my hand. "I understand."

I take a deep breath. "And I lied to you before."

"About what?"

"You asked me to admit that you didn't make me happy. But you make me happier than I've ever been, and I've decided that I need to be brave enough to not only accept that but reciprocate it." I take a deep breath. "So. . . my final truth is that I love you."

I set my glass down on his side table. "I love you, because there is no one like you. Who makes me laugh like you. Who sees me, and knows me, like you. And I see you, too. I see you show up for your family and care for your friends. I see you step into everyone room like a beam of sunshine. I want all of your chatter, all of your warmth." I wrap my arms around his neck. "I want your bad days, too. To take care of you and support you. I want to try all of it, with you."

Then he kisses me, hard, before holding my face in his hands. "I love you, Faye."

The kiss we share is so forceful we both lose balance, and he manages to catch my body as we roll off the couch. We laugh as we kiss and it's perfect.

He lifts his head up, looking down at me with those sweet, teasing eyes I will never get enough of. "I think we might miss that dinner reservation."

A piece of hair falls over his brow and I brush it back before pulling his mouth back to mine. I murmur against his lips, "Fine by me."

We do what we've done countless times before but

tonight is different. His hands on me are possessive, and my lips on his are finally home. We move together with no more doubts clouding the air between us.

I bury my face in the tender heat of his neck and whisper, "I missed you so much."

"I missed you more," he says before pressing his lips to my hair.

I'm so glad I won't have to miss him anymore.

—

47

FAYE

TWO MONTHS LATER

SOMETHING IS CLAWING at my toe. When I try to kick it off it only latches on harder. *Am I having a nightmare?*

I peek my eyes open and soft light pours into my bedroom through the sheer curtains. What possessed me to have sheer curtains in my bedroom, I have no idea. The clawing has turned to climbing and the little creature weasels its way up my leg, getting caught on the comforter along the way.

I'm not dreaming. It's just the kitten I got yesterday. She's a demon spawned directly from hell, but she's *my* demon spawned directly from hell.

"Come here, you little devil." I unlatch her from my legs and cuddle her up by my face, just like I wanted to do with Possum when I was little. Her little claws graze my cheek, but I don't care. "We've got to get you on a different sched-ule. I can't keep waking up with the sun."

I hear rustling in the kitchen, which means Eli is already up making some kind of chalky protein concoction for breakfast.

"I swear you two are conspiring to make me a morning person. Did he put you up to this?"

She answers by pouncing, and then chewing, on my hair.

Eli peeks his head in the room, and I do a double take because he's standing there wearing nothing but a pair of boxers with pink hearts all over them and a giant straw hat. He bought the boxers last week because he liked that they matched my underwear. "Sorry, did I wake you up?" he asks.

"No, this gremlin did." I point to his head. "What's with the hat?"

He comes in and kisses the cat on the head and then gives me a loud smacking kiss on the forehead. "I love my two little gremlins." He tightens the strap hanging below his chin before giving the brim a proud tug. "It's my gardening hat."

Eli and my grandpa have become best friends, and that's not even an exaggeration. They text each other every day, and I didn't even know my grandpa even knew how to text. Their latest project is cleaning up grandpa's garden beds. We're heading over there this afternoon to work on it.

"You're taking this gardening thing way too seriously."

"Tell that to the fall harvest we've got waiting for us."

"We? This has nothing to with me."

He leaves and comes back with another hat, which he deposits on my head. "Rumor has it that you haven't completed the hobby portion of your fun list."

"Dani and I took that pottery class last week, though."

"Doesn't count. She told me you complained the whole time about how the wet clay felt on your hands."

I shiver. "It was . . . slimy."

"So, you didn't have fun. So, it doesn't count."

"Gardening isn't fun either."

"You won't know until you try." He tightens my chin strap and uses the string to pull my face up to his. He kisses me on the nose. "You look cute."

I reach up to trace the latest tattoo he got a few weeks ago, on top of his left hand. Two swans with their necks entwined. When he came home and showed it to me, he said it was a spur-of-the-moment decision like all of his other ones, but that this one meant everything to him.

I have never felt so content with someone. To not question every word or action that I make. To feel security, but also anticipation for what's to come. Today it's something as simple as gardening, but tomorrow it could be anything we want.

And every night he holds me so tight, like the bedsheets are a tide threatening to wrench me away from him. But I don't pull away anymore.

I hold him tighter, saying *I love being here, with you. And I can't wait to see what we can do together.*

ACKNOWLEDGMENTS

It's true that writing a book is a very solitary endeavor, and it's true that no one will ever care about your story and your characters as much as you do. But I am incredibly lucky to have had some amazing people join me on this journey.

First, my writing group. My lovely fellow procrastinators and romantics. The way the stars aligned and brought us together is maybe one of the greatest things that's ever happened to me. Without your support, feedback, and encouragement this book would not exist. And it sure as hell would not be published. Thank you for being such a solid, warm presence on the other side of my phone and laptop screens.

I had a wonderful group of beta readers: Annie Adams, Rebecca V. Archer, Sanjana Basker, Andie James, Heather Varlow, Adaline D. Wright, and Jennifer. Your comments and suggestions were priceless to me in shaping this story into something I could truly be proud of.

Huge thank you to Katie Wolf, for witnessing me crashing out numerous times because writing a book is so fucking hard. Thank you for reminding me to be compassionate with myself, and for caring about Faye and Eli's story so much. Emily McNish, thank you for being such a cheerleader for me, and for helping me learn proper comma placement. Sarah T. Dubb, thank you immensely for the blurb help.

Mom and Dad, thank you for making me feel like

anything is possible. I wouldn't be a writer if it weren't for your constant support in finding my own path in life. Thank you to my family and friends for cheering me on along the way.

Adam, thank you for being my number one fan even though I've prohibited you from reading my books. Maybe I'll let you read this one, considering it's dedicated to you. I also want to thank my cats, Linus and Birdie, for disrupting my writing time in the adorable ways that only cats can.

And last, but certainly not least, thank *you*. Thank you for choosing to read this book out of the millions you could have picked up.

ABOUT THE AUTHOR

Hillary Noelle writes contemporary romantic comedies. She lives in North Carolina with her husband and two cats.

Connect Online:
Website: hillarynoelle.com
Instagram: _hillarynoelle_

www.ingramcontent.com/pod-product-compliance
Lightning Source LLC
Chambersburg PA
CBHW031114160726
47991CB00004B/1379